D1192290

St. Simons Island

A Stella Bankwell Mystery

Also by Ronda Rich

What Southern Know *(That Every Woman Should)*

My Life in The Pits *(A Nascar Memoir)*

What Southern Women Know about Flirting

What Southern Women Know about Faith

The Town that Came A-Courtin *(novel and a television movie)*

There's A Better Day A-Comin

Mark My Words a Memoir of Mama

Let Me Tell You Something

RONDA RICH

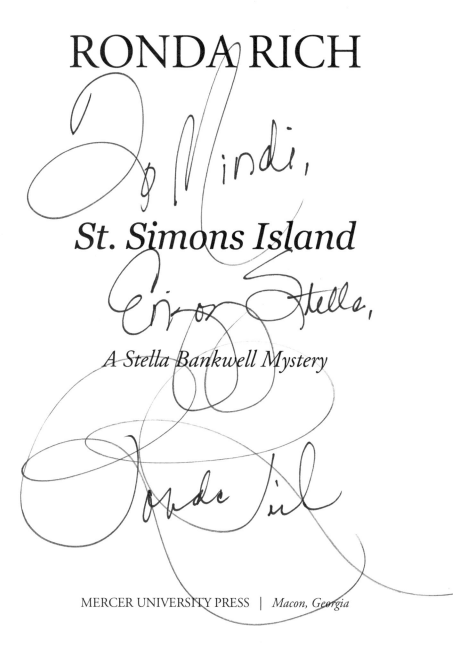

To Mindi,

St. Simons Island

Enjoy Stella,

A Stella Bankwell Mystery

Ronda Rich

MERCER UNIVERSITY PRESS | *Macon, Georgia*

MUP/ H1037

© 2023 Ronda Rich
Published by Mercer University Press
1501 Mercer University Drive
Macon, Georgia 31207
All rights reserved

27 26 25 24 23   5 4 3 2 1

Books published by Mercer University Press are printed on acid-free
paper that meets the requirements of the American National
Standard for Information Sciences—Permanence of Paper for Printed
Library Materials.

Printed and bound in the United States.

This book is set in Adobe Garamond Pro / Georgia.

Cover/jacket design by Burt&Burt.

ISBN (Print)   978-0-88146-896-0
ISBN (eBook)   978-0-88146-897-7

Cataloging-in-Publication Data is available from
the Library of Congress

Dedication

To Edward Armstrong

Who is my beloved Chatty

MERCER UNIVERSITY PRESS

Endowed by

TOM WATSON BROWN
and
THE WATSON-BROWN FOUNDATION, INC.

St. Simons Island

A Stella Bankwell Mystery

Chapter One

Chatham Balsam Colquitt IV was beside himself with joy. With a name like that, he could have been a law firm, but he was much more than that. He was Atlanta's chief purveyor of gossip, a task he relished with every fiber of his substantial size and one to which he was steadfastly devoted.

"As my butler draws my morning bath, I sip coffee from my great-grandmother's Wedgwood tea cup and saucer while anticipating what enticing news the day shall bring," he liked to say.

There was nothing that Chatham—or "Chatty," as he had been called since he first learned how to string words into endless sentences—loved better than a good scandal in which he could keep the coals stirred and glistening red hot. This one— *this one*, the most titillating he could ever recall—had the delicious added bonus of starring his best friend, Stella Jackson Bankwell. He had driven two hours from Atlanta through small towns, over winding, twisting roads, to find Stella at an old clapboard farmhouse with aged white paint that was beginning to peel and a somewhat rickety front porch graced by a swing and two weathered rocking chairs. The house, a hundred-year-old pile of sticks and stones, set down a long dirt road. It was framed by towering oak trees that were not majestic like the grandest trees in Atlanta but rugged because it takes more to survive a winter in the Appalachian foothills than one in tony Buckhead.

"Oh, Stellie, this is almost too good to be true," he gushed gleefully as they settled down to talk. He clapped his hands together like a child. His voice and words were an evenly mixed potion of softness, elegance, enthusiasm, and, above all, captivating charm owing to the educated, luscious tones of Southern aristocracy. For a moment, he closed his eyes and lingered, sweetly absorbed in the moment. He pressed his thick fingers against his lips and swayed slightly back and forth, a Chatty signature move that indicated complete bliss.

His eyes sprung open with sudden thought. A ramble of words gushed forward. "I *knew* that volunteering to call out the numbers every Thursday night for seniors' bingo at church would pay off. You reap what you sow. I forget where I read that but it's true. I've been sowing good for so long and now"—with this, he spread his arms—"here's my harvest: I have a scrumptious story to tell, but since it happened to you— my dearest friend in the whole, entire world, both the God-blessed and the God-forsaken countries—it's my exclusive scoop."

He dropped his voice to a dramatic whisper. "And I do pray for all those places that are far less fortunate than we who were born into wealth and privilege." He paused, raising an eyebrow. "And those who have married into the bosom of prosperity as well." He winked cheerfully at Stella, who rolled her weary eyes. "Anyway. Now that you've created Atlanta's biggest scandal in…" He placed a finger to his chin and thought for a second then spread his arms in a grand gesture. "Maybe ever. I am no longer obliged to pass along merely what I hear secondhand. I can actively participate in this juicy uprising by adding facts that no one else knows but me! I liken it to winning the Pulitzer." He smiled beatifically as he drew his shoulders up like a soldier returning from triumph. "It is a life-defining moment."

He reached over, took both of Stella's delicate, ivory hands, and squeezed them with the feeling of rapturous happiness that shuddered throughout his body. Then he pulled one hand back and placed the enormous paw over his heart, bowed his head, and said with false humility, "Thank you, Lord."

Stella, unamused and emotionally depleted, took a long gulp of the Chardonnay that he had smuggled past her teetotaling mother. She then pulled herself up from the faded chintz rocker that had been in this bedroom since she was six when her great-aunt Nellie died and left it to her. In the last several days—five to be precise—the only comfort she had found was here in her childhood home with the soothing, honeyed sounds of her Mama's words, reassuring her that she could rebound and put it all behind.

"Chatty, have you ever heard of pushing it too far?"

She was bone weary, so it was an enormous burden to force out her words. She cut her velvet green eyes over to him but he didn't notice. He was too content being happy in the role he had long coveted: Town Crier and Official Spokesperson of the Newly Disgraced. She walked to the window that looked out over the February rawness of the North Georgia mountains, with naked trees that displayed strong character in varying shades of gray and deep brown. She grabbed her thick, red-gold hair into a ponytail with her fingers, held it for second, then released the tousled curls to fall past her shoulders onto the faded blue sweatshirt she was wearing. She caught a glimpse of herself in the mirror, the same one where she had learned to apply mascara, practiced batting her eyelashes and memorizing passages from Shakespeare's Macbeth for her eleventh grade English final exam.

The pale, thin face in the mirror caught her off guard. Her eyes looked like they had been washed a shade lighter from all the tears. They had once been like dazzling, deeply dark emeralds but now they resembled discarded marbles, left to fade from rain and sun. She moved closer to the mirror and rubbed her hand across her high cheekbone, lately accented from the creeping fine lines scattered beneath her eyes.

"Maybe some moisturizer," she thought, then realized she couldn't remember the last time she put anything on her face. Oh, yes. Of course. She had applied face and eye creams before going out that night. *That* night. The one that would live in the collective memories of well-heeled Atlantans for years and possibly for generations. For the first time since she was sixteen, Stella was glad that her beloved Granny McAfee wasn't alive. Granny's continuing admonition to anyone in her family who might be considering an untoward or non-righteous adventure was always, "You ain't gonna do that. I absolutely forbid it. What would people think?"

She was gravely concerned that people always think highly of her family. They were hard-working farm people but they shared what they had, showed up for church every Sunday morning in clothes reserved for the Lord's day, and spent the summers tending gardens and putting up vegetables for winter's unyieldingly harsh days. Her family's solid, our-word-is-our-bond reputation meant everything to Eula McAfee, known as Granny or Miss Eula. Stella came from people like that on both sides of her family: good, decent, caring people. Then, in one moment of lost self-control, she had smudged the family name so thoroughly that it would be stained forever. No one would forget Stella Bankwell. Not after what had happened at the Buckhead Country Club.

Chatty paid no nevermind to her low spirits or the age showing on her face as her weight melted from her frame like butter in the hot sun. He continued on, trilling like a songbird.

"Do you know that Malinda Skarda called *me* yesterday? She never speaks to me. Just looks down her imperious nose—created, I might add, by her mother sleeping with her own first cousin. Everybody knows that's against the law in the state of Georgia."

"Chatty, that's rumor," Stella mumbled absent-mindedly, watching as two squirrels dug through the fallen, crusty leaves in the backyard, looking for acorns. One of them found an acorn then, as happy as Chatty was with his jewel-encrusted scandal, scampered across the yard toward the barn.

He waved away Stella's meager comment. "I have it on good authority. I don't just gossip. I fact-check. Don't forget that I come from a family of judges on my father's side and paralegals on my mother's." He held his head up haughtily as he always did when talking of his father's family that went back to the days when General Oglethorpe founded the colony of Georgia in Savannah. Chatty's profile was simultaneously austere and pleasant. He always carried too much weight and wore too many bow ties and seersucker suits, but his warmly colored brown hair was thick and quite fetching. His eyes were brilliant blue, his cheeks like dumplings, and his smile wide and friendly. And though he was known for the tales he carried, he was irresistibly likeable. His manners were gallant, and his dinner parties, always set with the silver that his family had buried in the backyard as Sherman's torching moved closer, were the height of fun despite the detailed etiquette.

Miss Caroline, the Bankwell family's matriarch and Stella's mother-in-law, at least for the moment, always said that Chatty's mother must have had a crystal ball when she named him because once he started talking, he had never stopped.

One night Chatty, in a rare bad mood during a cocktail party at Miss Caroline's stately English Tudor neighboring the Governor's mansion, took offense. "My name is Chatham," he said in a measured tone. "My ancestors were the founders of Chatham County where the grand old Southern city of Savannah resides. My mother did not have the prescience to name me Chatty. I am so nicknamed not due to my Christian name of Chatham but because when I was a child, still in knee socks and shorts, my favorite toy was my cousin's Chatty Cathy doll. We had the most glorious conversations together, that doll and I. Thus, my mother began to refer to us as 'Chatty' and 'Cathy.' We were, indeed, glorious playmates." He raised his luxurious brown eyebrows imperially. "And that is how I became known as Chatty."

He did not mean to be funny. Normally, he'd do anything to get a good laugh. On that particular night, however, he was simply in a foul mood, trying to condescend. It did not work. The group listened, absorbed his words, and then, as though someone pressed a button, they erupted in gales of laughter, their cheer wiping away any remnants of a bad mood he had previously possessed.

Now Stella, in thick mismatched socks, shuffled across the ancient wood floors of the farmhouse where she was born and raised, just as her daddy had been. She dropped down hard into the chintz rocker, sighed heavily, and started swaying back and forth while Chatty held court with his story about Malinda Skarda.

"So." He slapped his pudgy hands on his knees and pulled himself up as he always did when he was launching into a mighty tale. "Malinda called me, and wouldn't you know it, honey—sugar wouldn't melt in her mouth. You would have thought that our families crossed the ocean together with General Oglethorpe. Of course, that is neither true nor scientifically possible because the Colquitts are one of the oldest families in the South. Fancy Pants Malinda said, 'Chatty dear, I know you have all the details about that unseemly disturbance at the club with Stella. I shan't ever forgive myself for missing it, but Penelope had a fever and one must mother first. Especially when another nanny has resigned abruptly. But I digress. You are the only one in Atlanta who could possibly have heard from Stella, so you must, darling Chatty, divulge every delicious detail. I promise I shall be your best friend forever if you will only tell.'"

Chatty, like all deep-rooted Atlantans, pronounced the name as "Atlanna," dropping the "t." Of all the social engagements that Chatty attended regularly, because his trust fund was so plush that he would never have to work, the one he seemed to enjoy the most was the "Native Atlantans Club" that met at exclusive restaurants. To be a member required producing a birth certificate from one of seven hospitals in the Atlanta zip code.

"I was born at Piedmont," Chatty loved to boast. "I'm as native as possible." He had been simply aghast when someone once produced a forged birth certificate to sneak into the club.

"She was delivered of life in the city of Griffin. Can you imagine such deliberate deception? Why, she was closer to being born at the Atlanta race track than she was to being born in Atlanta proper."

Stella drew in her breath and summoned what little strength remained. "Chatham, my life is in shambles. I have embarrassed myself, my family, and the Bankwell family, though I do not mind one iota that I may have embarrassed Asher, my soon-to-be ex. However, Miss Caroline, while she was unyielding at times, has shown a degree of loveliness over the nine years of my marriage. Or sympathy. I'm not sure what it was. I am certain it is difficult to have a well-educated, aristocratic, handsome, rich son marry a mountain girl. I grew up on CorningWare, and Asher, quite simply, grew up with an entire sterling silver service in his mouth." She stopped, searching her mind. "Dadgum. I've forgotten what I was going to say." Her eyes filled with tears. "I'm losing my mind."

"Did it have anything to do with Malinda Skarda telephoning me and the certifiable fact that I know what others in Atlanta wish they were privy to?" he asked helpfully with a charming smile.

Stella looked at him and shook her head hopelessly. "Yes, Chatty. It had something to do with that."

"Do you recall what exactly?"

"Not exactly, but something to the effect that I ask you to not make this worse than it already is. Gossip, I understand, is the nectar of your existence, but I beg of you to please not discuss this!"

His eyes widened in alarm. "*Ever?*"

"Never!"

He slunk back into the straight-back ladder chair that he had brought up from the dining room when Mrs. Jackson had shown him in. His mind tried to absorb the gravity of his friend's command. Finally, he spoke.

"You cannot possibly mean that, Stella Bankwell. I was your friend when no one in Atlanta society wanted to open their tight-armed, firmly welded circle and allow you to place one of your red-mud-stained, country-girl toes in. I am now armed with the inside scoop on a dire gossip situation for *once* in my life and you are demanding that I silence my tongue. It is far more than I can endure." He wilted a bit as if he might faint. It was a well-practiced trick of his.

Stella pulled a lip balm from her jeans' pocket and smoothed it over her lips. She capped it, tucked it back in the pocket, then said firmly, "Yes. I mean it."

Chatty's blue eyes rested on her face for a moment, then, rather than retreat because neither the Chathams, the Balsams nor the Colquitts ever retreated, he changed his tack. A smile of Southern gentlemanly charm spread from ear to ear. He leaned forward in his chair and took her hand and patted it gently.

"Stella, my darling girl, do you not realize what you have done?" Her green eyes registered no emotion. He plunged forth. "Atlanta society quickly forgets the good girls who play by the rules. Those who are untouched by scandal are forever banned from the loftier heights of immortality and relegated to blandness, remembered only, *possibly*, by a name and date carved into marble and, in some cases, just plain run-of-the-mill granite." He shuddered, a ripple of blue oxford material shimmying over his chest. "But *you*, my girl, shall never be forgotten. One day, the legend of Stella Jackson Bankwell will be cast into a noble book filled with fine paper and bound with the costliest leather. It shall be emblazoned with golden gilt lettering. This book shall be filed in grand libraries and placed on exhibit at the High Museum. You do not seem to understand that I am the Edgar Rice Burroughs to your Tarzan or, more aptly, the Margaret Mitchell to your Scarlett. I was born, without question, in the Piedmont Hospital on a finely starlit spring night to perpetuate the legend you have so brilliantly begun."

Stella, though a bit entertained, refused to show it. Her gaze fixed on one of the dearest friends she had ever known while her mind flittered back over those few minutes at the Buckhead Country Club when she had made herself such a notorious fool. "A shame and a disgrace," her granny would've said. Her daddy, too, would never have recovered from the grief, Lord rest his soul. From the silence, Mrs. Jackson's voice rose up the pinewood staircase outside Stella's door.

"Stella! Chatty! Supper's ready. Y'all come on now while it's hot."

Stella picked up the fine crystal wine glass that Chatty had brought—he had rightly figured that he would find no tinkling crystal in the mountains—and drained the last drop. She stood up, walked to the solid three-panel door with the edges scrubbed by wear, and opened it.

Over her shoulder, she said, "I hope you like pinto beans and cornbread."

She knew, of course, that neither food had ever crossed his lips.

Chapter Two

With a pinging, the rain fell rhythmically on the farmhouse's tin roof while Stella, still awake as dawn pinked the sky, tried to still her mind and listen to the sound that had always been comforting and cozy.

"Oh, listen to that rain," her mama would often say to her husband and two girls. Many were the nights of Stella's childhood that Martha Annie Jackson would stand at the screen door, watching the rain fall between the leaves of the sprawling maple tree at the back porch. "It's gonna be good sleepin' weather, so you girls cuddle up good under your quilts and enjoy it. Nothin' sings prettier than a tin roof."

Mama was right about that. She was usually right, especially when she had expressed concern about Stella marrying Jasper Asher Bankwell III. Martha Annie could overstep, there was no doubt about it. Overstepping was as much a part of her mountain blood as her frugality and stoic demeanor. The problem turned out to be that she hadn't overstepped near enough in the days leading up to the wedding. If only she had put her foot down. But then, how do you stop a twenty-eight-year-old from doing as she pleases? Stella's mama was no more than slightly questioning as she pointed out the differences in their backgrounds and worried that those with money might look down on her little girl. Stella's big sister, Lynn, though, was right there rooting it on.

"You go, Freckles," she cheered. "No one in this family has ever lived in a mansion and it's time we started. I'm proud for you."

There was one worry, though, that Martha Annie Jackson hadn't been able to shake: Asher's nine-year-old son, Tennille, called "Neely" by all who knew him.

"He's such a sweet little boy, but I sense a deep trouble in him," Martha Annie had said to her husband Sims over coffee one morning. "And what child wouldn't have a troubled spirit after what his mother did?" Before Sims died, there were two daily points when he and his wife shared their stories, worries, and good news with each other—either at the breakfast table over coffee after the girls left for school, or after the night grew darkest and they turned out the lights. Martha Annie would lay her head on her husband's shoulder, and they'd talk of the day's events or the worries that the farm brought. During summer months, when all the doors and windows were opened to let in the cooling air, Stella and Lynn could sometimes hear their parents' voices drifting through the hall. It was a solid marriage, the kind sought by both daughters. Lynn got it by marrying her high school sweetheart, Ronnie Walton, and settling down on a nearby farm where they raised horses.

"I had to get too big for my little britches, and look where it got me," Stella murmured to herself as she pulled a quilt closer to her chin, trying to focus on the rain. Her mind refused to obey. It wandered and took her back over the past few days and years of her life. Asher, of course, was a problem. There was no disputing that. He was highly critical of Stella's inexperience in the sophisticated world, plus he was obsessed with trying to get richer. Since their marriage, he had invested significantly in an organic sweetener that never got out of the testing lab, been an investor in a racehorse that failed to make it to the starting gate, and poured money into his favorite restaurant that had been in Atlanta for forty years. After two fruitless years of funneling through Asher's money, the place had gone out of business. Now, for the past three years, he had been completely absorbed in co-owning a corporate jet leasing business. He was so involved, in fact, that he had gotten his pilot's license so he could fly if needed.

"Oh no, not me, honey child! I will not be placing my precious life in his hands!" Chatty exclaimed when he heard that Asher intended on piloting small jets. He had said this two years earlier, when Chatty and Stella were lunching at the Buckhead Country Club, the place where later she would come undone in a most public way and launch herself into infamy. "I attended Astor Academy for Boys with him, and I know for a fact, because I witnessed it with my own eyes, that he is incapable of adding the simplest of numbers. Take, for instance, two plus two."

Chatty was seldom without a story to back up his formed opinions. "One day, he insisted to Mrs. Guest that it added up to five. We were in the third grade, but if you don't know simple arithmetic by then, it is downhill from there. And one place I will not be going downhill is in a plane with Asher Bankwell, because he doesn't know his numbers. He told Mrs. Guest— and if I'm lying may Jesus take me now—that he wasn't required to add numbers because he, Asher, had a most capable accountant to do that for him." Here, Chatty stopped and allowed a sly smile to cross his face while the twinkle brightened his blue eyes. "Now, let's see. I believe that particular accountant of which he spoke with such devotion was Bennett Sutton, the same Bennett Sutton who made a dash out of town on a historically dark night—there was no moon in sight on that woeful eve—absconding with money from Atlanta's most elite. I myself lost $50,000 in grocery money to the scoundrel, but thank goodness that's only a year's worth of champagne and Tito's vodka for me."

Stella frowned as she stirred honey into her tea. "Miss Caroline and Asher lost far more than that." She pushed a lilt into her voice because she realized that, as of late, she was becoming too gloomy. "Some of it was recovered, though."

Chatty airily waved his hand. "Mere pennies on the dollar. I, due to the extremely healthy condition of trust funds from both the Chathams and the Colquitts—the Balsams mainly owned vast sums of land—was able to generously forego any retribution so that widows might be aided more substantially."

Stella rolled her eyes. "Chatty, do you realize if someone who didn't know you merely read on paper the things you say, you'd sound like the biggest ass in Georgia? Probably in the entire South?"

He was unfazed. "But those who know me are quite familiar with the fineness of my heart. I just donated two Saville Row, custom-made cashmere suits to the homeless shelter downtown."

Stella laughed. She couldn't resist. "Chatty, there's not a homeless man in Atlanta nor anywhere else who weighs 240 pounds and can wear your suits."

He was taken aback. "I don't understand."

"In other words, no homeless man has $50,000 a year to spend on groceries and retain that much poundage." She glanced at his belly spilling over his belt and causing the lower button on his perfectly starched white shirt to strain. He noticed her pointed look but, owing to a very pleasant disposition, was able to move past it quickly.

"Stella." He patted the edge of the white-clothed table with the tips of his fingers. "That's what I spend on champagne and vodka. I spend far more than that on groceries." Before she could retort, he returned to the subject. "Speaking of Bennett Sutton, do you know that he is in the same white collar federal prison with all those executives who defrauded healthcare and telecom companies? I'm sure they're all planning their next big heist together while playing cards and smoking big cigars. Thieving hearts never change." He took a quick breath. "And speaking of that, how is Neely doing?"

Stella's stomach flipped at the name of her stepson. The sweet boy she had adored and held such high hopes for at the beginning of her marriage had turned into a nightmare. They had enjoyed three lovely years together, often snuggling on the sofa to watch movies or attending Braves games, sometimes in a corporate suite, courtesy of a Bankwell friend. When he turned thirteen, though, it all changed. Over the years, it worsened. He became disrespectful to everyone—except to his grandmother Miss Caroline, who could still manage some control over him—and downright hostile to Stella. He was suspended from his private school so often for pranks, accelerating in degrees of seriousness, that the headmaster made it clear that the only reason he was not permanently removed was the Bankwell Endowment that had seeded the school 120 years earlier and still provided financial assistance.

"The Decatur police brought him home the other night after they arrested a couple of guys he was out with. Troublemakers, the police said." Stella sipped her tea. "Of course, Asher wasn't there, so it was left to me to deal with him.

Chatty, I don't know what to do. He despises me. He just turned from a sweet boy into a monster one day. He'll be sixteen soon, and that will be even more troubling when he can drive."

"My, my," Chatty murmured absent-mindedly, nodding as he rose to meet a gentleman passing the table. It was Edward Goldstein, one of the town's most prominent politicians.

"Howdy do, my fine sir," he said, shaking the man's hand. Goldstein turned to Stella, offered a bow, and said, "Good afternoon, Mrs. Bankwell."

After a bit of social niceties, Goldstein said, "There's the other gentleman I'm meeting. Y'all have a fine day."

Chatty sat back down, picking up right where they had left off. When it came to talking about other people, he never lost his place in the conversation.

"Poor Neely. I know he's a rascal, but there's one person primarily to shoulder the blame for his unruliness: Eleanor Collier Bankwell Piggs." A shudder of disgust ran over his body. "Who in their right mind would go from such elegant, worthy last names to one like Piggs? I shall always defend her in some small way because I believe she had a nervous breakdown. She deserves a certain amount of compassion and small sympathy." He paused to make his next words louder. "Asher seems to have that effect on his wives."

"I'm not having a nervous breakdown," Stella responded firmly, holding her lovely head up and tilting her exquisitely formed nose.

There was no question why all the society magazines once wanted to feature her regularly on their covers and in full-page layouts. She might be of humble beginnings, but she had a head-turning look. Her 5'5" frame was cushioned in fetching curves, her legs had once been pasted on a billboard that advertised one of the town's best shoe stores, her lips were full and usually turned up in a smile, and her hair the color of roasted carrots, eyes the color of the green velvet drapes that Scarlett O'Hara had worn, and her ivory-porcelain skin were a provocative combination. However, the stress of the last few years had taken a toll on her beauty, and now, rather than edging toward beautiful, she was more down-to-earth pretty. The lessons of life were clearly etched on her face and in her eyes, making her more solemn and less quick to laugh. The innocence of a young mountain girl had turned to a worldliness that she would have preferred never to know.

"I admit that my nerves are slightly frayed," she continued, trying not to sound defensive. "But I am a long way from any sort of breakdown. Why, even when I discussed this with my doctor, she insisted that I was nowhere near needing a prescription of any kind."

Chatty patted her hand. "Trust me, honey. I'm not formally trained as a doctor, but I do know when a little Zoloft should be called in. In your case, it is a 911 call."

She folded her arms across her ample bosom, which was particularly alluring in the DVF leopard print wrap dress she was wearing, and eyed him coldly. "So what were you saying about Ellie?"

"George!" he called to a waiter who had worked at the country club for more than thirty years. "Would you bring me a big slice of the chef's signature cheesecake? With cherries ladled on top? And a nice helping of whipped cream?"

Stella reached over and tapped the stiffly starched cuff of his shirt, which peeked out from his navy sports coat. "Chatty, you might want to cut back a bit on all that. Particularly as you are lecturing me on my own shortcomings."

"Funny you should mention that." He threw a forefinger in her direction. "Just this morning, I was thinking that one day—when I'm a good bit older than I am today—I am going to start forgoing the whipped cream." He smiled splendidly.

"Admittedly, that's a big step forward for a man as self-indulgent as you."

"Yes, it is, and I thank you kindly for acknowledging that. Now, back to Eleanor, or Ellie, as she was once affectionately known while she was still held in affection in this town. Neely was only five years old when she took up with that Bohemian pottery painter she met in an art class in the Virginia Highlands. I'm sorry you weren't around for that scandal. It was divine."

A look of pure rapture spread over his face. "One of the highlights of my life. It's all anyone talked about for six months, during which Miss Caroline took to her eighteenth century four-poster bed and refused to come out *until* Bennett Sutton sneaked out of town with a big chunk of Atlanta's money. That little escapade became even bigger news, far overshadowing a socialite running off with a pottery painter."

He leaned back in the pretty club chair covered in red and beige paisley as George set the cheesecake in front of him. "Thank you, George." Picking up the heavy silver fork and holding it mid-air, he said to Stella, "The Bennett Sutton story lasted for *over* a year because so many families had been taken."

He took a bite of cheesecake and as he was swallowing said, "I liken it to the time Clinton was President and the blue dress with its DNA suddenly appeared. Things were not looking good for him when he, Hillary, and Chelsea walked across the lawn to the helicopter that was waiting to take them on vacation to Martha's Vineyard. Oh honey, she was mad and it was showing. Then they get to Martha's Vineyard and what happens? Two U.S. Embassies in Africa were bombed and suddenly that's all the news. Just like that, no one is talking about the blue dress anymore." He lowered his voice conspiratorially. "A little too coincidental, I thought." He raised his voice again. "Or just the fabled good fortune of the Clintons. Anyway, that's what happened with Ellie's scandal after she took off to an arts commune near Asheville. Bennett Sutton took off with everyone's money so they no longer cared that *she* had taken off."

Stella did not want to get into a discussion about Asher's ex-wife. While Eleanor was not from a pile of old money, her lineage would rival Chatty's. Miss Caroline had been very proud that Eleanor was descended directly from three governors and one U.S. senator, and she was related, on her twisted family tree, to two presidents. She was raised well. She knew which to use in a ten-piece silver setting at a high society dinner party and did so confidently. Stella, on the other hand, had never seen a finger bowl until she met Asher.

Eleanor was a dark-haired patrician beauty who, though exceedingly rigid, was well liked by their social set and had been president of the Junior Service League four years in a row, a feat never accomplished by anyone else. She was society perfect until one day, out of the blue, she took up with her art instructor, David Piggs, and then took off with him. For the past ten years, she had worn nothing but paint-splattered jeans, a discarded man's shirt, no makeup, and now her hair was tied in a long, graying braid that fell down her back. If you listened to Chatty or Miss Caroline, they both declared that she rarely bathed, though no one could figure out how they would know such a thing since neither of them had laid an eye on her since she bolted for the commune. One thing was certain, though, she left her small son and appeared never to look back. She did not call nor write for five years, and then she started popping up from time to time in the form of a call, a note, or some absurd gift such as a tribal war doll or a piece of glass she had unearthed while hoeing her garden.

"Why would you dare to cast an aspersion toward the Clintons?" Stella asked, attempting to steer the conversation away from Eleanor, over whom she had only one triumph: Stella was not crazy. Yet. "You're a die-hard Democrat."

"Honey, I am not just a die-hard Democrat. I am a yellow dog Democrat. Do you know what that means?" As typical, he did not wait for her to answer before continuing. "That means that if the hallowed Democratic party put a yellow dog on the ticket, I would vote for said yellow dog. I have had this drummed into me since an early age. My great-grandfather and Franklin Delano Roosevelt were best of friends, beginning when Roosevelt started coming to Warm Springs in hopes of curing his polio and then built the Little White House. When he died, the Chathams and the Colquitts were there to watch his flag-draped coffin hoisted onto the black-crepe-draped train for the sad return trip to Washington. The train did not sound its whistle when it pulled out. My third cousin was appointed by Jimmy Carter as an ambassador to some country that no one could ever find on the map, but *still* he served."

He took a big bite of cheesecake, cast his eyes upward, and studied the ceiling for a moment. "However, there has been a changing in this state for the last good while. I certainly don't want to be the last one standing. That would be like wearing last year's Armani." Without stopping, he continued, "When was the last time Eleanor presented herself in any form to the Bankwell household?"

Stella sighed. "You're like a dog with a bone." She narrowed her eyes, glancing down at the cheesecake and then back up at him. "Or yourself with a piece of dessert. You don't let go."

"Your point?" he asked coolly. "You might as well tell me when last you heard from Eleanor because I will not silence myself on the matter until I have full disclosure."

Stella reached up to tighten the back on the large gold loop earrings she was wearing, a gift from the days when Asher still paid her attention. "Two weeks ago. She called because she had heard—I don't know how, maybe through smoke signals—that Neely was being problematic. He happened to answer the phone, and when he heard it was his mother, he let out a string of language I couldn't believe. He used words I had no idea he knew, then he slammed down the phone. She called Asher at the office but, as you can imagine, he has no sympathy for her."

Chatty swallowed his final bite of cheesecake then washed it down with coffee laden with heavy cream. "My advice—and remember my advice is well regarded in Atlanta town—would be this: Don't let all of this drive you to crazy. We have already seen that happen with one Bankwell wife. It would be unseemly for it to happen twice. Rise above it."

It's interesting the things a troubled mind recalls when it is most troubled. That one conversation with Chatty, over the countless others they had had, was what Stella kept remembering for the past week since returning to the mountains.

"Rise above it," Chatty had cautioned. Yet Stella hadn't. She had not only not risen above it, she had sunk to a level that made Eleanor look regal. And it wasn't just the public shaming she had garnered that bothered her. Her heart was broken because the fairy tale was over.

⌀

As Stella laid in the full-sized bed of her childhood home, staring up at the ceiling, clothed in a floral flannel gown trimmed in lace that had been a Christmas gift when she was sixteen, her mind tripped back over the last ten years, then took a roadside stop at the night she met Asher. That night of their introduction, she had also found herself sleepless, but then it was from excitement and not from anguish as it was now.

Besieged with grief, she turned her head from side to side. When she gathered her emotions, she faced toward her bookcase filled with the stories of her youth: Nancy Drew, *Wuthering Heights, Jane Eyre,* and at least a dozen Victoria Holt English romance novels. On top of the bookcase were the blue and white pom-poms from her high school cheerleading days. Those Friday night football games, Thursday night pep rallies with bonfires, and all the excitement they wrought was what started her journey. She and her best friend, Marlo, had such thrilling times at football and basketball games that when Stella graduated from the University of Georgia with a marketing degree and a business minor, she had decided to seek a job in sports marketing.

That decision led her to Atlanta, led her to Avalon Sports Marketing, led her to Veni Vidi Vici Italian restaurant for a client dinner, led her to Asher, and, ultimately, led her right back to the farm where now, instead of being a young girl with high hopes, she was a thirty-seven-year-old woman with no hope at all. She was a boomerang with the story of an unexpected journey. She couldn't stop thinking about that night. It all came back so clearly, down to the detail of the deep, luscious pink color of her fingernails.

She had recently been promoted to account manager. Since the International Olympics in 1996, Atlanta had become a mecca for sports marketing, with firms suddenly rivaling those in New York, Los Angeles, and Chicago. The offer to enter the management program of the city's top firm had been a dream come true. For the past five years, she had been moved throughout the company for a sampling of mail room, accounting, public relations, hospitality, and advertising. She had even worked a full month as a receptionist. Owen Dupree, the company's president, wanted all who went through the management program to know details of the firm's work. She handed out hot dogs at baseball games; strung banners up at hospitality events at the Indy 500; booked hotel rooms—often at the last minute in a city where rooms were sold out—for sponsor executives who were intolerant of anything but success and never grateful; trudged through ankle-deep mud at steeple chase races; thrown herself between a professional football player and a sports reporter whom he aimed to slug; and, once, she had even ridden in the Goodyear blimp as it floated over a stock car race in Sonoma, California. Through it all, she had proven herself to be tough, resourceful, cheerful, appreciative, and unfazed by hard work in 100-degree heat. Some of this had been born in her and some had been taught by her daddy in the searing hot hayfields and freezing, muddy barn on the farm where she was raised in Turner's Corner, two hours north of Atlanta. Hers had been a well-rounded raising, taught by humble, God-fearing people. From books to cooking to sewing to gardening to tractor driving, Stella's mama and daddy made sure she could always figure things out and be independent.

She had recently been promoted to an account—Foster's Homemade Baked Beans—and oversaw all facets of their sports marketing: events, graphics, advertising, hospitality, and public relations. She now had three people who reported to her, a small, windowless office with a big desk, and a generous expense account—which is why she was at Veni Vidi Vici, one of the town's more exclusive restaurants, that night. Henry Foster, the Chief Executive Officer of the family-run company, was passing through Atlanta from headquarters in Birmingham, on his way to Hilton Head for a golf retreat.

"Let's have dinner," he suggested by phone. "I'd like you to meet my wife, Stephanie, because this is a family company so you should know all the family."

Stella, as was her habit, arrived fifteen minutes early and was seated. It was one of those days—she remembered this clearly—when she felt confident about her appearance. She was wearing a deep butter-yellow, high-neck dress with three-quarter-length sleeves and ruching from the bustline to the hips, which flattered her curves beautifully yet was professional and elegant. It was a good hair day. She only had five or six a year because her curly hair often had a mind of its own. That day, each loose curl was perfectly wound without one bit of frizz, quite an accomplishment in late August in the South. Her lips were coated with Twinkle, her favorite shade of gloss, and her well-shaped legs looked longer thanks to the nude shade of the four-inch heel pumps she wore.

Mario, the assistant manager, showed her to a corner table with a fabulous view of the lights that brightened midtown. Directly across was a row of red leather-covered booths. Stella and Mario chatted for a moment until he was called elsewhere. She opened her purse to put away the valet ticket and then paused a moment to admire the Chanel classic, nine-inch-long, light beige caviar leather bag she had bought with her first bonus. The frugal raised-in-the-mountains side of her had argued that she should put the $2000 bonus in savings to go toward a down payment on a house or condo. The frivolous side argued that she was quite happy renting the tiny but adorable carriage house on Lenox Road and should have a reward now for the five-year journey to account manager. Through a friend's mother, she had found the purse in an upscale consignment shop—never used, with the Neiman-Marcus sale tag still attached to prove it had cost twice as much when brand new. That settled it. She happily bought it and satisfied both the frugal and frivolous side of her size-six self. She was trying to decide where to situate the purse—she didn't want to put it on the floor—when Mario came back over.

"Miss Jackson, I regret to inform you that I just received a call from your guest, Mr. Foster, and he sends his apologies. His wife is suffering from a migraine. She obviously cannot dine and he does not want to leave her. He asked that I tell you that he will call you tomorrow."

Stella's heart sank. Her first official client dinner, called off. It had felt wonderful to prepare emotionally for it. Too, she had her stomach set on a good house salad and the creamy pancetta and pea pasta that she loved. She pulled herself up to professionalism.

"Mario, thank you. I do hope that Mrs. Foster will recover quickly." She glanced around the table. "Well. Hmm. Uh." She thought for a second. "I guess I'll just be going, then."

He put his hand out to stop her. "Why not stay and have a lovely dinner?" he asked. "You can even stay at the table for four because it's Tuesday night, light business for us."

Stella didn't mind eating alone. She had done it many times while traveling, though usually not in an elegant, candle-lit restaurant. She was also on the expense account and the company would pay. Why not?

She sighed gratefully. "Mario, that's exactly what I'll do. I haven't had a decent meal in a week. I've been living on cheese and crackers. I'll start with a glass of Merlot and some of that heavenly bread you bake with the delicious olive oil."

He smiled broadly. "Right away."

And just like that, all twists and turns converged to bring her to a new road. She placed her purse in an empty chair and sat back to relax and listen to Dean Martin singing "That's Amore."

⤙

Stella was absorbed in thought and eating her salad. She pulled a pad and pen from her purse and started making notes on the upcoming Cleveland Grand Prix, where Foster's would entertain their Midwestern sales representatives. All would be treated to a tented hospitality area and tickets to the race, but the ones who had achieved certain sales incentives would watch the event from a fully catered luxury suite. She was in charge of all the details. Completely in another world—after all, if the company was paying for her dinner then she should rightfully earn it by working as she had been taught—she did not see Mario seat three people in a booth a few feet away. She jumped a bit when a man's voice said quietly, "Excuse me. I apologize for interrupting."

He put his hand on her shoulder lightly and said, "I do apologize. I'm sorry to have startled you."

Stella looked up to the distinguished, older man with salt and pepper hair and a pleasant face. He was dressed in an expensive navy suit, starched white shirt, and red silk tie. Had she had time to think, she would have immediately sized him up to be a banker. Or from Coca-Cola. The executives all dressed the same.

"My name is Walter Thurston." He handed her a card, and, sure enough, it was emblazoned with the SunTrust Bank logo. Executive Vice President. "My wife and I are dining with our friend tonight." He motioned to the booth where a stately woman with puffed blonde hair and elegant gold jewelry sat across from a tall, dark-headed man who was clearly uncomfortable. He glanced up, their eyes met briefly, and then he looked back to the cocktail in front of him.

"We saw you here, alone, and since it's a table for four, we thought you might have been expecting someone who didn't show up. We would love for you to join us." Stella saw the woman smiling broadly and discretely motioning her over.

"Oh no, I'm sorry. I couldn't," Stella said. She didn't know why exactly she couldn't, but she felt awkward. She patted the pad. "I'm working. I was to have dinner with a client who encountered a problem, so I thought I'd make the most of the night."

Stella always gave more detail than needed, but it was the way of her people. They were honest and always answered questions before they were asked.

Walter Thurston pressed gently. "Are you certain? We'd enjoy the additional company."

She smiled. "No, thank you very much. You are kind to offer."

"If you should change your mind, please, do come over."

He went back to his table and scooted in beside his wife. Stella smiled at the wife then at the man across from her. Azure blue. She would never forget it. The guy wore a cashmere sweater in the prettiest shade of blue she had ever seen. It was so stunning that it seemed like the rest of the restaurant and patrons were in black and white, and only that one shade of color stood out. It would forever linger in her memory.

She returned to working. Her pasta arrived and, as expected, was delicious. When the waiter came to clear the plates, she passed on dessert and asked for her check as she retrieved her lipstick. It was 9 P.M. and she wanted to get home for a good night's sleep. The waiter smiled and leaned toward her.

"Your check was paid." He motioned with his head to the booth behind him. "By the Thurstons."

Meanwhile, the Thurstons and their guest were trying not to look her way. A feeling of dread hit her. She had no choice but to go over and thank them, in person. Honestly, she was a bit aggravated by the ploy. To herself, she sighed heavily. She left an additional tip on the table, then picked up her purse, stood, and walked over to them.

"You are much too kind. You shouldn't have," she said.

Walter Thurston jumped to his feet. "Please meet my wife, Joyce Ann." The woman, whom Stella later discovered was Miss Georgia 1961, offered a beautifully manicured hand attached to an arm that jangled with several 14-karat gold bracelets.

"I'm sorry," said Walter. "I didn't get your name."

"I'm Stella Jackson." She shook Mrs. Thurston's hand.

Walter took her arm and turned her slightly toward their guest. For the first time, Stella saw what a handsome man he was. "Please meet our friend, Asher Bankwell."

Asher slid out of the booth, stood, and took her hand gallantly. He did not shake it. He took the tips of her fingers, held them gently, then made a slight bow. "Miss Jackson, it is my pleasure."

If Hollywood was casting for a new James Bond, someone ought to call Asher Bankwell. He was six feet or taller, with hair so darkly brown that it was almost black and swept back like John F. Kennedy, Jr.'s. He was strikingly thin, like a runner. His eyes were a golden brown, light, almost hazel. As handsome as he was, it wasn't his looks that captured her—it was his bearing and elegance. In the mountains, when someone met you, they thrust out their hand and pumped heartily. Her people were big, robust, and exuberant with conversation and gestures. Her people hollered. Not Asher Bankwell. He was debonair. His motions were small and gentle. His presence whispered.

She couldn't speak. She was swept away. That had never happened in her life. A one-sided smile slid up his face.

"Please, join us for coffee," he said. "We were just getting ready to order dessert. The crème brûlée here is sinfully good." He winked, and still she couldn't speak. He stepped aside, put his hand gently on her back, and gestured to the seat. "Please. And if you'd rather sit on the outside so you can make a quick escape, that will be fine. Just as long as you join us." Charm sprang forth from every one of his pearly white, perfectly straight teeth.

She nodded, thinking at the same time that she was so glad her hair looked great *and* that she had reapplied lipstick.

"Thank you," she said in her best imitation of a cultivated voice. She smoothed her pretty yellow dress under her and slid into the booth.

By the time the crème brûlée arrived, she was madly in love.

❦

Stella jerked the quilt over her head and turned her face into the pillow as small tears dribbled from her eyes. She had already used up the big tears. Hers had been a storybook romance—simple girl marries well. Well above herself, for sure. On the roof, the pinging turned to more of a drumming roar. Rain became ice. At that moment, her bedroom door opened and her mama peeped in.

"Hey," Mrs. Jackson said softly. "Just checkin' on you."

"I'm listenin' to the rain." When she came home, Stella always took back to dropping the "g" from the ends of words. She tried to clear the frog from her throat. "It sounds like it's turnin' to ice."

Her mama pushed the door open a bit more and stepped in. "It is. I'm glad I insisted on Chatty spendin' the night. The roads to Atlanta have been a mess."

Stella sat up, tucked her hair behind her ears, and sniffed, "That's right, Mama. The roads to Atlanta have been a mess."

And, again, the tears poured down her cheeks.

Chapter Three

The day that Stella Faye Jackson married Jasper Asher Bank-well III was the second happiest day of her life. The happiest day had been three months earlier when he bought out the entire dining room of Veni Vidi Vici so he could propose.

Stella was so crazy in love, so caught up with the charming Asher, that she paid little mind to her surroundings that night. By osmosis, because she had been there so many times, she knew that the wood was dark, the walls a light beige, and the arched doorways a nod to Tuscany architecture. Soft lighting, candles, and piped-in music of Italian singers and songs added to the atmosphere. She and Asher were side by side in the same booth where they first sat together one year earlier. She did not then, now, or ever want to make a hasty retreat from Asher.

Dressing for her dates with Asher became an anticipated happiness. She loved planning what to wear and took a pleasure in her beauty that she had not known before. Her mama always said, "Pretty is as pretty does," and pushed both of her daughters to concentrate on inner beauty and kindness rather than outer looks. Asher, however, made it clear that her beauty was what had drawn him to her initially. She didn't mind. Whatever she had that made Asher love her was just fine. The previous week, while shopping at Nordstrom, she had come across an ankle-length sheath dress with tight sleeves in a deep Irish green. With her red hair and deep green eyes, it was quite fetching. She was also wearing a strand of pearls with a diamond clasp that Asher had given her for Christmas along with the matching earrings that had been her Valentine's Day surprise. Their salads finished, they pulled themselves out of the hand-holding, snuggling of young lovers when the waiter came to deliver their pasta. It was only then that Stella realized the restaurant was quiet. She looked around.

"Asher! There is no one else here except for us! How can that be? It's Wednesday night."

He smiled sweetly. "It's also one year, two weeks, and one day since the night we met here." He took her hands in his. "I paid the restaurant to close to everyone else. I wanted it to be just the two of us."

She drew back in surprise. "That must have cost you a small fortune!" Her frugality and sense of money was so different from that of this man whose great-great-great-grandfather had built the family wealth on railroading. Then, each Bankwell generation had increased that money in different ways: commercial real estate in the late 1800s, Coca-Cola investments in the 1930s, residential real estate in post-World War II America, and the stock market in the boom years of the 1970s and 1980s. Asher's father, Jasper, was the last one to add significantly to the family's worth, which put a great deal of pressure on Asher to prove his merit, particularly to his mother, Miss Caroline. He was still looking for the right opportunity. Stella had absolute confidence that he would find it. Meanwhile, the Bankwell family, despite Bennett Sutton's thievery, was doing just fine. Miss Caroline, to quote a song from the movie *Funny Lady*, "had a wardrobe to choke Mrs. Astor's pet horse." And diamonds. And pearls. Her Buckhead estate, on five acres of prime real estate, brimmed with antique silver, sets of expensive China, fine paintings—she even owned a John

Singer Sargent—and furniture from the eighteenth and nineteenth centuries. She turned up her nose at anything from the twentieth century, forth.

"Art Deco ruined the aesthetics of civilization," she said as she sniffed imperiously over a family dinner that included her friend, Beatrice Persephone, who was visiting from London. "It began an unappetizing march to the appalling modernistic designs of Mid-Century. It is truly sad what those who are not more properly trained view it as 'attractive.' The living rooms of America have become nothing more than a Salvation Army-like depository for ugly, faux leather sofas and ghastly oversized televisions. I do hope the situation is not as dire in London as it is here. You English have always been such a civilized society. Far more than the gauche Americans. Especially those who are nouveau riche." She wrinkled her nose slightly as though there were a foul smell nearby.

Stella knew nothing of Art Deco or Mid-Century designs, but as soon as she returned to her little stone carriage house with the character-strong enormous windows and French doors, she researched both. There was so much she didn't know, but she was willing and eager to learn. Asher was proud of her. He was patient with the trepidation she sometimes demonstrated when pushed into society gatherings as unfamiliar to her as a river baptizing was to him. They had been dating for only a month when he escorted her to a white tie benefit for the High Museum, which was initially funded in part by Robert Woodruff, chairman of Coca-Cola, after a plane filled with Atlanta arts patrons had crashed at Orly Field in Paris in 1962. The Atlantans had been on a grand tour of the European arts communities and had just taken off when the plane crashed and exploded, killing 122 of Atlanta's most devoted arts patrons. Of the people on board, Caroline Bankwell knew 97, including her best friend and bridge partner. In her grief, Miss Caroline had promised to fervently support the High after Mr. Woodruff and others raised the money to build a museum in the honor of their fallen friends. Stella's introduction to Atlanta society was the High benefit dinner chaired by Miss Caroline for a record tenth time.

Asher had bought her a dress at Saks, one he had selected. "Trust me," he said. "I know these people and what they will view as acceptable, particularly from an outsider." He addressed her worried expression by taking her in his arms and reassuring her. "You will be, unquestionably, the most beautiful woman there. You captured my heart the moment I saw you and I believe everyone will be equally enthralled." He pulled back, took her chin in his hand, and gave a small chuckle. "The most difficult will be my mother. She is highly critical of everyone. You won't be the exception. But after Ellie ran off with, as my mother says, 'such an uncivilized savage,' she is particularly harsh to anyone on whom I might cast an eye." He shrugged. "You might say that she doesn't trust my instincts. But I will defend myself by saying that Ellie's lineage was of the highest importance to Mother."

What a dazzling couple they made when they entered amid a group of well-turned-out folks, including women dressed in designer originals, each of which cost more than Stella earned in a year. Asher wore his custom-made tux with tails, starched white shirt, white waistcoat, and tie. A white silk adorned his breast pocket. He looked like the hero of every English drama series Stella had devoured on PBS when she was growing up watching one of the four channels their farm got by antenna. Her dress for the benefit was long, and its silver sequined fabric clung to her curves in the most ladylike of ways. Her mane of red hair was stacked in a pile of tousled curls with wispy pieces that framed her face. From his aunt, Asher had borrowed a pair of large earrings with pear-shaped diamonds that dangled from large pearls.

The room stopped. You could hear it. Feel it. They were an undeniably dazzling pair. Asher also had that "first wife" drama attached to him, so for three years his circle had hoped—some had even bowed their heads and prayed—that he would find happiness again and, at the same time, find a loving mother for poor Neely. Suddenly, from the side of the ballroom swooped forth a large man whose formal tailcoat fit perfectly across the girth of his stomach. He did not walk. He waltzed, carrying a full martini while not spilling a drop despite his rapid approach.

"My heavens to Betsy!" exclaimed the cherubic man with a huge, radiant smile. "Venus has arrived! Who knew she had red hair? I always assumed she was dark, like Cleopatra." He took a sip of the martini and eyed Stella from head to toe as if she were a fine piece of art he was studying. "I have always been of the high opinion that this is exactly how Maud Gonne looked. She must have been this ravishing to have a bevy of men madly in love with her." He stopped, took a breath, and placed a hand to his heart dramatically. "Yeats. He loved her so." He cast his eyes upward. "*I spread my dreams before you. Tread softly because you tread on my dreams.*" He placed one hand across his waist, held the martini glass high, and bowed. "I am Chatham Balsam Colquitt, IV." He winked. "But most importantly, I, henceforth, am your mere lowly servant, one who is now a prisoner captured by your beauty."

Asher placed his left hand over Stella's, where she clung to his right arm. He leaned closer to her. "This, dear Stella, I offer to you as the crown jewel of characters in our treasure chest. Chatham speaks frequently in italics and most often about himself. His wit is quick and his trust fund vast."

"Trust *funds*," Chatham interrupted, then made a sweeping motion with his unengaged hand. "But do go on. It's not often that one can hear what Buckhead's Prince Charming has to comment about him."

Asher cleared his throat. "As I was saying, he has far too much time and money on his hands, which has made him the encyclopedia and the directory of the entire 404 and 770 area codes. His specialty is 404, since that is old Atlanta within the perimeter."

"Now, Asher, please do not fail to acknowledge that I have an abundance of knowledge on those in the 912 area code since my family roots go deep into Savannah. Chatham County. Colquitt County." He took another sip of martini. "It is the 706 area code—those mountain hoodlums to the north—of which I know little. We count our inheritance in fine silver pieces. They count theirs in cast-iron skillets."

Asher's face paled. He glanced sideways to Stella, who held her shoulders back, offered her hand, and said, "Nice to meet you, Chatham. I am Stella Jackson." She paused for a beat. "Of the 706 area code. I rise up from a tribe of hoodlums north of Cleveland." She smiled beatifically. "I have two cast-iron skillets. One from my grandmother Jackson—it was her favorite, she used it every day—and one that Mama bought me, which she spent weeks seasoning in the oven. So it would cook perfectly."

Chatham began choking on a sip of martini while Asher, grinning from ear to ear, slapped him on the back, laughing. "What a glorious day this is!" Asher proclaimed. "Chatham has been given a much overdue comeuppance, and I have fallen deeper in love with the woman who wrought such an unexpected joy."

It began like that, a friendship of two unlikely people who became as thick as mountain-made molasses. To ward off his embarrassment, Chatham recovered quickly and insisted that they sit at his table, then promptly switched place cards to make it happen.

"I put the Wighams over there. I only invited them to fill out my table because everyone else I knew was already coming."

"Are they from the 706 area code?" Stella smiled coquettishly.

"678," he shot back quickly. "The worst. It started out as an area code for cell phones, and then so many new people—many of them Yankees—moved in that it is now used residentially. Stella, please, sit by me. It will be my earnest endeavor throughout the evening to repair your first impression of me. You will find me, I am certain, to be immensely entertaining. One of life's great sins is to be boring."

Stella barely had any time to spare for her beloved Asher that night because Chatham—who insisted that she call him "Chatty"—filled her ear with commentary on the people around them.

"There is the most honorable Andrew Young," he said, throwing a salute toward the former mayor and ambassador. "When he ran for mayor, I did more than just contribute a copious amount of money. *I stuffed envelopes.* I took myself right down to his campaign office and I worked for, oh, I don't recall how long. Maybe forty-five minutes or an hour. A *long* time."

Before Stella could reply, Chatty nudged her, turning his eyes toward an elderly woman who was shuffling by. Her hair, a shampoo and set, no doubt, was teased into a bouffant and dyed jet black. Her face had been lifted so many times that it was hard to see character, only stretch. Her eyebrows were penciled darkly and her lipstick was shockingly red.

"Dora Vandergriffin," he mumbled from the corner of his mouth. When he was quite sure that she had passed out of earshot, though she was half-deaf, he continued. "She was a great beauty, people say. She claims that Warhol once did a lithograph of her, similar to the ones he did of Jackie and Marilyn. Back when Dora was a high fashion model in New York. Yet no one has ever seen hide nor hair of it. I saw a photo of her with Jean Shrimpton, and at that point she was fifteen years past her prime, yet she was even more beautiful than the much younger Shrimpton. That was a long time ago. About a hundred years. In fact, I am certain that it was *before* Pickett's Retreat at Gettysburg."

"Pickett's Charge," Stella corrected him.

"You say to-may-to, I say to-MAH-to," he quipped. Stella was to learn that Chatty's high intelligence and profound education equipped him well with words and observations. It was hard to outduel him. Asher was engaged in conversation with a gentleman to his left, so Stella and her new friend kept "discussing" people. The master of ceremonies began asking everyone to please move to their seats, and slowly they drifted to their tables.

"Hello, Chatty." A long, gorgeous arm bathed in diamond bracelets and rings floated down between Stella and Chatty and rested on his shoulder. He turned his entire body toward the arm, not just his head, and then suddenly jumped to his feet.

"Annabelle!" He air-kissed each cheek. "You are positively stunning."

And she was. But it was a bit too much. She wore a halter dress of red shimmer with red feathers along the hemline and a neckline that plunged to her navel area, which wasn't to be noticed since she was amply spilling out of it. She wore a diamond rope necklace with an enormous solitaire hanging from it so that it dangled between her substantial breasts. Diamonds of equal size hung from her earlobes. Her makeup was thick, accented by two pairs of false eyelashes and tons of thick, blonde hair cascading down her back. She looked like a movie star. Or a Las Vegas showgirl. Or perhaps...

Annabelle smiled demurely, which was necessary to tone down the loudness of her presentation. "Chatham, dear, you say the sweetest things. The words just flow from your mouth."

Chatty continued to fawn over her until Annabelle glanced down at Stella, then over to Chatty, indicating she wanted an introduction.

"Where are my manners? Stella Jackson, please meet the sweetheart of Atlanta. This is Annabelle Zimmerman."

"Honeycutt." She smiled and batted her eyes. "It's been Honeycutt for over a year. Can you believe I've had a whole year with that wonderful, adorable Lyndon? Oh, here he comes, now."

The wonderful, adorable Lyndon stretched in height only to her formidable bosom and wore a toupee that sat at a slight angle on his head. He was at least thirty years older, though it was hard to guess Annabelle's age. Botox. Fillers. Stella turned in her seat to see them both better and shook hands with them. Annabelle's shake was weak and unwelcoming, as though she really didn't want to touch Stella. Chatty continued to effuse over both until the emcee said firmly, "Please take your seats. We will begin in two minutes."

The wonderful, adorable Honeycutts said their good-byes, and Asher, who had not seen them because he was immersed in conversation, was interrupted by Annabelle, who placed a bejeweled hand on his shoulder as she started to go.

"Hello, Asher." She lingered, waiting for Asher to see her. The look on his face was a mixture of emotions—awe, intrigue, uncertainty. It was hard to say, but Stella knew this: it was an odd expression. Asher stood. He was a gentleman. He bowed slightly.

"Good evening, Annabelle. You look lovely as always."

She feigned a blush. "And you look handsome as always." She placed her hand on his broad shoulder and fluttered her two pairs of eyelashes at him.

"Annabelle, please!" wonderful, adorable Lyndon snapped hatefully from several feet away. A fury crossed his eyes. "Now."

She did a wiggle with her bronzed, beautiful shoulder. "Oops. My husband is calling. I'm an obedient wife. As long as I'm a wife." She winked. "Ciao, y'all." She prissed off but stopped and glanced back. "We've just returned from two heavenly weeks in our villa in Rome."

"Rome, Georgia, or Rome, Italy?" Chatty teased then smiled innocently. A huff poured over Annabelle's face, but she said nothing. She just stomped off, leaving a trail of red feathers flying behind her.

The moment she was gone, Chatty started in on her. "You have just come face-to-face with the biggest jezebel in Atlanta. I would call her something a bit racier but my mother raised me to be a gentleman." He rolled his eyes. "Her reputation stretches from here to New York with plenty of rest stops in between. I must say she is dressed quite appropriately to represent who she is."

Stella already felt comfortable with Chatty, so her sense of humor emerged. "Really? Well, by the way you were flitting around and flattering her, I would have thought you were her best friend on earth."

He waved her off, then picked up his napkin and placed it in his lap with particular care. "It is better to be friends with the beast than to be chewed up by the monster. She is not merely a man-eater. She *devours* men. I am one of the few men in Atlanta who will neither date nor marry her." He paused and smiled. "Because I am a *confirmed* bachelor, a choice I made long ago when I saw how women dilly-dally with your emotions and buy, buy, buy. I will not have a woman going through all my money at a rapid pace of spending. I can do that on my own."

"How long have you known her?" Stella asked. Asher had reached over and placed his hand lovingly on her knee while he spoke to the couple across the table.

"Since she first stormed into Atlanta like Sherman. She is on her *fourth* husband. Maybe fifth, come to think of it. She marries for a lot of money then keeps it when they divorce. I would think she has enough money to fund her 401K now, so that she could quit her job of marrying. Honey, I am certain she fills out her marriage license in pencil then just erases it and puts in a new name."

Stella was quiet. She looked at Asher, who felt her gaze and leaned over to touch her cheek with his forehead. He squeezed her hand. She was somewhat disquieted by the encounter with Annabelle.

Still, she did not know that she had just met her undoing.

Chapter Four

"If you ask me," Chatty said as he poured cream into his coffee, "this *disaster* all began with that homemade wedding dress."

Stella loved Chatty, and in good times he was a constant enjoyment because of his wit and colorful view on life and people. But she did wish her mama had not asked him to spend the night. Her nerves, what little was left of them, needed a break. And as long as His Highness was in the farmhouse, that was not going to happen. He meant well, but he just didn't know better. Apparently, his parents had neglected to teach him that he was not the center of the universe. Chatty had already pressed Stella's mama into service, asking her to iron his clothes, then ambled into the kitchen, stretching his back and moaning as though he had slept on the floor—allowing as to how he would never take for granted his luxurious Porthault sheets or his 1,000-thread-count down comforter or his goose-feather pillows.

"At a much later point in my life, when I recollect on the night spent here, I am certain I will be grateful for the experience of roughing it. My territory of understanding has been enlarged." Stella shot him a look but Martha Annie ignored him. She quite often spoke her mind frankly, so she could take as well as she gave. She knew the farmhouse was edging toward rustic compared to Chatty's Colonial estate. Even his carriage house, with its gleaming marble kitchen and sunken tub, was nicer than their house with its bathroom fixtures from the

1960s, which they considered modern since the farmhouse was 100 years old.

"Chatty, you sit here." Mrs. Jackson gestured toward the well-worn Windsor chair that had once been her husband's. She opened the oven and pulled out a pan of steaming, home-made buttermilk biscuits. She had already set the eggs, bacon, grits, and sawmill cream gravy on the table. Chatty inhaled a lungful of the delicious aroma and began shoveling eggs onto his plate.

"On second thought, perhaps roughing it is gentler than I once supposed." Once he had scarfed down his breakfast—an unusual sight because he normally ate with the most precise manners, taking small bites and eating French style with a knife and his fork turned down—he launched back into a discourse on Stella's troubles and how she had gotten there in the first place.

Stella did not, at the moment, care how the trajectory began; she only cared how she would survive it and rebuild her life. Her heart was broken, her life shattered, and, worst of all, she was certain she had written her obituary. This absurd notion had run through her mind for a week. Where she came from, obituaries were cherished, clipped from the newspapers, and often tucked into a treasured book or the Bible. She kept torturing herself with the thought that when she died, the *Atlanta Journal Constitution* and the *White County News* would both begin the story with something like this:

> *"Stella Jackson Bankwell, 98, has died. Though hers was a long life of varying adventures and accomplishments, she is, perhaps, best remembered for the night that she had a very public breakdown at the austere Buckhead*

Country Club. At the time, she was married to Jasper Asher Bankwell III, whose grandfather had once been an Ambassador to St. James Court (the highest honor among embassies), and she had been a quiet but productive member of Atlanta society. Later, in a memoir she published when she was 80, she explained that numerous legal and behavioral problems with her stepson as well as the suspicion that her husband was having an affair with a well-known, multi-married beauty had driven her off the edge. In her book, she wrote, 'If I could take back any 15 minutes of my life, it would be that night at the country club. I did not relish the fame—infamy, if you will— that those 15 minutes brought. I am quite certain that those few minutes will be the lead paragraph of my entire life when I die. The sensationalism of that night will follow me to the grave and will be mixed with the dirt that covers me.'"

Chatty had finished breakfast and was on his fourth cup of coffee—caffeine ramped him up to a place that made him almost unbearable—when he made the comment about the wedding dress. Mrs. Jackson had gone outside to feed the dogs.

"Yes ma'am." He folded his arms across his broad chest, rested his chin in his hand, and studied on it for a second. He nodded firmly when he was convinced of his theory. "It was the homemade wedding dress. I went on record *then* as saying I did not think it was a good idea for you to stroll down the aisle of the revered Peachtree Presbyterian Church in front of Atlanta's elite in a dress that you and your mama stitched up on a Singer sewing machine using thread you bought from Walmart." He took a pinch of golden crust from another biscuit and, with his normal precise manners, placed it in his mouth. "Truth be told, that homemade wedding gown was more of your undoing than your public, unseemly meltdown."

The phone on the kitchen wall began to ring. In the hallway, Mrs. Jackson answered the extension while Chatty added another barb. "Honestly, Stella, in our circle of designer couture, no one ever heard of 4-H. You certainly did not have to parade it down the streets of Peachtree in a peasant dress. Our people *do not care* about 4-H sewing ribbons or how many you have accumulated. They care only about which group of debutantes you were in and which designers you favor or, rather, favor you."

Stella, standing at the counter about to pour herself another cup of coffee, slammed down the mug. She was dangerously close to something else unseemly. Chatty did not have the sense to realize that she was a long way from her formerly pleasing personality.

"Chatty! SHUT UP!" It was loud and hateful, something akin to the tone she had used with Asher and Annabelle Honeycutt, whom Stella had long called "Fancy Panties," but Chatty, from the start, had contended that Stella overestimated Annabelle's inclination to wear underwear.

As was her misfortune of late, she was screaming at Chatty just as her mama walked in the kitchen.

"Stella Faye Jackson," she said sternly with that don't-cross-me look that all mamas have at one time or the other. "Chatty is a guest in our home, and you won't speak to him in that manner. This is *not* the Buckhead Country Club." She arched one eyebrow as her final warning.

Stella's shoulders sank. She put her elbows on the counter and leaned forward to drop her face in her hands. She rubbed her temples while Chatty, acting like the naughty little boy who had been blessed rather than blamed, smiled happily and picked up another biscuit to reward himself.

"Marlo's on the phone," her mama said. "She's worried sick." As Stella shuffled by on the way to the hall phone, Mrs. Jackson said, "Try to act right with her. Don't bite her head off as you just did with Chatty." She caught Stella's arm. "Don't forget, young lady, that you got yourself into this mess. We're all just doin' our best to get you through it."

Normally, Stella would have commented, but her mama's words chastened her. She had been raised that you took responsibility for the problems you caused and the people you hurt. Stella, however, was still trying to reconcile who had actually caused the problem and who had simply reacted to it.

"Hello," she said glumly into the receiver to her best friend since childhood. "I hope you haven't called to join in on beatin' me up, too."

The day that Stella Jackson Bankwell fell from grace in a most public manner was unusually warm for February in Atlanta. It felt like the beginning of a false spring, the time of year that would cruelly trick the city's famed dogwoods, hydrangeas, and azaleas into blooming early, only to kill them in a sudden deep freeze a week or two later. It was Saturday before Valentine's Day, so she and Asher planned to attend the gala dinner that evening at the country club. After a restless night, she arose at 9 to discover a note near the coffee pot from Asher saying that he had an early tee time at the club. She threw a thick red shawl around her shoulders, pulled on a pair of warm boots with her black zebra-striped flannel pajamas, and went out to the veranda to settle into a cushioned rattan rocker. She sipped her coffee and absent-mindedly stared at the enormous magnolia tree to the right of the expensive pool that was built to resemble a lagoon. A small stone waterfall usually flowed into the pool, but both were without water for the winter. They always opened it by mid-May. Now, though, random dead leaves were scattered across the custom-made cover, and the landscaping looked bare, void of foliage, except for the magnolia with its glistening green leaves. Stella was drained, emotionally spent from the constant friction with Asher and the serious problems with Neely. The latest debacle included the Bannisters who lived next door, on Peachtree Circle, separated by a hedge of holly bushes. Two nights earlier, Neely had "borrowed" Devon Bannister's new Porsche, then crashed it into a light pole on Clairmont Road when the car overpowered him. Six stitches, four police charges, and an all-night go-around between Asher and Neely resulted in Asher's cousin, George, suggesting that Neely stay at their house for a few days while emotions cooled. That was a reprieve from one upsetting situation, but there was still excessive tension between Asher and Stella.

Though she could no longer recall exactly, it had all seemed to start with the disagreements over Neely. Asher refused to apply a firm hand to Neely's growing rebellion, always saying, "It's just a phase. He'll grow out of it," or "Cut him some slack. His mother left him when he was five. He is damaged."

Neely took out plenty of anger on Stella, who, after years of successful stepmothering, had become his target. His actions were hurtful and his words, which he chose to be deliberately mean, wounded deeply. In fact, they broke her heart. He berated her for her red hair, her mountain upbringing, and how she talked. These were his favorite topics, but there were others. One night, he went into a rampage over her grocery purchase of skim milk as opposed to whole milk.

"You should leave the grocery shopping to Lana Banana," he spat, referring to their longtime housekeeper. He had called her that since he was a child. "She has enough sense to know how to buy milk!" When Stella would collapse into tears, Neely would triumphantly grin and turn on his heels to leave.

Peachtree Cat, their rescued yellow tabby who lived in the abandoned car house that was now storage, ambled across the backyard. Stella remembered the night when she and Asher had found the kitten tucked under street curbing near their ivy-covered, white-washed brick Georgian in fashionable Ansley Park. It was about five years ago, before all the trouble started. They were out for an evening walk. Asher cuddled the poor, frightened kitten inside his jacket for comfort. That was the Asher she loved. The one who had romantically proposed at Veni Vidi Vici, pledging his forever love, and then watched as the manager of Tiffany at Phipps Plaza arrived with a tray of seven diamond rings of substantial size.

"My beautiful Stella, the choice is yours," he had said, lifting her left hand and kissing the ring finger. "As long as you choose me."

It was the most gorgeous feeling of her life, followed by three years of similar joy, one year of somewhat joy, and then five years of gradual unraveling, none of which had any joy. The past several months had been painful in a new way. Asher's irritation had subsided a bit. He smiled more and was more gregarious when they were out with friends. He even tolerated Miss Caroline with more patience. Normally, her motherly bossiness drove him to distraction. At first, Stella was grateful and began to relax. It was nice to see a truce in the war zone. Then, one day when Lana was out sick with the flu, Stella had gone into Asher's dressing room to get his laundry. She picked up his white tee shirts and a slight fragrance rose up. She put a shirt to her nose and sniffed hard. Perfume. And it wasn't hers. She went through every tee shirt and discovered that at least half of them had that fragrance. Suddenly, his good mood made sense.

There had been other small signs. Once, he had claimed to be playing golf with Devon Bannister, but that same afternoon, Stella had pulled into her driveway while Devon was getting the mail next door. She rolled down the car window.

"I thought you were playing golf this afternoon," she said after greeting him.

"Golf?" He looked quizzical. "I haven't played in two months." He opened his mouth as though to ask "Why?" but a sudden, knowing look crossed his eyes. "Oh, I'm helping Bonnie today. Honey-do-list, you know. And I'd better get back to work. Bye." And with that, he scooted up the drive before she could say another word.

All of this troubled her, and her nerves were frightfully on edge. She had refused Chatty's constant admonishment that she should get an antidepressant.

"I'm not depressed," she often responded. "I'm upset. There's a difference. I need to keep my wits about me so I can deal with everything clearly." Still, often were the early evenings when Asher had not returned from his office, she'd taken a single strong shot of Jack Daniels to calm the jitters. Until that point six months ago, she had never tasted whiskey.

Peachtree Cat loped after a bird, jumping up and pawing at the air. The bird was smarter and quicker, easily making the escape.

"I'm just like that cat," she said aloud to herself. "I'm chasing something I can't catch."

She did not know it then, but a catch was awaiting her inside the house.

&

Stella had finished her coffee then dragged herself back inside to the coffee pot. She was meandering through the breakfast room when she heard a phone buzzing. She could seldom keep track of her cell phone—it meant little to her and she asked people to call the house phone if they needed her—so she assumed it was hers and began looking. It stopped while she was in the midst of her search. A few minutes later, as she was making cheese toast, it began buzzing again. This time, she found it where Asher always laid his phone and keys: in a red, ceramic basket on a counter in the mud room. It was Asher's phone. The call ended before she could answer. In a moment, an unfamiliar number came up as a missed call, and her blood ran cold. She knew, she just knew that the number would lead her to something she didn't want to know but something she should. She paced the floor for fifteen minutes, wringing her hands, fretting and tearful. Finally, she decided to call the number from their home phone, which was unlisted so it would not show up on caller ID.

It took several seconds before she could push the last number. When finally she did, her heart was pounding in her ears and she felt swimmy-headed. Someone answered.

"Good morning, Five Points Hair Drama," a young girl said. Stella hung up and dialed Chatty.

"You know everything," she said as soon as Chatty picked up.

"That is correct," he responded.

"Where does Annabelle Honeycutt get her hair done?" Stella was breathing hard.

His reply was quick. "Jonathan Milford's salon in Five Points. Hair Drama."

The drama, it seemed, was just beginning.

Chapter Five

When, on that Saturday of the Valentine Gala, Asher returned late from his "early golf game" in an exceedingly good mood, Stella said not a word. She had decided to wait and get her ducks in order since she didn't have hard evidence. Too, she could be wrong. That's what she told herself. That's what she tried to believe, anyway.

This, in retrospect, probably led to her undoing. She was, after all, a pressure cooker with steadily mounting steam, waiting to explode just like the day when her mama's pressure canner had exploded on the stove. It was a terrifying sound—this was in the days when you had to watch the jiggling of the gage—but, just as bad, they had spent two days cleaning the potato pieces from the ceiling, walls, cabinets, and all the crevices.

Stella was somewhat curt but mindful to keep her tone even. Asher noticed nothing, such were his high spirits. Each headed toward their separate dressing areas that bookended the large master suit. His was manly with black marble countertops, black and white tile, a shower, and dark wood. Hers was feminine and light with white marble counters and floor, deep pink-striped wallpaper, white cabinets, a lighted vanity area, and an enormous tub. Both had generous-sized, walk-in closets, and each had a small, discrete safe to hold valuables.

"I'm going to dress," she said nonchalantly, passing through the bedroom where he stood in front of the television, watching sports scores. He nodded without a glance, and she went into her bathroom/dressing area and closed the door. She slumped onto the rich, rose-colored velvet slipper chair, trying to gather her emotions. Despite the finger of whiskey she threw back a bit earlier, she was shaking. Her heart hurt so much that it made her physically sick with an upset stomach and pounding head. The gold filigree clock on her vanity reminded her it was time to dress. She pulled herself up and went into the closet.

At that moment, she both cared and did not care what she wore. She wanted Asher to admire her, but she also had no heart, especially since she realized she had gained eight or ten pounds over the last few weeks while stress-eating. The red velvet cupcakes from the high-priced bakery on Juniper Street had comforted her daily, while Lana's homemade chicken and dumplings felt like a warm blanket in the midst of a chill.

Finally, she chose a deep blue, floor-length sheath encrusted with iridescent sequins of the same blue. It had always looked terrific on her, but it was form fitting. That was the problem. The form it used to fit was not the form she had now. It wouldn't even consider zipping closed. If there was any way to feel worse about herself than she already did from a verbally abusive stepson and a probably-cheating husband, it was failing to fit into a favorite dress and then looking in the mirror to see a contorted version of a once-familiar body. She sniffed back the tears and rummaged until she found a Carolina Herrera that was diaphanous and flowing. It was four layers of tissue weight chiffon, each a different color: beige, red, deep pink, light lavender. A floating layer of chiffon, dyed in stripes of those four colors, attached to the back shoulders, draping heavenly and fluttering softly behind as she walked. It was very

Grace Kelly. She supposed the cape would hide her rear end that had expanded and any rolling folds of flesh on her back. It was more generously sized than the blue dress, but when the zipper got to the waist, it wouldn't go further. It was a situation where she knew she could help push the dress together while someone finished zipping it. The only person that could be was Asher since he was the only other person around.

"Oh, no, I can't," she thought in despair. "I can't possibly let him know how much weight I've gained." Frantically, she searched through her closet but could not find anything else that would zip. She had no choice. She did her makeup and hair, spritzed on perfume, selected a pair of long, dangling gold earrings studded with diamonds from her safe, then took a deep breath to compose herself.

She walked out into the bedroom where Asher was putting black onyx studs in his tuxedo shirt. She tried to sound casual.

"Asher, I need a little help getting this dress zipped, if you don't mind." She smiled sweetly then cast her eyes away as soon as she saw his eyes dart with the truth of her situation.

Wordlessly, he moved toward her while she put her hands on her waist and pushed with all her might. Still, he struggled to zip it.

"Can you push your waist in more?" he asked through his grunts. She wanted to cry. But she pushed harder, and finally he got it through the stubborn spot and zipped it to the neck. It was an uncomfortable fit, but she would suffer through it. Asher picked up his onyx cufflinks and fiddled with one.

"How many cupcakes does it take to make a dress that tight?" There was undeniable sarcasm in his tone.

The words shot through her heart as she swirled to face him. His expression was cool with a wicked glint in his eyes.

He chuckled unkindly, then returned to his cuffs. With arms dropped to her side, she squeezed her hands into balls until her nails cut into her palms. She held her tongue and walked away.

The pressure cooker gathered more dangerous steam. The explosion was less than an hour away.

∾

The Bankwells, nursing a serious strain between them, walked into the grand ballroom of the country club, where cocktails would be served before dinner in the main dining room. Asher was still James Bond handsome, and Stella, despite a thickened waist, was elegant and strikingly pretty in the vividly colored, flowing dress.

The first to approach was Devon Bannister, who extended his hand and asked with compassion about Neely. They exchanged a few uncomfortable words—it's embarrassing when your teenage son steals your neighbor's sports car and wrecks it—then Devon patted Asher on the shoulder before moving on. "It'll be alright, pal. Just hang in there."

Miss Caroline glided over, dressed in a matronly black dress with long sleeves and wearing the elaborate diamond collar necklace that she favored with a plain neckline. It was a stunning complement to her glistening silver hair. "Hello, dears." She lifted her cheek for her son to kiss then reached over and squeezed Stella's hand. "You make me so proud. You are such a beautiful couple." Until what happened a short time later, looks and money mattered the most to Miss Caroline. Later, she would decide, dignity should be placed above looks. She glanced over at Devon and then back to Asher and Stella.

"Was he creating any discomfort?" she asked with an arched eyebrow. Miss Caroline was a fierce matriarch of the family, and even if her grandson had caused the problem, she would find a way to turn the blame.

"Actually, no," Stella replied tartly, her nervous condition overcoming her good sense. "He was taking the higher road and comforting *us*." Levelly, she eyed her mother-in-law. "I would think that all of Atlanta has grown weary of viewing us sympathetically since we are the ones who are unable to get Neely under control. Surely, at this point, sympathy is running out." Stella had never spoken to Miss Caroline that way. First, she had been taught to respect her elders. Second, she was normally intimidated by her mother-in-law. She couldn't believe what she heard coming out of her mouth.

Fury leapt into Miss Caroline's deep blue eyes, but Asher stepped in before she could speak. "Mother, Esther Marcus called my company yesterday to reserve a jet for a New York shopping trip in April. She said she planned to invite you. Has she called yet?"

Miss Caroline's stare was icy. "She has not. I am uncertain that I would accept the invitation because she cheated at bridge the other day."

"Mother, you think everyone cheats at bridge unless you win."

Chatty breezed up, a libation in hand. "This is fabulous. Two of my favorite women. You both look marvelous." He glanced down at Stella's tight waistband, and she knew that he saw the weight gain. He never missed a detail. He looked back up at her and smiled knowingly. Chatty knew more than just what he saw in her waistline. He knew she suspected that something was going on between Asher and Annabelle. Of course, he had refused to allow her to end their call that morning until she had told him about phoning the beauty salon. And she had told him about finding the fragrant scented tee shirts.

"Lovely dress, Stella. Oscar?"

"Carolina Herrera," she replied, throwing an eye toward the bar. She certainly could use something to steady her nerves.

"Oh yes, they are so similar in style. Both refined and classy."

"Chatham, you, as always, look healthy." Asher grinned and winked at his childhood friend.

"Thank you, Asher, for noticing. I walked for five minutes this morning around the garden," he shot back. "It was such a lovely day. I am pleased that the results are immediately evident. Perhaps I'll try it again, another time."

What happened next would be a blur for Stella in the days that lay ahead, but she knew this: she would forever regret it. Annabelle Honeycutt, aka Fancy Panties, wiggled over, looking like a million dollars. Her mass of blonde extensions fell over her fake boobs, which were covered by a dress at least one size too small. By choice. Not by cupcakes. It was a deep red, sequined dress with a jewel neckline and long sleeves. The dress was emblazoned with pink, yellow, and green floral appliqués, also in sequins. The body-hugging part stopped at mid-thigh and then long, shimmering strands that looked like Christmas tree tinsel fringed to the ankles. Her sleeves, too, were festooned in tinsel, beginning at the elbows. Dolce & Gabbana. It was her "go-to" designer. She flashed dazzling teeth bleached unnaturally white. She was comfortable with the power of her beauty and allure. Asher eyed her with appreciation, a look that did not escape Stella.

"Hellooooo," Annabelle shrilled, dancing three fingers in the air. "Y'all all are looking wonderful tonight."

Miss Caroline gave her a frosty look then turned and walked off. Asher watched his mother, Stella watched him, and Chatty watched Stella. Annabelle watched no one, oblivious to it all. There was a moment of silence before Chatham Balsam Colquitt, IV spoke up.

"Annabelle, your hair is beautiful tonight. It seems a little different. Am I correct?" He smiled wickedly, glancing over at Stella before fixing his eyes on the woman who could never resist a compliment.

"You're the sweetest. Thank you for that observation. Jonathan added brighter highlights around my face. Just this morning, in fact. You're the first to notice." Her gorgeous lips formed a pout. "Lyndon never pays attention."

A chill shivered over Stella. Her heart, already low, plummeted to a new low. Chatty was quite pleased with himself, but when he saw the thunderstruck look on the face of his best friend, he immediately regretted his boldness. Asher noticed nothing other than Annabelle, who continued on. She never knew when to quit.

"Oh, Stella, how delightful to see you! Aren't you just the cutest thing?" She cast a knowing eye from Stella's head to her feet. "Marvelous shoes. Did you buy those from Ronnie at Saks? Isn't he the best personal shopper? Not a day goes by that he doesn't text me with photos of the most scrumptious treasures. And I always buy *everything*. I am his best Chanel customer." She paused. This was hard because she loved to talk. "Is that a Chanel dress?"

Asher smirked. He SMIRKED. "Whatever it is, it's too small by at least 10 pounds."

That was it.

Five years of suffering, three of sheer torment, including two of which were filled with despair and sleepless nights collapsed into one horrible moment that would forever be discussed and recalled at the Buckhead Country Club. Something snapped. The pressure cooker exploded. Stella glanced to the bar directly behind Asher and saw the bartender as he finished filling tall glasses of mint julep. She stomped to the bar, snatched a glass in each hand, charged back toward Fancy Panties and Asher then threw one each in their faces, the mint-accented bourbon landing on Asher's face a second behind the Botoxed face of Fancy Panties. Stella took two seconds to observe their stunned looks and then grabbed Annabelle's hair, pulled hard, and jerked a handful of extensions from her head. She threw them down and stomped on them.

"I HAVE HAD ENOUGH!!!" Stella screamed while the entire ballroom came to a stunned stop. "I am not as *stupid* as you two think I am! I know what's going on!" She stepped forward and pushed Annabelle's shoulders with all her might, causing Fancy Panties to tumble backwards over her five-inch-high Christian Louboutins and land hard on the hardwood floor of the Buckhead Country Club. Chatty would later report that he had been correct, as he always was: she wore no panties. Quickly, Annabelle scrambled up on her knees in a mass of tinseled disarray, trying to crawl frantically away from the raving lunatic who had just attacked her and seemed intent on coming after her. Meanwhile, she continued showing her tail to the crowd.

"Damnit, Stella! You've lost your mind!" Asher snapped as he rushed to help Annabelle to her feet.

Chatty slammed his fleshy hand over his mouth, his eyes bulging with shock. When he had jumped back to get out of Hurricane Stella's way, he had thrown the contents of his wine glass over his shoulder, and the Chardonnay—Chatty would tell everyone that it was an excellent year—drenched, of all people, Miss Caroline, who had turned at that moment to see what the commotion was all about. Before he could respond, retort, or retreat, his best friend turned on her heels and stormed out of the country club, looking for all the world like the Queen of Sheba as she held her head high and her chiffon cape fluttered gracefully in a cloud of disgraced glory. Behind her, several men, besides Asher, rushed to comfort the sobbing Jezebel.

"Rob, bring me our car, please," Stella instructed the valet. "We're in the silver sedan." Once safely inside, she called "Good riddance!" out the window then pressed the gas pedal on her new Jaguar, squealing her tires and leaving the opulent life behind.

That's how the socialite life ended for Stella Jackson Bankwell, but it's also where another story began.

Stella had a plan. Of sorts. She stopped by the Ansley Park house with its generous yards and long, brick-paved driveway. She disarmed the alarm, pulled off her high heels, tossed them in the midst of the grand foyer, then ran up the majestic staircase to the master suite and straight to her closet.

She pulled off the too tight dress and, without a second thought, wadded it up and tossed it in the nearby wastebasket. That went against every fiber of her frugal upbringing, but even given the wild state of her mind, she knew she would never want a reminder of her little escapade at the club. Goodbye, Grace Kelly. Hello, Country Girl. She grabbed a pair of boyfriend jeans that felt comfortable after the ill-fitting dress, an expensive white tee shirt, and a loose chambray shirt. She slipped into a pair of navy leather loafers from Tod's and grabbed a large navy Chanel bag. She opened the safe and pulled out $10,000 in cash—Asher had always insisted they keep cash in each of their safes, and thank goodness now for that—her marriage license, passport, four letters her mama had written to her in college, four pairs of Tiffany earrings, two antique necklaces (one handcrafted by Cartier's grandson for Marjorie Merriweather Post), a childhood photo of herself and her daddy, and the title to the Jaguar that Asher had recently gifted her. She dumped the cash, the valuables, and the contents from her usual purse, including credit card case, lip gloss, and a lovely red jeweled compact, into the Chanel bag. She was working at rapid speed, her heart pounding. She figured, at least she hoped, that it would take Asher a bit to snap out of the surreal experience, get his wits together, and figure out that she was gone in the Jag. Once he did, he would assume she had gone home and, most likely, come looking for her. She had to get out of there before that happened.

Earlier that day, after the beauty shop call, she had packed a bag with a few clothes, toiletries, cosmetics, and electronic tablet, then shoved it under the bed. While she was on the floor, lying on her bloated stomach trying to reach the suitcase, a sudden thought occurred: Asher's phone would receive a notification that she had disarmed the alarm. Her heart raced. She grabbed the Chanel bag and her suitcase and ran, as best she could with the weight of the haul, to the car. She opened the back door, threw everything inside, then jumped into the driver's seat. Her hands shaking, she turned the ignition, threw the car in reverse, and backed around so fast that she missed hitting a light pole in the turnaround by only two inches. She sped down the driveway—it seemed longer than it ever had—screeched to the left, and headed toward Peachtree. Before she was at the end of their street, she met Devon Bannister coming toward her in a black BMW. The streetlights were bright, giving her the opportunity to see that Asher was in the passenger seat. Devon was looking straight ahead, and Asher's head was turned toward his window.

Neither appeared to see her. She had escaped by no more than sixty seconds. Under her breath, she mumbled, "Thank you, Lord."

Within twenty minutes of creating the biggest scene ever enjoyed at Buckhead Country Club, she was turning from Peachtree Street onto the I-85 entrance ramp and heading north.

"North, toward home," she whispered, remembering the name of a memoir of Mississippi's Willie Morris, who had written that New York had become his true home. She, too, in a way, was leaving the South and heading north. To Turner's Corner, a small speck of a place where farms rollicked and the Appalachian Mountains and enormous trees grew together as closely as buildings in Atlanta. She glanced down at her dashboard clock. 7:47 P.M. Yes, that would be right. They had arrived at the country club—Stella tugging at her tight dress on the two-mile drive—around 6:45. In the length of one hour, her life had gone south, and now she was headed north.

She hit the button on her phone, gave it a voice command, and in a moment a gentle voice answered.

"Mama," she said. "Turn down my bed. I'm comin' home."

Chapter Six

"Asher called." Marlo plunged right in when she heard Stella's voice on the phone.

Stella and Marlo, who grew up on adjoining farmland, were cousins and best friends since childhood. Their mothers had been double first cousins because two Cain sisters had married two Satterfield brothers. They were solidly rooted together in family, memories, and similar journeys that had taken them from the Appalachian foothills to satisfying careers and marriages into noted families. Back before the true drama of life set in, back before they were adults, they always prepared the other for news by saying excitedly, "You will never believe what happened!" or "I have the biggest news!" or, as in this case, "Guess who called me?" It used to start with preamble and buildup, but over the past several years the news was consistently dramatic enough that each would get straight to the "headline," as they called it. Two days before the country club meltdown, Stella had called Marlo at her home in South Georgia and said simply, "Neely stole our neighbor's car, crashed it, and the police have him." A story like that needs no buildup.

Now, at the news that Asher had phoned Marlo, fear pushed its way up Stella's throat, tightening into a chokehold. Not that she wasn't expecting it. He had called the farmhouse three times. Martha Annie would not admit that Stella was sheltering there but assured him that she was okay. This was a big step for Martha Annie, who had always refused to lie to boys on her daughters' behalf. One night during high school, Stella was avoiding Edwin Hester after a horrible first date. She knew he'd call again. When the phone rang two days later as she and her mama washed up the supper dishes, Stella said urgently, "If that's Eddie, tell him I'm not here."

Her mama answered the phone, listened for a second, then said, "Yes, she is." She handed the phone to Stella, gave her a no-nonsense look, and said firmly, "I am not gonna lie for you."

But Asher Bankwell had met his match in Martha Annie Jackson. She was definitely from a different world, but in her hardscrabble life, nothing was more important than protecting family. She was not intimidated by him or his wealth. She did not avoid his calls. She answered, spoke in few words, then said, "That's all I'm gonna say. Good-bye, Asher."

When he called the third time, Martha Annie Jackson went on the offensive. "Instead of talking about Stella, let's talk about you, Asher, and what you've been up to. Your son has needed a father and you've been off skirt chasin' while drivin' my little girl to a nervous breakdown. You take care of your child and I'll take care of mine."

That was the last time Asher had called the farmhouse. "I put his little cart in the road," she claimed, using a mountain expression for getting rid of someone.

He had called Chatty, too, which he had told Stella the previous evening. "Chatham, if anyone knows where Stella is, it's you."

"Asher, it's so nice to hear from you," Chatty had replied in a saccharine voice. "Why does it seem like you only call when you need something?"

Asher ignored the sarcasm. "As you were witness to the other night, Stella is not stable. I'm concerned about her and need to find her so I can help her. Her mother won't tell me anything." He tried to make the words convincing, but the heart was missing. Chatty could see there was more involved than Stella's health and well-being.

"Stella will be more stable without you anywhere in the nearby vicinity."

"Chatham, please."

"I shall not tell."

"That would be the first time you have known something you didn't tell."

"I'm team Stella. She is my best friend." Chatham was stubborn when he wanted to be. And also when he wasn't trying.

"We've been friends since kindergarten," Asher reminded him.

"We've *known* each other since kindergarten," Chatham said pointedly. "Stella is my friend because *she* did not let the air out of my bicycle tires when we were ten. *She* did not short-sheet my bed at summer camp, and let's see…who was it who asked Julia Brandeberry to the tenth grade homecoming dance before I could? Who was it who knew I was going to ask her but stepped in before I could? Let me see." He paused dramatically. Chatty did not like to miss an opportunity to be theatrical. "Who was that? Oh, yes, it was Asher Jasper Bankwell the *third*." Chatham enjoyed poking at Asher for being merely a third when he, himself, was a fourth in his family line.

Asher was getting plenty exasperated but didn't want to show his hand. He needed Chatham's help. "I've never known you to hold a grudge," he cajoled. "You're always the bigger person."

Chatty ignored it. "And then there was that rare occasion when I went out into my garden and, upon that rare occasion, was bitten by a mosquito that resulted in me getting the West Nile virus. Stella was there."

"You had the flu."

"Misdiagnosed. Nonetheless, Stella never left my side through the grueling days of my touch-and-go, lingering between here and eternity. She held my hand. She comforted me."

"You were at Quick Care for two hours. At most."

"I shall remain loyal to Stella always. Good-bye, Asher. Please, do not tell Annabelle that I said 'hello.'" He replaced the receiver into the cradle with a hard thump and sighed with the satisfaction brought on by a phone that you can slam down. He smiled and said to himself, "I shall always have a landline and phone for that very reason: so I can hang up with purpose on irritants like Asher Bankwell."

❧

After Marlo's news, Stella let the silence hang in the air, strung through the phone lines between Turner's Corner and the Georgia Golden Isle of St. Simons. When Marlo's grandparents, Lester and Mozelle Mincey, retired from General Motors in Atlanta, they had moved to what was then a sleepy little island covered in live oak trees with hanging moss, shimmering beaches, a beautiful blue ocean with white, billowing waves that entertained them for hours, a village of small shops, and a rich history that included Christ Church, Fort Frederica, a lighthouse, the King and Prince hotel, and the 1200-acre Musgrove Plantation that had been owned by the RJ Reynolds family for decades. Stella and Marlo were allowed to spend two weeks there with the Minceys every summer, then ten days after Christmas. These trips began when they were six and continued until college ended. It was their happy place, sealed in their memories forever as the perfect plot of earth on which to tread, particularly barefooted. Marlo had married an island native, Tatum Sloan, and settled into the beautiful sunlit paradise where fishing boats and freight ships, each carrying foreign-made cars to drop at the nearby Brunswick port, dotted the coast daily. The Sloans were a much-appreciated, highly regarded real estate family, but Tate had ventured off the path and become a veterinarian, graduating from Auburn. He returned to the island to practice with old Dr. Pike. When Pike retired a few years later, Dr. Tatum Sloan bought out his practice while Marlo worked with her in-laws, Alton and Evelyn, selling real estate and managing the rental properties they owned.

"Hello? Are you still there, Stellie?" Marlo asked.

"Yes." She sighed. "What did you tell him?"

"I haven't talked to him. I was showing a cottage for sale near the lighthouse. Remember the little white one with the light blue shutters, the tiny front porch, and the screen door? It was one of your favorites. Sweet ocean view, but it's near a public access for the beach so it's a harder sale than you'd imagine."

"Oh, yeah," Stella replied with no enthusiasm.

"Anyway, he called and left a message. I wouldn't have taken his call anyway. I am far smarter than that. He wants me to call him back. I'm not planning to unless you say differently."

"Good. Don't. I turned my phone off the moment I got on the interstate and haven't turned it back on since. I don't want to hear from him, or most anyone else in Atlanta, and I don't want him to locate me through the phone's tracking."

"I understand, my dear one. But you're going to have to talk to him sooner or later."

"I prefer to wait until the statute of limitations has run out," Stella shot back.

"What?" Marlo sounded puzzled. "What are you talking about? Surely, Fancy Panties won't be dumb enough to press assault charges."

"I hadn't even thought of that." Another worry clouded her mind. "Marlo, I'm afraid Asher might try to commit me for psychiatric reasons. What I did was completely unlike me. It was so public. So many witnesses. This is certain: he is not calling to apologize. Or to sincerely check on my well-being. He has a plot of some kind. I look back at all the businesses he's gone through, now this jet service, and I realize he's always scheming. I preferred to see it as industrious but now I realize he's not who I thought he was. Or he has changed. Do you think he can have me put away in a mental facility?"

"That never occurred to me." Stella imagined that Marlo was chewing the corner of her bottom lip, which she often did when perplexed. If both hands were free, she would sometimes run her long fingers through her straight, glossy black hair, then shake her head as she mulled over a question. "You're overreacting," Marlo finally said. "That's easy to do when you're upset like this."

"Have you ever known anyone who was put away?"

Marlo seemed to respond quickly without thinking. "No, everyone I've ever known who was crazy was born that way. They didn't go crazy later in life." The moment the words were out, Stella could tell her friend wanted to pull them back. Though she tried to stifle the sobs, they came anyway.

"I am so sorry," Marlo said. "Please forgive me for such insensitivity. You are the sanest person I know. What you did was *brave*. Not crazy."

"You're the only one I've told," Stella sniffed, determined to dry her tears. "It's a terrible situation. I think about all the worst things that could happen—like being institutionalized, divorce, settlement, my future. And Mama is just about past any enduring sympathy. By this afternoon, the whole thing will have become my fault. I'm wearing out both my welcome and her compassion."

"That's the way of our mamas because of how they were raised. They dole out love and protection until they decide it's time to be stoic and face the music. Honestly, though, you should give your mama some credit. She has petted you for four days longer than normal."

"That's true. I've gotten almost a full week out of it. But Marlo, I don't think I can make myself be through with crying yet."

Marlo glanced out the large plate window to the right of her desk. Their offices were on Mallery, the street that ran through the center of the village and went straight to the pier. The soft morning sun bathed the ocean in sparkling light and caused brightness to rise up and illuminate the buildings. Behind their office was the lighthouse, its museum, the community theater center, and a park with a playground and a gazebo. There, the Methodist church would hold Sunday services on occasion. Folks would bring their lawn chairs and listen to the preacher less than usual since the soothing sight of the sea was such a distraction. The Baptists wised up to the distraction and stopping having church outside.

"I know," Marlo responded. "You can't hurry healing."

Suddenly, Stella wanted to change the subject. "Chatty's here," she said. She shared how she had just bitten his head off. Marlo listened, and Stella could hear her shuffling through some papers.

Marlo opened a manila folder marked "Beachview" that was filled with properties for sale and rent on that street or nearby. Her eye fell on one that the Sloan family owned and were in the process of fixing up, but the last hurricane had left a year-long waiting list for non-mandatory renovations. They had finished the outside but the bathroom, powder room, and kitchen needed to be updated from the 1950s look. It would be months before a contractor could get back and finish. Meanwhile, it sat empty. As Stella carried on about Chatty, Marlo chewed her lower lip and studied on the house. It was a cheerful two-bedroom cottage painted a light aqua blue with yellow shutters and matching door. Its little white-trimmed porch ran the length of the house. It was a block from the beach, which made it perfect for vacationing families that couldn't afford beachfront houses.

Stella pattered on but cupped her hand around the receiver and whispered. "Then he had the nerve to say that my homemade wedding dress started it all! Can you believe that?"

When she took a breath, Marlo grabbed the opportunity. "I have a great idea. Why don't you come down to St. Simons for a while? Come to your happy place. You're wearing out your welcome with your mama, so come down here. I promise I'll let you cry all you want."

The idea instantly appealed to Stella, but she began to think of why she couldn't. "I don't have many clothes with me."

"Are you still a size six?"

"After all this dehydration and lack of food, yes. But did I tell you about Asher having to zip my dress the night that—?"

Marlo plunged forth. "I have plenty of clothes you can wear."

"We're iced in."

"It'll melt by tomorrow. I grew up there, too, you know."

"I have no place to stay, and Asher has cancelled all my credit cards. I found that out when a standing monthly charge for data on my tablet was denied."

"Aw, I have the perfect place. It's a cottage we own that needs interior remodeling. We finished the outside, but it'll be a while before the contractor can get back. Hurricane repairs. It's on Beachview. It's idyllic. It's walking distance to the beach, to Crab Trap, Beachcomber, the King and Prince. You can even walk to the village in twenty minutes. Say you'll come, and it'll be ready and waiting."

Stella opened her mouth to protest further, and then a tumble of memories cascaded over her: the harmony of waves colliding and melting into each other; colorful floats gliding up and down; laughter tinkling through the salt-kissed air; the way the light hit the marshes when the sun set; fresh fish tacos; two girls with sunburned noses collapsing into their beds at night, exhausted from the fun and adventure; dancing on the beach with summertime boyfriends; the sand that invaded everything from shoes to underwear to beds; and Grandma Mozelle's big hugs and hot suppers.

Stella gave in. "As soon as the roads clear, I'll be there. I could use a dose of sunshine and a little sand and sea. St. Simons has always been my happy place. I hope it still is."

Chapter Seven

"Marlo, it's absolutely charming!"

Stella stood before the little cottage in St. Simons, swept away by its sweetness even though it was a far cry from the Ansley Park mansion she had recently departed. The aqua blue wood planking and soft yellow shutters were welcoming at first sight. Inside, she found a small living room and an old French country kitchen with yellow cabinets accented with blue trim and knobs. The appliances were vintage but working, though there was no dishwasher.

"Big deal," she said, shrugging. "I still remember how to wash and dry dishes."

There were two small bedrooms. The main bedroom, dressed in white eyelet curtains and chenille bedspread, had a cramped half bath. The small full bathroom off the hallway, floored in tiny white tiles, had a footed bathtub but no shower.

"It might be problematic to wash your hair," Marlo said worriedly.

Stella waved it off. "I'll either lean over the tub and shampoo or I'll do it in the kitchen sink. I love baths." Stella's normally optimistic personality had begun to return, albeit slightly, when she turned from Highway 17 onto the causeway that stretched over the marshes of Glynn County and led her onto the island where she had spent many of her happiest days. She had rolled down the windows to smell the air, which filled her lungs and began to revive her spirit. She recalled how excited they had always been when the car, taking them to Marlo's grandparents, had made this approach onto St. Simons. In those days, most people vacationed on Jekyll, the other nearby island, so St. Simons felt quainter and more isolated except for the families who chose the King and Prince hotel, a resort that had been on the island since before World War II.

Surprisingly, a calming of spirit had swept over her. She reveled in the first peace she had felt in many months. After pulling into a parking space on Mallery near Marlo's office, she had taken a moment to survey the little village of restaurants, boutiques, tee shirt shops, an ice cream shop, and the used bookstore that had been there for years. She walked down the street far enough to see the pier, with children fishing from it, and the ocean that shimmered with an invitation to laugh and enjoy. Now, this cozy cottage added to the sense of well-being that seemed to crawl slowly back toward her.

The second bedroom was situated with twin beds, sheer curtains, and an old-fashioned braided rug atop the heart of pine floor. The slightly musty smell of drywall that was seventy-five years old mixed comfortably with the fragrance of pine.

"This must have been a happy house," Stella commented. "I feel a spirit of warmth and cheer."

Marlo smiled and nodded. "It was built by a couple named McElhaney, just as World War II ended. They came here so the husband could work at Liberty, the shipyard that built merchant ships to patrol the coast during the war. After Pearl Harbor, it was feared that there would be additional attacks on ports or naval ships. But they loved it here and stayed. Dot McElhaney died about fifteen years ago. After Mr. McElhaney went into a nursing home, Alton and Evelyn bought the house from their children. At first, we rented it well, then it became apparent that we'd have to update it to stay with the market. But to address your question, this was a very happy house. They were the sweetest couple. They raised two daughters here and then their grandchildren visited often. Mrs. McElhaney was always baking cookies and welcoming the neighborhood kids in."

For the most part, the house was outfitted like a storybook cottage with its pale blue interior walls, white trim, built-in china cabinets, and a round pine table with a lazy Susan in the center. There was no separate dining room. The windows were plain sashed and opened up and down except for the one over the kitchen sink, which could be thrown open vertically. The window box beneath it caught the mild morning sun. Most of the yard was shaded by old oak trees with hanging moss, so there was no harsh sunlight.

"No air conditioning," Marlo informed her. Both of them had grown up without air conditioning, so neither considered it to be a big deal under the right circumstances. These were the right circumstances: screen doors, ceiling fans, shade trees, and a box fan to use in the bedroom if needed. The ocean was only a block away, so the sea breeze also helped.

The living room was mostly dressed in a floral blue and yellow chintz that complemented the house design, except for a deep royal blue velvet sofa. It looked invitingly comfortable with big down-filled cushions and pillows.

Stella eyed it. "That's a wonderful sofa but it seems a bit out of place here."

Marlo laughed. "Evelyn. She bought it at an estate sale a few months ago to use in their den but Alton said, 'Absolutely not. I will not have velvet in the room where I watch ball-games.' She moved it over here until she can figure out what to do with it."

Stella flopped down and sunk into it comfortably. "This is an expensive sofa." The Buckhead Stella knew that. The country girl would never have had a clue. "It's a bit different with the other furniture." She glanced at the rough-hewn coffee table and side pieces. "But it adds interest, and I like that."

She swung her legs up. "Oh! Do you mind if I put my feet on it?"

"Not a bit. If it had been a precious piece, it would not have gone to Alton's den in the first place and then been moved over here. A velvet sofa isn't exactly what you want for a rental property."

Stella hugged her legs and looked at her lifelong friend. "Marlie, I promise that when I have a job again, I'll pay you for every second I spend here. And the utilities."

Marlo put up a hand. "No, Prissy Missy, you certainly won't. We can't rent without finishing the renovations. Meanwhile, it helps us to have someone here. A house, especially a sweet, welcoming one like this, should be lived in." Stella opened her mouth to protest, but Marlo continued. "Was Chatty Colquitt sad to see you leave?"

Stella rolled her eyes comically. "I love him so much. He is a loyal friend, without question. He told Asher in no uncertain terms that he was 'Team Stella.' But he can drive me up the wall. He has no filter. If he thinks it, he says it. Especially with me. He watches his tongue a bit more with people like Miss Caroline. But, to answer your question: Yes. He hated to see me go." She laughed and cast an eye toward the large picture window where a bluebird had landed on the window sill.

"Of course, I'm not sure how much of that has to do with me personally and how much of it has to do with being a firsthand witness to every second of this sorry, sordid business. I really think the joy of being an up-close spectator has increased his life by several years." She then told Marlo about Chatty's parting words.

They both had stayed until the ice melted, which was the day following Marlo's call. Chatty had helped Stella load her few things into her car. He planned to follow her to Jefferson, where he would then take I-85 back to Atlanta and she would head for Athens and Route 15. It would have been forty-five minutes quicker to go through Atlanta and take I-75, but she didn't want to pass Lenox Road, Cheshire Bridge, Peachtree. She didn't want to awaken the emotions that were napping for the moment. Instead, she'd quietly drive the back roads, take her time, and listen to satellite radio.

Chatty, manners precise as always, had opened the door for her. He hugged her then drew back, firmly grasped her shoulders, and said, "Just remember, whenever you hit a low point—and there are many more low points to come—remember these two words: Bennett Sutton."

Stella blinked and looked at him blankly. "Bennett Sutton? Why on earth would I want to think of him?"

"Because as long as Bennett Sutton is alive and remembered by the hallowed members of old Atlanta society, he shall always be the number one scandal. And a villain to all."

"And that should comfort me how?" she asked.

"Oh, Stella, darling, it's quite simple. If he's the number *one* scandal then you will always be no higher than number *two*."

Marlo chortled loudly, hearing the story. "I don't know why I'm laughing because I don't have a clue who Bennett Sutton is, but Chatty is always entertaining with his assessments of life. Who is Bennett Sutton?"

"An accountant who ran off with his clients' money years ago. Including a bunch of Miss Caroline's and some of Asher's. They managed to recover a portion of it and redistribute it, but he put a hurting on the old money society. Most of the funds were never recovered."

"Just a second." Marlo went over to the cabinet, pulled down a couple of wine glasses, and opened a bottle of Merlot. She handed a glass to Stella. "Cheers to Bennett Sutton." They clinked glasses. "May he always be number one and may Stella Bankwell move further down the list." They laughed merrily, just like they always did when they were together. Stella was surprised by the lightness of her heart.

Marlo took a sip then said, "Oh, I got enough groceries here to feed you for a week." She opened the fridge to show that it was filled with milk, ginger ale (Stella's favorite), cold cuts, cheese, bread, mayonnaise, fresh vegetables, and salad. "A bag of coffee and coffee maker. Soap, laundry detergent. The stacked washer and dryer are there in the pantry. Shampoo, paper towels, toilet paper. I think I've gotten everything. Do you need cash?"

Stella shook her head. "I took $10,000 in cash from the little safe in my closet. Asher always insisted we each keep that much."

"I bet he's regretting it now," Marlo commented wryly. "Why don't you keep a couple hundred and give me the rest to put in the vault at the office? Just to be safe." She reached in her purse and pulled out a credit card. "This is a company credit card that my assistant uses, but she's out on maternity. I called and added your name to our account. Use it when or if you need it."

Stella's eyes filled with tears. Not from her usual sadness but from appreciation. She grabbed her best friend, hugging her tightly. "Thank you," she whispered in her ear. "Thank you so much."

Marlo squeezed her tight. "This is the moment that our years of friendship has prepared me for—to be here when you need me in a big way."

Marlo stayed another hour as the two old friends chatted about things that were of little consequence, such as the two boxes of colorful resort wear that Marlo had brought over.

"Now, I know you're used to Tom Ford and Versace, but this stuff is mostly from Steinmart's and Belk's. However, it's just what you'll need on the island. There are a couple of cardigans in there as well, and a lightweight coat."

"A Lilly Pulitzer!" Stella exclaimed, pulling out a pink, white, and green floral shift. "I love these floral dresses. And look—a green cardigan to match. These are perfect."

They talked about high school friends and folks on the island that they both knew and how Marlo's ten-year-old daughter had read over a hundred books in a year. Finally, Marlo stood up.

"It's after four. I need to run by the office and return a few calls." Stella pulled herself up from the comfort of the velvet sofa and trailed her friend, the screen door banging behind them. Marlo started down the front porch steps, then suddenly snapped her fingers and said, "Oh, I forgot to tell you. Cager Burnett sent word that he wanted to see you as soon as you stepped foot on this island." She smiled and shook her head.

"Doesn't that sound just like him? Commanding and demanding?"

Stella's heart flipped and sank to its previously low level. "Governor Burnett wants to see me? He's here?"

"At their house on Sea Island. The doctor sent him down here to recuperate from pneumonia he had a couple of months ago."

Her upset was roaring so heavily in her ears that she could barely think to speak. Former Governor Burnett was a tough man, both in his younger days and as he had grown older. Now he was ornerier than ever. He had no time to put up with foolishness, he liked to say.

"How does he know I'm here?" she managed to ask, her dry tongue sticking to the roof of her mouth.

"News travels fast between Atlanta society and Sea Island. I have little doubt that he has heard all about the country club. He called Tate yesterday and told him, in no uncertain terms, that you were to see him when you got here."

"But only y'all, Mama, and Chatty know I'm here," Stella protested.

"They don't call him 'Cagey' Burnett for no reason. He figured it out then tricked Tate into admitting you were coming today. Tate is very intimidated by him. As are most folks, so it didn't take much to unnerve him and get your ETA. He won't tell anyone. You've always been a favorite of his. You know that."

She sighed miserably. "I *was* a favorite of his, but that's before I scandalized myself. I'm sure he wants to give me a stern talking to about the unseemliness of my behavior." She thought for a second. "I'll just avoid him for the time being."

She brightened at the thought. "I'll call him next week. Or maybe the next."

Marlo was about to step into her white SUV. "He's expecting you at his house tomorrow promptly at 4 P.M. He'll leave your name at the gate."

"What!" She started to panic.

"Tomorrow. Four P.M. at his house. Don't be late. Call me if you need anything. The phone is on the kitchen wall. Bye!"

Stella sank into the porch rocker, and for the next hour she fretted and wrung her hands over the meeting with the Governor. This, she told herself, was going to be most unpleasant.

"I'd rather see Asher or Miss Caroline than have to face the Governor," she mumbled.

McCager Alistair Burnett did not suffer fools. That was well known. And whenever possible, he liked to make fools suffer. Or, at the very least, squirm until death seemed like a welcomed release.

A realization was beginning to dawn on her: it was time to quit hiding and face the music. She just wished she didn't have to start with a full orchestra.

Chapter Eight

The sun was setting—always a lovely sight on St. Simons Island when the sun turns to tangerine and casts streaks of orange and yellow against the white-clouded blue skies. By that time of day, the sea has darkened and the waves are growing increasingly restless and loud. Together, it creates both the light and dark side of beauty.

From a block away, Stella could hear the coming of night by the ocean's loud sighs. She had spent two hours agonizing over her meeting with McCager Burnett the next day. Finally, she pulled herself up from her chair of misery and decided to go over to the beach for a walk, perhaps stop into the King and Prince for a tropical drink. She was dressed in the same outfit she wore the night she left her other life behind—jeans, chambray shirt, white tee shirt, and navy Tod's—but she decided to take along a sweater from the clothes Marlo had brought. She found a beautiful, heavy cotton cardigan in navy and tied it around her shoulders. She put a twenty-dollar bill in her back pocket along with a tube of lipstick then shoved her purse under the bed. She picked up the key that Marlo had given her and ensured that all windows were locked. After switching on a lamp in the living room that sat on the table by the royal blue velvet sofa, she pulled the front door shut. It felt like something was missing. She stopped. She thought. Oh yes! A phone. She had turned hers off, stuffed it into a bag, and never thought about it again. Until now. And when she did, she sighed as though a burden had lifted—no more constant contact from others, some she welcomed, most she didn't. It was time, Stella had decided in the last two hours, to start seeing the good in everything. Not being anchored to the phone or living in anticipation of some news—good or bad—that it might bring was liberating. It felt like a rain cloud had brightened.

"I can get used, quite nicely, to not having a phone," she thought. The cottage had a phone, so she'd do fine.

Stepping off the porch, she noticed two azalea bushes in the first blush of bloom. One was a deep, fuchsia pink and the other was a rich pastel pink. Then, her ears honed into a sound she couldn't place. Water dripping? Lips smacking? It seemed to come from the side of the house so she quietly walked around. There, at the outdoor spigot, was a white dog trimmed in black spots. She had one white ear and one black, a smudge of black ran over one eye, and her nose was peppered in black freckles. She looked to be about twenty pounds and was a mixture of something. Perhaps beagle and Jack Russell? Some kind of terrier, for sure, with that wiry hair. The dog was licking eagerly at the dripping spigot, but she looked around when she heard Stella. Her ears pricked up and if dogs can, in fact, smile, that dog looked like she had just seen her favorite person. She ran to Stella, looking up at her happily. She danced in a circle.

"Well, hello there." Stella squatted down to pat her. "Who are you?" The dog was overcome with joy, licking Stella's hand and then giving her a big lick across the cheek. "I'm glad to meet you, too," Stella said, laughing. "Do you live around here? You must be one of the neighbor's dogs." Stella patted her and played with her for a few minutes, determining that the dog was definitely a she, then stood up. One last pat on the head. "You come back and see me. Okay?"

Stella was about to cross Ocean Boulevard when she felt someone behind her. She turned and there was the eager pup.

"No! No!" Stella scolded in a stern voice. "You cannot cross the road." There wasn't much traffic but it was best to teach her now. "You go home. GO. HOME." The sweet girl was saddened but she obviously understood. She dropped her head and dragged back toward Beachview. She looked back over her shoulder with such a sad expression that Stella wanted to pop into tears. She had promised herself, though, that tears were a luxury she would allow only on rare occasions from now on.

The last streaks of daylight faded quickly toward the early nightfall of winter as she sauntered toward the public beach access running between the King and Prince and its South Villas. The hotel's Mediterranean style with rounded arches, cool beige stucco, heavy artistic doors, rounded tower, custom-made green canopies, and red tile roof reminded Stella of the Mission Revival style in California. She thought particularly of the Pacific Palisades home once owned by 1920s actress Thelma Todd, the place where Miss Todd was found murdered in the garage. Its style as well as the fact that it sat as close to the Pacific Ocean as the King and Prince sat on the Atlantic made them feel akin to each other. Once, she and Asher had toured the house while they were in Los Angeles for a business meeting about yet another of his fruitless projects.

She meandered down to the shore, took her shoes off, and walked the crunching beach, watching thoughtfully as the thirsty sand sipped from the frothy waves. The water danced toward the beach then quickly pulled back like the gestures of a coquettish, flirtatious girl. The thought of flirtation led her, naturally, to Annabelle Honeycutt.

Annabelle. The gorgeous, self-indulging Annabelle who gave Stella a stomachache whenever her beautiful face crossed Stella's troubled mind. She stepped away from an approaching wave, pulling the sweater tighter and hugging her stomach, and thought, "At least, through all of this, I've lost that extra weight." That did make her feel better. Then something else captured her thoughts and sullied her mood. She darkened as she hovered on it.

They—Atlanta society and a few wannabes—had attended Amber Sutherlin's wedding back in late summer at Waverly Plantation. It was an expensive affair, rumored to have cost over a million dollars, where every possible whim was addressed including the brightly colored array of cashmere wraps tied with bows and waiting on a white-clothed table, should the weather turn chilly. Chatty, elegant in his tailored tuxedo, had glided over to Stella, who was admiring some extraordinarily large magnolia buds placed fetchingly in a towering silver vase.

"That magnolia bud is as large as your head, Stella Faye," he said, laughing. "Not that you have a big head, but it certainly is bigger than most magnolia buds." He studied the buds for a brief moment. "Do you think they injected them with steroids?" He was quite serious.

"No," she replied, laughing. "Nor hormones, either."

"Speaking of hormones." Chatty took off in another direction. "Did you see that ghastly dress that Amber's Aunt Dora is wearing? If I couldn't dress any better than that, I'd just stay home."

"What does that have to do with hormones?"

"She needs them. She's sweating like a pig at a county fair in July. Though I have never seen such. I have only heard tell of such unseemliness." Something caught Chatty's eye and he watched carefully before leaning over to Stella and saying in a low voice, "I believe that Annabelle has her eye on Asher."

Stella blanched. Her composure had already taken a shot the previous day when Neely was sent home for having a stolen exam in his possession. She hadn't recovered from that rattling. "What do you mean?" she asked, nervously.

"I mean exactly what you think I mean. She's eyeing him for her next husband." A pause. "Or she wants to be his concubine. They look at each other like they don't want to look at each other but they really do want to look at each other." He dropped his voice lower. "Just a second ago, they passed each other closely and each said something out of the corner of their mouths. They lingered for a fleeting second then moved on."

Stella rolled her eyes and waved him away. "That means nothing." She was talking braver than she felt.

Chatty shrugged. "You're right, perhaps. Maybe they were discussing where she could buy a good Cuban cigar."

As Stella trudged the beach now, she tried to push away the image of Annabelle, focusing instead on a shrimp boat in the distance. The chill grew as the sun sank, so Stella decided to head over to the hotel. She passed teenagers chasing each other while laughing loudly, older couples holding hands, and one harried man who was trying to round up two little girls running in opposite directions. As she reached the wooden steps leading up from the beach, she stopped and eyed the strands of big, bare bulbs that hung jauntily over the outside dining area. It was just dark enough to look romantic and remind her of the summer dance when she was eighteen. She and Marlo had learned to Carolina shag that night, taught by an older couple who competed in shag dancing contests. They had recently won one in Myrtle Beach. Stella closed her eyes and began to hum the old classic "Under the Boardwalk," then danced a sand-covered foot in the six-count, eight-step motion. She lingered in time, remembering the happiness and how Tatum had taken Marlo in his arms and danced under the lights. They were so in love, so right for each other, that Stella had watched with a bit of envy that August night and thought, "One day, I want to be loved like that."

"Maybe I still will be," she whispered quietly.

She was jolted out of the moment by a black Labrador who gave a mighty shake to free himself of sea drops, throwing an abundance of wet her way. The lady to whom the dog belonged said nothing to Stella, just hurriedly put a leash on the dog and commanded, "C'mon, Samson."

And just like that, Stella was back in the real world.

The King and Prince lobby was buzzing. A big banner welcomed the Floral Designers of Georgia. People stood, chattering and laughing, many with a glass of wine in hand. Stella started across the beige and black marble floor toward the sunken bar. It had, for many years, been an indoor swimming pool. Granny Mozelle had been in a Bible study with Mrs. Trotter, the hotel's bookkeeper at the time. As was the way of Southerners, this meant that Marlo and Stella were always welcome to swim there. Of course, they preferred the sun, sea, and beach, but rainy days found them splashing in the indoor pool, having fun and making new friends.

Stella was not a proponent of change and would never have voted for the pool to be removed, even though it did create humidity that smacked you in the face upon entrance at the front door. The lobby was newly renovated with sleek marble and glistening woodwork. It was, she had to admit, quite nice, even if her childhood memories had been thrown away with the redoing. One bartender was working frantically between customers, standing two or three deep at the bar, and all the chairs and tables were filled.

"Not worth the trouble," Stella thought. Besides, with Asher and Neely a long way back in Atlanta and Chatty not around to stir her insecurities, her nerves were feeling better. She turned to leave, but instead of going out the front door, she chose to go out the side door through a short hallway. On the right-hand side were the men's and women's restrooms. To the left was a wall filled with the resort's history. An old ad caught her eye and she stopped to read it.

Telegraph Location: St. Simons Island, Georgia

Airlines: Eastern from New York City. Delta from Atlanta and Chicago.

Railroad Service: Southern, out of Atlanta to Brunswick

Atlantic Coast Line from New York City to Nahunta, Georgia

Seaboard Railway from New York City to Thalmann, Georgia

Dancing, Free Bath Privileges, Golf, Fishing, Saddle Horses, Autos for Hire

Stella read the ad carefully, completely absorbed. She had never heard of Nahunta or Thalmann. She was studying the rates when a hand reached past her face and pointed to the prices.

"Doubles. Ten dollars with ocean view," a man's voice rumbled gently. "I wonder what year that was."

Stella glanced up to see a good-looking man, several inches taller, who immediately reminded her of the stereotypical boy-next-door, all grown up. His dirty-blond hair was trimmed close to frame an angular face with a healthy tan. His eyes resembled her favorite blue marble from childhood. He was broad shouldered but trim. Muscular but lean. He wore a white sports shirt with short, banded sleeves and khaki slacks.

He grinned, and she would have declared that sparkles bounced off his teeth. "Now, seriously," he continued. "That had to be the 1940s or '50s. I don't know when this place was built."

"1935," Stella responded without thought. "During World War II, the government took it over and used it for naval training purposes and to watch the coast. The U-boats posed a serious threat to all our U.S. coasts. A German submarine torpedoed two oil freighters just off the coast here. One was the *Oklahoma*. The other was an oil tanker coming from Texas." She smiled proudly. "Local shrimp boats and fishing boats sailed out into the dark waters to rescue the men. And Candler—I forget his first name, but he was the son of Asa, who founded Coca-Cola—he used his yacht to bring in survivors. A while back, the commander of the U-boat came back here and met with survivors. Everyone made peace. It was nice."

The man had an exaggerated look of being both taken aback and impressed. "That's quite interesting. Do you work here?"

She laughed. "No. I didn't even grow up here. But I did spend time here every summer when I was growing up. And Christmas break. I love the island and I love history. St. Simons is historic. Do you live here or are you visiting?"

"I'm here on business. I'm staying in one of the villas."

"Is home a long way away?"

"A bit of a haul, but I like the time alone in a car," he replied. "I'm from Memphis. Originally. And now."

She perked up. "Memphis? We love Memphis!" It had always been a favorite city for her and Asher. A weekend at the Peabody with a trip to Graceland was divine. When Neely was younger, they had taken him several times to enjoy the hotel ducks, and once he had even been the Duck Master, joyfully following the ducks to the elevator where they rode to their penthouse retreat for a good night's rest before emerging the next morning to more pomp and circumstance and a day's float in the lobby fountain. He had been the most precious child. Always entertaining and kind. Those were happy memories, but as soon as Stella said, "we," she realized what every divorced or widowed woman does at some point: she had become an "I" and no longer a "we." It was the beginning of discoveries that a newly single woman learns: grocery shopping and cooking for one; no anniversary to celebrate; no longer part of a couple to attend wedding and parties.

She stumbled over her words to correct herself, a bit flushed. "Uh, I mean, uh 'I'...*I* love Memphis." Clearly puzzled, he eyed her as she continued, trying to move past the rough spot. "I'm a big Elvis fan."

He brightened. "Me, too. My mama's cousin dated him a couple of times. She was Miss Mid-South Popcorn or some such. Every beauty queen of a certain age in Memphis dated him." They laughed together. "But you know, everyone always speaks highly of him. No one says an unkind word. When I was a kid, my granddaddy used to take me to Lansky's men's store where a young Elvis bought his clothes. He was very loyal.

He continued to buy from them over the years. Mr. Lansky told great Elvis stories and how he always called him 'Mr. Lansky' and said it wouldn't be respectful to call him anything else."

"I met him once," Stella said cheerfully and, suddenly, for some reason, wished she had combed her hair and powdered her nose. "Mr. Lansky. Not Elvis. Though I wish I'd met Elvis. The Lanskys have stores in the Peabody. He was probably ninety years old."

"Yes, I believe he lived well up into his nineties and was pretty spry, too." The man offered his hand. "I'm Jackson Culpepper. I'm sorry. I'm acting formal because I'm still in my business frame of mind where we use formal names. Some people call me Jack but most call me Pepper, short for Culpepper."

"Jackson," she repeated softly. "Your name is Jackson?"

He angled his head, his handsomeness showing more from the light behind him. "Why?"

She smiled, captivated. He seemed captivated, too. "My maiden name was Jackson." If she had been more clued in, she would have seen a flicker of disappointment cross his clear blue eyes.

"What's your name now?" he asked gamely, rising above any disappointment he might feel.

"Bankwell. I'm Stella Bankwell."

"Nice to meet you, Stella Bankwell."

They shook hands, then she folded her arms across her chest. He put his hands on his waist and they relaxed to talk a bit.

"What do you for a living that brings you on business to St. Simons?" Her voice trailed off at the last two words because, out of the corner of her eye, she saw a pile of blonde hair she recognized too well. It was tossed upwards in an unsightly mountain of hairpieces, teasing, and hairspray. Mona Windsor. The biggest gossip ever to draw breath in the city of Atlanta. What she didn't know for a fact, she made up. There were times she would have made Chatty look like a rank amateur in gossip, except that Chatty's gossip was usually accurate.

Pepper was saying something, but whatever it was, Stella didn't hear. Her mind was spinning. She had to get out of there before Mona came out of the ladies' room and saw her. If she were discovered, Asher would know within the hour. Mona and Miss Caroline were in the garden club together, which was a way of saying they sipped tea together and talked about whoever wasn't present.

"Uh, I'm sorry. I just thought of something." Her words tumbled out randomly. "Uh, I gotta go." She practically pushed him aside in the small hallway in a scramble to disappear. All she could think was to get past that doorway before Mona Big Mouth emerged. "It was nice to meet you," she called behind her, heart pounding as she practically ran to the door, leaving a stunned man behind her.

Once outside in the crisp air, she took a breath, but she did not stop until she had crossed Ocean Boulevard and returned to the cottage on Beachview. She collapsed on the porch, put her elbows on her knees, dropped her head into her hands, and tried to slow her heart. She felt a gentle tugging under her arm. It was the spigot dog, pushing her head up into her lap. Once that was accomplished, she looked at Stella happily and nuzzled her nose to her neck. A calm flowed over Stella. Her heart slowed to normal. She hugged the little creature tightly.

"Hello, Spigot," she said, the name popping out unexpectedly. "You waited for me. You must have known I was gonna need a friend."

It was exactly what Stella needed at the moment. Truthfully, it was what they both needed.

Chapter Nine

Stella followed Alva Burnett down the cheery hallway bathed with light from the high windows and the sheen of freshly polished wood floors. Stella focused, though, on the bobbed haircut with bangs that Miss Alva had worn since she was a young woman. Only age had changed it by turning the raven-dark hair to varying shades of silver. There was never a hair out of place on this woman who had been the Governor's right arm since the day he met her. The curled-under ends were tucked behind her ears, displaying the simple pair of pearl earrings she wore always. For formal occasions, she wore similar pearls but with a single diamond attached to the bottom.

"Hello, Stella," Miss Alva had said cheerfully when she opened the heavy wood doors to the two-story white brick cottage on Sea Island, set in the midst of a meticulously manicured yard. She had made something of a show by opening both doors, since the other was usually anchored in place. It seemed odd at the time, but Stella later surmised that it meant the Burnetts were fully opening their doors to her. Politics are composed of such sly indicators.

Miss Alva gave the anxious young woman a hug while Stella tried to choke out a few courteous words. With her arm around Stella's shoulders, Miss Alva whispered softly, "Come with me. He's waiting for you in the library. Just remember the man who roars like a grizzly bear has the heart of a teddy bear." She smiled and winked.

Within seconds, she was pushing open the ornate pocket doors to the library. Stella stepped in to see McCager Alastair Burnett with his back to them, his seventy-two-year-old shoulders hunched over an old rolltop desk as he sat in a high-back, swivel wood chair with a black cushion tied to the seat. Sun streamed in from ceiling-high windows and poured straight onto his silvery hair. It looked like something in a movie, like when Joan of Arc was chosen and illuminated by a beam of light.

Most telling, he did not turn to greet them, even when Miss Alva, tall and elegantly turned out in a skirt, sweater, and flat loafers, said in a strong voice, "McCager, Stella has arrived." Most people still called him the Governor. Some old friends called him Cage. His enemies called him Cagey, but only Miss Alva and a few closest to him called him McCager, a name he had inherited from a great-great-grandfather killed in the Battle of Franklin during the Civil War.

He took a moment, continuing to study a page he held in his hands, then put it on the table and signed it. When he finished, he threw his hand out to the right, motioning to a library chair with vertical slats, back posts, and a hard bottom that was next to the desk. He still did not face them. "Have a seat."

Stella moved slowly to the execution seat while Miss Alva said, "I will bring in a service of coffee shortly."

"We need nothing," the Governor replied gruffly, taking off his black-rimmed glasses and rubbing his eyes.

Miss Alva smiled sweetly, and though he didn't see the smile, he could hear it in her voice when she replied, "I think you do." Then she stepped into the hallway and pulled shut the doors.

Finally, he glanced over at Stella. She sat rod straight, in the horribly uncomfortable chair. Her red hair was pulled into a ponytail with tendrils falling around her face. She had purposely chosen that hairstyle because when she was nervous, she twirled her hair around her fingers. Needless to say, she was nervous. The Governor glanced back at the top of the desk, took a moment, then sat against the chair and swiveled it slowly to face her. His gaze was steady. He shook his head.

"Life brings a great deal of disappointment. No one is immune to that. If one is foolish enough to enter the bloody arena of politics, that disappointment is multiplied many times. The swords are numerous and are quite willing to be drawn to slash at a moment's notice. If one is an idealistic, moralistic boy from the North Georgia mountains, where people tend to put a high price on righteousness and common decency, those disappointments are savage."

He paused. She squirmed.

"Many a time in my career have I felt that I was on the last heartbeat of my life, that I had been beaten and bloodied until little remained. Savage. Brutal. That is the way of politics. Yet none of what I have faced over the last fifty years of public stonings prepared me for the disappointment I felt when I heard of your disruption in the somewhat civilized yet often frivolous dining room of the country club. Granted, it is no stranger to people who make fools of themselves, but it was never meant to be a public stage where a well-raised mountain girl could disgrace the dignity of her people." Pause. "Of our people." His eyes were grave, filled with a mixture of disappointment, judgment, and reprimand. He furrowed his brow and frowned deeply, the folds around his mouth hanging sadly, voluminously.

Stella slid down in the chair, tugging at the long-sleeved, below-the-knee blue knit dress she had chosen from Marlo's boxes. She knew his words were genuine. Cager Burnett spoke solidly and forthrightly. Always. In a state filled from its colony beginning with admirable politicians, he was ranked at the top. His words were elegant, poetic, powerfully painted with Shakespearean words and King James Bible phrases. Cager Burnett was heavily influenced by the oratorical style of Dr. Martin Luther King Jr. Truth be told, the Governor had learned much of his dramatic delivery from Dr. King, who often used the children of Israel as an example for the civil rights movement. "We have left the land of Egypt, traveling to the Promised Land."

At the moment, Stella wished she was in Egypt, the Promised Land, anywhere but in this house on Sea Island, facing the music of a man who liked to fiddle for an unbearable time.

McCager Alistair Burnett had been born in Gilmer County, outside the mountain town of Ellijay, in a community called Turnip Town.

"When I decided to come down outta them mountains and represent the good and decent people in my district, I determined I would never change one iota. I would not say I was from Ellijay, fine place that it is, when I, in truth, was raised in Turnip Town. I would stay true to my roots." He said this repeatedly, and he had been true to his word.

Many times, he had stood to address the United States Congress and said, in some form or the other with a strong mountain drawl, "Now, I'm just an old barefoot boy from Turnip Town, and sometimes I don't always understand things the way you well-polished, highly educated city folk do. Where I come from—in the North Georgia mountains—it's either smart or it's dumb. No two ways about that. No in-between.

Smart or dumb. Good common sense or a fool's errand. But from what I see here in Washington, there is a whole lot of in-between going on. Now, I aim to be on the smart side. The side with common sense. I aim to do what a country mule would do—set my ways and stick to 'em. Do you know how smart an old mule can be?"

One of his fiercest political opponents once said, "McCager Burnett gets what he wants by playing country dumb. He's smart enough to do that and people fall for it. His 'country boy from Turnip Town' spiel has won more votes in the United States Congress than all the speeches from Harvard graduates combined. I call him 'Cagey' and that's all I'll ever call him. Because it's the truth."

Now, Stella fully understood how it felt to be under his dreaded microscope of moral scrutiny. She glanced nervously toward the doors. He watched her.

"Lookin' for a way to escape?"

"No. I'm wondering how close the bathroom is in case I get sick at my stomach." She paused and added humorously. "I ate light."

He seemed tempted to smile but did not. He held his rigid glare and said, "Down the hall on the right. It will take you about four seconds to get there if you time it right."

She nodded. "Thank you."

"I'm disappointed in you," he restated. And she knew he was aware that no words from anyone could have hurt more. "You're a mountain girl. You know better than to act a fool in front of people. It's not just your dignity it takes away; it robs you of leverage. People see your weakness, and they view you mighty different from then on. You can build yourself back. I guarantee that. I know you have the grit to do it. But that little scene will be forever remembered by those who were there and those they've told. Thirty years down the road, folks'll be sittin' 'round, having a few drinks, and someone will bring up the day that Stella Bankwell caused a ruckus at the Buckhead Country Club."

He paused. She was overwhelmed. But McCager Burnett was not finished. He was of hearty stock that did not quit or retreat. "We mountain people suffer under a stigma. People just start off thinkin', right outta the gate, that we're backwards and uncivilized. And damn if you didn't prove them right."

She wanted to cry. Tears swelled, but she knew the Governor. If she cried, he'd only get madder.

"You're strong, Stella. This is just a moment in time. You'll get through it," she told herself.

His gray eyes bore into hers. At that moment, she knew what she had to do. She had to go toe-to-toe. She had to bear up with bravery and not coward down. If she withdrew, she would only make things worse. Mentally, she closed her eyes and plunged in. She was quaking, but he would never know that.

"You heard the whole story?" she asked in a confident voice. "Because if I'm gonna get my head handed to me on a silver platter like John the Baptist, I wanna make sure it's for something I really did and not over embellished gossip. I admit that my behavior was not pretty, but it is probably not as gruesome as it has been made out to be."

"I heard enough of the sordid tale. I'm fairly adept at separating tomfoolery from fact." His eyes seem to soften a bit. Her approach was working. He liked sturdy people who stood up and admitted their shortcomings. "I did hear that Caroline wound up with a glass of wine poured atop her head." He chuckled. "Now, I would have paid good money to have witnessed that moment, I'll give you that."

Stella saw her chance to divert and leaned forward, putting her elbows on her knees in a conversational way. "It was Chatham. He stumbled backwards and threw the whole drink on her head. I didn't see it because, of course, I was giving my full and undivided attention to Annabelle. But later, Chatty said it was the most glorious experience, that he had always dreamt of bringing Miss Caroline down a notch or two but never suspected he'd have such an opportunity. Then, it happened. He claps his hands with such childish joy when he recounts it. The best part of all, he said, was that I got the blame for it and he was completely innocent." She squeezed her shoulders together and smiled impishly. "For once, I gave Chatty as much joy as he has given me all these years. It was almost worth it."

The Governor couldn't seem to help himself. He laughed. He had always had a soft spot for Stella because he knew she was a lamb cast among lions as he once was. But unlike him, he thought, she did not have the internal fortitude to stand up to them. She was a good and decent person who wanted to avoid conflict whenever possible. She was not battle strong as was he.

"You and Chatham are quite the pair," he commented. "I'm pleased for you both. Chatham puts up a happy façade, carrying on about all his trust funds and jolly times. Deep down, he was painfully lonely until you came along. His mother was a jet-setter, a typical heiress of her day, who never stayed home, and his father drowned himself in either work or too much whiskey. Chatham has long needed a good friend like you. He has needed to be truly important in someone's life."

She smiled. "I needed him, too." Then, she relaxed. She thought it was over, but the Governor was too smart for that. He was quite adept at switching between tough and soft. It was an oft-used tactic in throwing off his opponents.

"Let me tell you somethin', young lady. You've got to pull yourself up by the bootstraps and get outta this mess. How you behaved was shameful, but put it behind you and rebuild yourself." He pointed a straight but somewhat wrinkled finger at her. "I'll be watching you. Understand that." She nodded. "And I'll be here for you. Whatever you need, I'll help you." He winked. "I have a few connections here and there."

She sighed. "Thank you, Governor. There has been so much that is horrible about this, but knowing that I let down you and my mama has been the worst."

His eyes misted. "That means a great deal." He leaned forward. "Now tell me, when was the last time you were at church when it wasn't either Christmas or Easter?"

Stella and the Burnetts sat around the cozy, warm fire, all comfortably seated. The Burnetts sat together on a white mid-century sofa, with Stella in a cushioned white swivel rocker. On the coffee table between them was a silver service of coffee, a plate of homemade muffins, and delicate china cups and plates.

"Is coffee always served in the White House with silver and china?" she asked curiously.

"Yes," the Governor replied. "And most of it is as old as our great nation. It is of tremendous interest to an old country boy like me. I find myself wonderin' who sipped from the same china that my lips have touched. Washington, perhaps?

Kennedy? Or my favorite president, Franklin Delano Roosevelt? No wonder people get up there and get the big head. I decided I'd better get on back home to Georgia and run for Governor before I got too big for my britches. Then I'd be no good to nobody and certainly more of a pain for Alva."

Alva was steadfast. Wherever her husband was, she was within reach of his shadow. "It's nice to be retired," she said. "I loved our public service but we're both worn out. That's why we're here for a few months. The doctors said that McCager needed the warmth right now instead of the icy cold of mountain winters."

"I was there last week with my mama and an ice storm came in," Stella said. "There's nothing like a mountain chill."

"I long always for those mountains when I'm not there." The Governor set down his cup. "Stella, I know I've been rough on you today. But you needed it. You need a cold splash of water to the face to get back to the genuine person you are. What on earth drove you to your breaking point?" His voice was kind and Miss Alva's face filled with sympathy. That made it easier for Stella to be honest.

"Have you heard of the problems we've been having with Neely for quite some time?"

"I have."

"It's been trying, to say the least. Asher ignored it and Neely took his anger out on me. We were once so close." Her voice cracked. "I tried to stay calm and push it down. Chatty kept telling me I needed Zoloft and I refused."

"Good for you. Too much of that being used over the least little thing. You're a stoic mountain girl. You can rise above whatever confronts you. Our ancestors went through much worse."

She sighed then frowned. "That's what I thought. But I was wrong. I should have taken something to settle myself. I was of the mind that I'm stronger than I am. Governor, everyone has a breaking point, and thank goodness there are medications that will keep people from making a fool out of themselves." She paused and pointed to herself. "Case in point. I had suspected Asher of an affair. On that Saturday morning, I accidentally stumbled across more proof and knew it was most likely Annabelle. I should have confronted Asher. I didn't. So I got to the country club, the explosion button was pushed, and I ignited." She dropped her head. "I'm very ashamed. And, most despairing of all, I feel like I could have avoided it. I should have taken something for my nerves or, at the very least, not allowed the pressure to build inside me."

The Governor was quiet for a moment then stood up, walked over to her, and placed a strong, reassuring hand on her shoulder. "I'm too quick to rush to judgment sometimes. It's the politician in me, I suppose. You often have to choose your side quickly when the enemy is approaching. Sometimes, I have to ask forgiveness for my shotgun ways. Now is one of those times."

She reached up and placed her hand on his, grateful that she had faced up to this uncomfortable get-together. She was feeling better.

"Thank you, Governor."

"Have you heard from Asher?" Miss Alva asked as her husband settled back in beside her.

"Not directly, but he has called Mama, Chatty, Marlo, and who knows who else, looking for me." Pause. "Has he called y'all?" She punctuated it with a comical look.

"Asher Bankwell knows better than to call me for any-thing," the Governor replied in a strong, sharp voice. Stella was taken aback. She had never known of any friction between the two. They had always been amicable toward each other as far as she could tell. She couldn't think of anything to say.

"Stella, I've known Asher since he was born. His daddy, Jasper, was a close friend of mine." He stopped, studying her carefully for a moment. "Why does Asher go through so many businesses?"

She shrugged lightly. "He's not good at business, I guess."

"Apparently," the Governor retorted briskly before laughing.

"Jasper was an admirable businessman, wasn't he?" his wife asked.

The Governor nodded firmly. "His father, though born to wealth, could take a nickel and squeeze it into two dimes. It is a long-held trait of the Bankwell family to be good with money. Jasper's grandfather made a killin' off Coca-Cola stock, and Jasper was a king among Atlanta commercial developers. But Asher? His apple fell a long way from his family's tree, I guar-antee you that."

Stella felt an uneasiness in her spirit. She wondered if the Governor knew something she should know. She grappled in her mind for a way to ask, but before she could form the words or thoughts, the doorbell rang. Miss Alva excused herself to answer it. Within seconds, they heard delighted laughter. She came rushing joyfully into the room.

"Look, y'all, who has come to pay us a surprise visit! Our favorite neighbor," she exclaimed.

A man strolled leisurely into the room, his hands thrust comfortably in the pockets of his well-pressed khakis. He acted for all the world as though he was the Second Coming, something he probably believed.

He grinned broadly. "Have y'all missed me?"

Chapter Ten

The next morning was the first time in two weeks that Stella had not awakened to a world shrouded in despair and hopelessness. That morning, she did not open her eyes and quickly squish them shut tightly and pull the covers over her head, as usual. She did not roll up into a pitiful ball of flesh, nor did she cry. Most importantly, she did not fear what the new day dawning might bring.

Instead, she felt the soft morning sun on her skin and then, rather than turning away from it, she turned her face toward the light. She tilted her head back on the pillow dotted with small yellow flowers and basked in the warmth that greeted her there in the airy bedroom painted the color of a clear blue sky. Like a prescription, the island was working its magic on her, just as it always had.

What a difference from the previous morning when she woke up ragged from a night of thrashing about and worrying over what the Governor would say to her. Her dreaded nightmare had crossed an invisible dividing line from dark desperation into the beckoning of a better day to come. She had faced up to her shameful behavior, looked into the eyes of the living man she revered most, and owned up to the fool she had made of herself.

And she had survived. He was tough as a mountain lion, but she withstood the encounter. Then, he had offered his hand of friendship and loving support. If McCager Burnett and her mama could offer her such grace, then she could start anew.

"I might even be able to call Asher today," she thought brightly. But when that idea threatened to darken her happy beginning, she quickly pushed it aside. "Maybe tomorrow. I need to take it slow with this newfound cheerfulness. I don't want to scare it away." She threw back the fluffy, down-filled comforter and pulled herself out of the bed that Marlo had thoughtfully made splendidly comfortable. That was the first time in thirteen days that she had not lingered in a tangle of sheets, tears, and worry.

She pulled her thick, red-gold hair into a top ponytail, washed and moisturized her face, and headed to the kitchen for coffee. She longed for a newspaper. She always like to read the news with her coffee. Maybe she could afford a subscription to the *Brunswick News*, but she would have to be careful about money. No frivolous purchases.

Marlo, bless her heart, had thought of everything. She had left a thick earth-colored pottery coffee mug emblazoned with "Best Friends Forever." Stella poured coffee, added cream, then decided to drink it on the porch. She pulled on a pair of flannel-lined jeans, a heavy sweatshirt, and furry bedroom boots, all courtesy of Marlo's generosity. She pushed open the screen door and was immediately met by Spigot jumping down from the porch swing to eagerly greet her. No tag and no owner had been found, so Spigot was welcomed with water, hugs, and food purchased by the first few dollars Stella had spent from her stash.

"Little girl, it's so good to see you." Stella squatted down, put her mug on the porch floor, and swept the darling into her arms. "I'm afraid to get attached because what if you belong to someone? And who wouldn't own an adorable puppy like you?" Spigot nuzzled into Stella's arms. "But you do bring joy right now, and I'll take what I can get."

The air held a slight chill, but with a hot mug of coffee, warm clothes, and Spigot nestled into her lap in the rocker, she was comfortable, even peaceful.

"Good morning!" called an older gentleman who was walking by. The baby blue sky that hung over the ocean was a glorious backdrop. "Looks like it's gonna be nice today."

She smiled. "Yes, it does." She said it firmly. It was time to start believing in the good to come and stop dreading and even expecting the bad. What was done was done. Asher could have everything, including Annabelle and all the problems that Neely brought. That thought saddened her. Neely had been immensely unkind to her for a long time, but it was true what people said about folks like Neely: hurting people hurt people. She hoped he would straighten up and quit hurting himself and others.

The only thing that Stella wanted from her marriage was her car, sentimental pieces of jewelry, clothes, the sideboard her grandfather had built in his woodworking shed, and a bit of money to see her through until she could figure out what to do for a living. Her immediate plan was to build up gumption to face Asher. At least by phone. She felt like she had taken the first step toward that. Her coffee finished, she sat Spigot down and headed for a refill. The door banged behind her, and immediately she heard whining and scratching at the screen.

"Sweet little Spigot," she said from the other side. "You can't come in. This isn't my house." Spigot's eyes grew compelling as the dog seemed to summon every emotion from the bottom of her tippy tail. Stella knew the indoor company would be nice. Hmmm. She looked around at the blue velvet sofa and then back to Spigot.

"Wait here a minute." While the dog whimpered, Stella hurried to the second bedroom and searched the closet, where she found two large quilted blankets. She took one down from the shelf, carried it to the living room, and fixed it rather prettily over the sofa, which it covered almost completely. She flung open the door. "Welcome!"

Spigot did not need a second invitation or even a second to think about it. She trotted in and immediately jumped on the sofa, where she sniffed, scratched, pulled the blanket into a pile, then settled down happily. She looked at Stella as though she was the greatest person in the world.

Stella smiled. "Thank you, Spigot. I needed that look from someone."

She poured a second cup of coffee, then went to her nightstand and picked up an old copy of a Grace Kelly biography. The cottage had a well-stocked bookcase filled mostly with autobiographies and memoirs, which were Stella's favorites. With book in hand, she settled in the corner of the sofa while Spigot nudged as close as possible. Stella read as she sipped coffee. Her soul felt soothed. After about an hour, she was startled by the ringing phone. The shrill noise scared her. First the sound, then the thought of who could be on the other end. Asher? Had he found her? She wasn't ready to talk to him, so she decided not to answer. After a dozen rings, it stopped. She took a breath, but in seconds the phone began ringing again. Hesitantly, she rose from the sofa and approached the handset that was situated on a little table between the hallway and kitchen. Her hands trembling, she picked up the receiver.

Maybe she wasn't doing as good as she thought when she awoke. She put the receiver to her ear but said not a word.

"Hello?" came a voice, followed by, "Helloooo? Stellie, are you there?"

Stella heaved a sigh of relief and held a hand to her pounding chest. "Oh, Marlo, that scared me. I was afraid it was Asher. We need to get a signal so I'll know it's you. This old phone doesn't have caller ID."

Marlo chuckled. "You can't buy a phone like that anymore. Speaking of phones, do I need to get a cell phone for you? I could get you one with a burner number." She meant it both as a joke and a serious thought.

"No, I don't think so. I like not having one. My nerves are getting better. I need this phone number, though, so I can call Mama and give it to her."

"It's right there inside the front cover of the phone book. When was the last time you saw one of those?"

Stella flipped to the front page and saw the number. "It's been a while, but I rather like it. I've been living in a world far removed from the true Stella Jackson. It's good to be jerked back so hard."

In the background, Stella heard the door of Sloan Coastal Realty open as the bell jingled.

"Hold on," Marlo said to Stella. She called out from her office to the person who had entered. "Hello! If you'll take a seat, I'll be right out."

An elderly woman's voice replied, "Take your time, honey. We'll just sit here in the warm sunshine and read a magazine. We've got all the time in the world."

"Thank you, ma'am," Marlo said. Stella heard her get up and close the door before she continued their conversation.

"Listen, Stellie, we're in a real jam."

Stella perked up. "I was in a real jam when y'all helped me. What can I do?"

Marlo took a breath. "Our receptionist/assistant is on maternity leave. We thought we could make it fine because she was only going to take six weeks, but she called this morning. She's four weeks in and has decided she wants to take three months. We will go nuts. It'd take us two weeks to interview and hire someone, and we need someone now. This very moment. Would you consider helping us out?"

Stella's first response was, "Absolutely. Anything you need." Then, second thoughts flew through her mind. Was she capable, considering her feeble brain? Would she run into people—people from Atlanta with second homes—who would know her and of her country club performance? Would it lead to Asher finding her? Could she operate an office computer? She was fretting but trying not to let it show.

"Oh, sister-friend, you are the best! Are you sure?"

"Uh, yeah. Sure." If Marlo noticed the hesitancy in her voice, she ignored it. "When do you want me?"

"Now."

"Now???" Stella's heart flew into her throat.

"As soon as you can get dressed and get here. We wear resort dressy to the office, so you'll find several outfits in the boxes. A dress. Slacks, top, sweater. Anything like that."

Stella tried to find the words to back out. She was scared. The fear hung in her chest like lead. Before she could get the words out, Marlo said, "I gotta go. Someone else just came in and I'm the only one here. Alton's at the doctor and Evelyn is out showing property. I'll see you as soon as you can get here. Thanks, my dear friend! Hurry!"

Stella held the phone for a second then gingerly replaced it. Well, this wasn't exactly the day she had imagined when she woke up like a chirpy little bird. Dread choked her throat. But instead of pushing away, she used the full measure of her mountain stubbornness and leaned in. Somehow things had to change, and this was certainly some kind of a start.

✑

Stella turned the car off, checked her lipstick in the mirror, picked up her keys, and took a deep breath.

"I am not going to worry about what could happen. I am only going to do this." She stepped out of the car and smoothed away the wrinkles from the pink and white Lilly Pulitzer dress—a simple shift but tremendously fetching on her newly slender body. "Lord, help me," she whispered as she stepped onto the curb. When she opened the door, she was immediately flummoxed and forgot her anxiety. Marlo was engulfed by people. She was showing photos to a couple, well into their seventies, perhaps eighties, while a middle-aged man studied properties on a bulletin board. A young couple with a twisty toddler was flipping through a listing book. Two phones rang at once. Marlo's hair was disheveled and her lipstick was long gone.

"Stella!" she called urgently across the room. "Please get the phones."

Stella ran to the nearby desk facing the full windows that showcased the village. She set her purse down, never thinking how odd it might look that a receptionist was carrying a Chanel, and answered the first phone. "Good afternoon." She glanced at the wall clock. 10:47. "I mean 'morning.'" Sloan Coastal Realty. May I help you?"

"Yes. Alton Sloan, please."

Thankfully, she knew the answer. "I'm sorry. Mr. Sloan is not in at the moment. May I take a message?" A tiny bit of ease slipped across her as she realized that all she had to do was help people and she'd be fine. She just had to practice Southern courtesy and manners as her mama taught her.

It was almost 1:30 before the flurry of busyness stopped. During that time, Stella had answered the phones, taken messages, talked with folks waiting to see Marlo, and offered coffee to everyone. Finally, the office cleared and both women collapsed in Marlo's office.

"Girlfriend, I'd be done for if you hadn't showed up. Thank you!"

Stella waved it aside. "Glad to help."

"I hope you mean it because we could sure use you for a few days. Maybe you'll even stay long enough to see us through Courtney's maternity leave."

"Why not? I have nowhere else to go and no one else who wants me." She said it jokingly, but it hurt to hear the words.

Marlo got up from her chair, crossed from behind her desk, and hugged Stella. "You are always wanted and needed here. The cottage is yours for as long you want to stay there. Consider it part of your payment as our new receptionist."

Stella teared up. One problem solved. Then she thought of another. "Uh, Marlo, is there a pet policy for the cottage?"

Marlo looked surprised. "Normally, no pets because, for some reason I can't fathom, everyone seems to own dogs that weigh over a hundred pounds. That's flirting with disaster and damage. Why?"

Stella shrugged and gave her friend a bashful look. "I don't know. This little terrier mix has been staying at the cottage since I got here. I found her licking for water so I named her Spigot. No tag. I've knocked on doors and no one claims her. I let her in this morning." She quickly added, "But I covered the sofa with a quilt first." Stella dropped her head and looked at her folded hands. "She's been a comfort to me. I haven't had a dog since I went to college. I forgot how calming they could be."

"Unconditional love." Marlo was smiling. "Well, it looks like Spigot has found a new cottage, too. Just try to keep her out of any trouble or chewing. The backyard has that sweet picket fence. Maybe you can make her a bed in the garden shed when you're gone all day." She frowned. "I hope you don't get attached and then someone claims her."

Stella nodded quietly. "Me, too." Then she looked up at her kind friend, studying her like she was seeing her for the first time.

Marlo was an attractive woman with thick, long, dark brown hair, large eyes, and an open smile. She had always been a bit tomboyish. When they were kids, she climbed trees in jeans and tee shirts while Stella wore either a dress or a cute shorts outfit that her mama had sewed. Since high school, Stella had worn her nails polished and filed to a medium-length oval. Marla's nails, though, were au natural and filed close. Occasionally she agreed to a clear coat of polish, but mostly she didn't bother. She was handsome with the dark complexion and high cheek bones of her Cherokee ancestors on her daddy's side. She wore mascara, a light blusher, and a dab of lipstick. Stella, always fully made up in a tasteful way, envied Marlo's natural beauty and how comfortable she looked in slim floral slacks—Stella would never look right in those—a twin sweater set, and Tod's.

Marlo shifted, and Stella could tell she wanted to change the subject. "How did things go with Governor Burnett yesterday?" she asked. "Boy, I'll tell you that ol' Tatum Sloan owes you big time. Tate feels awful that he let the Governor trick him into admitting you were coming here. Just tuck that away"—she tapped her temple—"and use it as a 'get out of jail free' card when you need something from Tate. Was it bad?"

Stella shook her head and reached for a strand of hair to twirl around her finger. "He didn't give me any breaks, that's for sure. It was a serious talking-to, but you know, Marlo, it was more like a father who loves his daughter and wants to make sure she doesn't trip again. It made me miss my daddy. He and Miss Alva were very loving after the chewing out was over, though. I had coffee with them." She perked up, remembering. "Oh, and you'll never guess who showed up at the house while I was there. Just came waltzing right in."

Marlo's mouth was forming "Who?" when the front door jingled and in whirled the force of nature known as Evelyn Maria Sloan, Marlo's mother-in-law.

"I sold a house!" she sang. "A *big* one. Oceanfront. Hello, new patio furniture!" Evelyn was a large woman. Tall. Wide shoulders. A considerable girth. All of which was covered in bright colors and flowing fabrics. Today, she wore wide-legged black pants, flat heels, a roomy black tunic, and a multi-colored, knee-length chiffon duster. Her dark blonde hair was teased into a bouffant bob. Her costume jewelry, "statement pieces" as she enjoyed saying, was a pair of enormous gold earrings and a collar necklace that was four inches wide. She whirled merrily around Marlo's office. She was a bossy person but a happy one.

Suddenly, she realized Stella was there. "Stella!" She held out her arms. "I'm so glad to see you. Give me a big hug." Stella felt so tiny as she was wrapped in Evelyn's ample flesh. "It's so good to have you here. You're at the Beachview cottage, right? Why are you here at the office? Y'all goin' to lunch?"

Marlo loved her mother-in-law despite the fact that she got on her nerves sometimes. But Evelyn was a good woman. A hard-working go-getter. She did everything she could to help Marlo, Tate, and her grandchildren.

"Stella has graciously agreed to help us out while Courtney takes baby leave. She's been a big help already. You wouldn't believe what this place looked like an hour ago…wall-to-wall people."

Evelyn clapped her hands. "Marvelous! This is marvelous. We'll show you how to use the MLS and FMLS systems." She winked. "We might even make a realtor out of you before it's over. The island is booming! Everyone wants to live in paradise."

The door opened and the bell sang. Evelyn motioned her hand toward the door and winked merrily. "Practice makes perfect, sweet girl. You take this while we're here to help you with the answers."

Stella straightened her shoulders, tossed her hair back, pulled a broad smile onto her face, and winked. With confidence, she marched through the door into the reception area. A man in a navy shirt and light slacks stood with his back to her, thumbing through a real estate guide.

"Hello!" she called cheerfully. "May I help you?"

He turned around, and her eyes, for some reason, went immediately to the embroidery on the left side of his shirt. "United States Marshals Service," it said. For a moment, her heart thumped. Her first thought was that she was about to be arrested for her public conniption fit. She struggled to maintain her composure, and then looked up to his face.

"Stella Bankwell," he said, his face breaking into a charming smile. "What are you doing here?"

It was Jackson Culpepper.

Chapter Eleven

Stella's heart sputtered, partly a flutter because of Pepper's handsomeness and his appealing personality and partly a stutter because her mind tried to tell her heart that she didn't know how not to act any way other than awkward.

She took a second to think before coming up with a terrific opening line. "Hello, Pepper."

He laughed, seeing her discomfort.

"Don't worry, Stella, I'm not here to arrest you." He laughed, meaning it as a bad joke that he often used. She did not laugh. She did not even smile. Being arrested, she feared, was a strong possibility. The worrisome thought of being extradited back to Atlanta crossed her mind.

She saw him watching as a frown clouded her face.

"As a federal officer for twenty years, I know that look," he said. "You haven't done anything I should arrest you for, have you?" He flashed a smile full of flawless, white teeth while his eyes searched her face. She was taken again by his strong, manly appeal and, at the same time, drawn to him, sensing that he could provide a haven of emotional and physical safety. She wasn't some feminist who didn't want help from a man. She'd take less worry, more love, and a hand up from anyone who could offer it. Whether it was an adorable little dog or a strong, handsome man.

Her mouth was dry. She cleared her throat and tried to joke. "Do I look like a criminal?"

"Yes," he deadpanned.

Her tongue stuck to the roof of her mouth.

He studied her wide-eyed look, fringed with a bit of fear. "I deal with a lot of white-collar crime, so I've seen quite a few folks trade an Armani suit or a Chanel dress for an orange jumpsuit." He glanced toward her Chanel bag. "The appearance of a criminal takes many forms, and that means the most surprising lawbreakers, to many people, are never a surprise to a U.S. Marshal."

"Hopefully, no one I know," she responded in a fake, light tone as she tried nonchalantly to pick up her purse and slide it under the desk. He noticed but did not let on. "But I did know Bennett Sutton by name and reputation," she continued. "His photo was in the country club directory the first year he was put away, the same year I became a member through marriage, not natural selection. Those little white-haired committee women couldn't get any photo or mention of Bennett out of the directory quick enough. When there was a delay in reprinting, they just took the old books, cut out a black paper square, and pasted it over his face." She was trying to distract Pepper so he wouldn't think of her as a doer of wrongs.

"Bennett Sutton," he repeated, looking out the window and studying the sky for a moment. "That name is familiar but I can't quite put my finger on it."

"Atlanta accountant. Stole from the rich and gave to himself."

"Oh, I'm sure I've met him or at least a thousand like him." He laughed then paused, looking around the office. "Do you work here?"

"Oh no," she started, then caught herself. "Actually, I do. I just agreed to take the job an hour ago, so I'm not use to saying I work. I've been a stay-at-home wife, stepmother, and patron of the arts for the last few years." She fluttered her eyes comically at the last comment. "Marlo, whose in-laws own this company, is my best friend. I'm staying on St. Simons for a while. Their receptionist is out on maternity leave, so Marlo needed help and here's her help." She pointed a thumb toward her chest.

He eyed her knowingly. Clearly he could seize up a situation quickly. Her Chanel bag. Her obviously expensive hairdressers, designers, manicurists, and the like. And then the large chip in the pale pink polish on the thumb of her left hand and a dress that wasn't quite up to the standards of a Chanel bag. She imagined him deciding there was more to the story than what he'd thought.

Phones were ringing, and Evelyn and Marlo were talking as two more folks came in jabbering, yet in the clatter, Pepper leaned closer and said softly in her ear, "I'm sorry for whatever you're going through. I hope it is as easy for you as it can possibly be."

She stared at him, puzzled. Completely confused. He watched her expression then said quietly, "In my line of work, I see a lot of situations. It's amazing what similar situations have in common."

"Mr. Culpepper," she began, resorting to the tone of comeuppance always employed when Southerners want to step away from the casualness of first names and draw boundaries. Of course, he could tell what she was doing. After all, he was from Memphis. She tried anyway. "I haven't a thought in my head as to what you could possibly be talking about."

Sympathy colored his eyes bluer, and he spoke with such kindness. "Please forgive me if I sounded like a smart aleck.

That would be the duty of my younger brother, not mine. I'm the nice one." He smiled sweetly. "It appears that you may be headed either for a divorce, in a divorce, or finishing with a divorce."

Her face melted into surprise. "And you know this how?" He shook his head. "Let's forget it. Again, sometime I'll tell you." There was no reason to mention that he noticed a slight indention on the ring finger of her left hand where once a ring had been. "But right now, I am here on a bit of business. Is it possible that you have a short-term lease for an apartment or condo? Is there anything available near where I'm staying? It's for a friend from Virginia. She will be arriving in three days."

Stella absolutely hated herself for the feeling of disappointment that stabbed her heart. She wasn't divorced yet, wouldn't even speak to her husband so she could obtain a divorce, wasn't healed emotionally, yet here she was with her eyes on someone else only to find that he had someone else. At that moment, she thought what all women going through a breakup think at one time or the other: It was is so much easier being a couple; that way you don't have to worry about liking someone who doesn't like you back or is unavailable.

"I will need to check with Marlo," she replied somewhat briskly. "I'm so new that I don't even know where the coffee maker is or if there *is* a coffee maker."

Marlo hurried by them, headed to the copier. Stella stopped her and introduced Jackson Culpepper, who insisted, "Call me Pepper." Then Stella explained his rental need.

"I think we have something, but let me make sure. Stella will let you know later today."

Pepper turned to Stella and smiled. "Why don't we meet in the lobby of the King and Prince around five? We can look over what you've found, and perhaps I can talk you into a glass of wine before you leave."

Stella opened her mouth to decline. She sure didn't need to add wounds and humiliation onto her pathetic being, but Marlo spoke first. "Perfect! She will be there at five." Marlo turned to her friend and winked.

Stella threw a look of annoyance at Marlo, but Pepper never saw it. He just called over his shoulder as he started out, "Thank you, Marlo. See you soon, Stella Bankwell."

❧

Spigot was cuddled up on the blanket, holding in her paws a plush ice cream toy colored in brown, blue, and yellow. She either toted it everywhere she went or laid with her chin on it. She was happy to see Stella, jumping down from the sofa and running in circles until Stella snapped the leash onto her collar.

"C'mon, baby girl," Stella said, again grateful for someone to love when it felt there was no one to love her or anyone else she'd ever love. She knelt down and petted Spigot. "Let's take a quick walk then settle you down because I have somewhere to go."

It was lovely outside. A breeze was blowing, and though it had been a chilly a few hours earlier, it had settled into the perfect beach wind. When they returned to the sweet cottage, a shiver of happiness crossed Stella's spirit at the cheerful blue and yellow colors. She fed and watered Spigot and gave her a chew treat.

Then she studied herself in the mirror, wondering if she should change clothes. She chuckled sarcastically to herself. "First, that'd be trying too hard. Second, he doesn't care. He already has someone." She did reach into the closet to pull out a knee-length yellow cardigan. She picked up her Chanel bag, thinking she needed to get a more subtle purse. Just as she put her hand on the doorknob, the phone on the kitchen wall rang.

She walked the few steps to blue trimline phone. "Hello?"

"Good. I caught you," Marlo said. "I know you've got a little dreamy eye on Jack Culpepper so..."

"I do *not* have an eye, dreamy or steamy, on Mr. Culpepper," Stella replied with an unusual snap in her voice.

Marlo laughed. "Okay. When you sound like that, it means I'm too close to the truth. Not another word until I tell you this: Mr. Culpepper is single."

Stella's eyes widened, and a slip of a smile came to her stubborn lips. "Are you sure?"

"As sure as I am that somewhere, someplace near Atlanta, Georgia, Neely Bankwell is up to no good tonight."

"How can you be so certain? About Jack Culpepper, I mean. Neely, for sure."

"I called Bud over in marketing at the King and Prince and asked since Culpepper is staying there."

Stella slapped her hand on the kitchen table in a gesture of aggravation. Those were not the kinds of things to ask a guy. At least in her experience, guys seldom knew what was going on with other people, particularly in their romances, and if they did know something they were bound to get wrong some vital piece of information. This was a very iffy source. Other than Chatty, Stella never relied on a man for pertinent information.

"Marlo, you would have been best served to ask the front desk or a housekeeper. Surely, there's an observant woman you could have asked." A brief pause. "Discretely."

"Oh ye of little faith. Bud had his rental contract on his desk, and it was right there in black and white: Single. Bud said he's been staying with them for years whenever he comes down to Glynco on Marshal business, and he has always been single."

Still, Stella was afraid to get her hopes up. Maybe he wasn't drawn to romantic relationships for one reason or the other...like being married to his work or burned by a bad experience. "He's probably not interested," she said. "Besides, if he gets ordered to arrest me, that could kill a good potential romance right there."

Marlo started laughing. "Stella, U.S. Marshals have much more important work to do than arrest a rich woman for throwing a drink in the face of the Jezebel loving on her husband. You need to calm your mind down when it comes to your high opinion of your illegal offenses."

"Well…." Stella mused. Then quickly added, "Well, he's finding an apartment for a woman who is coming to visit. Did Bud know anything about that?"

Marlo's tone was soothing and reassuring. "What we do know is that he's not married, and that's a good start. If this is a girlfriend, maybe the relationship is on a slippery slope or maybe it's just a friend. Maybe he's bringing her down here to tell her it's over. Not everyone runs away from a face-to-face breakup like some people we know. Now. Exhale and shake negative thoughts from your mind. Comb your hair, put lipstick on, dab some perfume behind your ears, and get over there."

Stella, her long, pretty legs showing in the dress that skimmed her knees, slipped from a pair of flats to high wedge espadrilles, shook her hair until it was thick and voluminous, used a coral-colored gloss, then headed out for the one-block walk.

The hotel was always so pretty as night began to fall. The castle-like, cream-colored stucco exterior featured just enough lights to give the place a romantic hue. With the palm trees swaying in the light breeze, it looked like a movie set from the 1940s. Suddenly, her confidence was back. Surely, a false note of some kind. Stella was certain that it would pass rather quickly. She had been playing mind games with herself, telling herself that Pepper would be swept away by her allure. Then, maybe, after talking a little business, they'd take a walk either on the beach or on the miniature boardwalk that ran around the outside of the hotel just inside the wrought-iron railings. Full of spirit and a dash of optimism, she hurried in the front door and headed toward the massive dark wood bar in the center of the room.

Pepper saw her, and she knew she did not imagine how brightly his face lit up—the face of a man who sees *the* woman he wants to see. She straightened her back and stood tall. She glimpsed the shoulder of another man sitting at the bar, talking to Pepper, but a young couple standing behind him obstructed the view. She paid no never mind to any of those things. She just walked straight to Pepper, her smile broad. He wore a blue striped button-down shirt opened at his long, tanned neck, a navy jacket, and khaki pants. She sashayed over to him and said, somewhat flirtatiously, "Hello, Jackson Culpepper."

He jumped from his chair and looked over her face and hair in admiration. "Hello, don't you…"

Before he could finish his words, Stella felt the lightness of three fingers tickling across her shoulder. "Helloooo, Stella Jackson Bankwell."

Without turning around, her stomach flipped. Goodbye, romance.

"Dahlin', aren't you gonna speak? To your most beloved?"

She took a deep sigh and turned around. "Chatty, what are you doing here?"

Chapter Twelve

Chatty, always the good sport, heard the touch of hatefulness in Stella's voice, and still he laughed. "Stella, I am your best friend and have been ever since that terrible twist of fate dumped you in the roiling bowels of Buckhead society." He leaned over and fake kissed each cheek, then pattered on.

"Should I not be getting an inferiority complex—if I could figure out how to do that—after seeing you at the Governor's house yesterday when you didn't seem overly enthused to see me? Thank God the Burnetts simply adore me. Otherwise, I could have been crushed."

She ignored that ramble. "Should I take it that you two have met?" Her stomach was in such a twist that she hoped the two men had just sat down by each other and that, by the time she got there, had not yet gotten past chitchat such as the weather or who won the golf championship.

Pepper revved up her heart with his brilliant smile. "Oh, we've been sitting here for a little while. Long enough for me to know the names Asher, Caroline, and, uh, oh yes, Annabelle."

For the first time in the years she had known Chatty, she wanted to grab his head full of thick hair and drag his substantial girth off the barstool, through the lobby, and all the way to the Atlantic ocean that was currently displaying the possibility of a riptide.

Chatty shrugged playfully and smiled. "Well, he explained he is a friend of yours. He was obviously very interested to hear about your soon-to-be former life." He tilted his head back as though he was a Greek posing for his likeness to be placed on a coin. "I was happy to oblige. I want to always help others as I was taught by Mrs. Faughtenberry in Sunday school when I was six years old." Chatty turned to Pepper. "Mrs. Faughtenberry always said I was destined to do great works of helpfulness in my life." He spread wide his hands between Pepper and Stella. "As I have just done."

Stella was so mad that her blood was roaring and she could barely get her breath. "Chatham Balsam Colquitt the FOURTH, how could you? You have told him all about my heartaches and the most embarrassing episode in my life, the one that will follow me to my grave. The one that, after everyone has left the graveside and gone back to my house for casseroles and deviled eggs, will be the single subject they discuss endlessly, with each person weighing in." Had Stella not been so mad, she might have noticed the funny, goggle-like thing that Chatty did with his eyes and how he snapped back his head when he was trying to comprehend the incomprehensible. But she didn't notice. She just plunged forward.

She, in fact, moved closer and took her cute, little tipped-up nose close to his broad, patrician one. "You told him that I physically assaulted Annabelle with a mint julep at the Buckhead Country Club?"

Now, Chatty's goggle eyes spun wider and his mouth popped open like a spring from a Jack-in-a-box. Before he could utter a defense, Pepper took Stella by the shoulders and turned her to face him.

"Stella, I have no idea what you're talking about. All Chatham has told me is about Asher, who, as I think I recall accurately, is a good-looking sneaky snake of a guy, and how his mother, Miss Caroline, is the doyenne of Buckhead with money and power. All I know about Annabelle is that she's from Memphis, and Chatham, who says that all Southerners are separated by a mere two degrees, wondered if I might know her."

Chatty folded his hands over his stomach and smiled angelically. "The only imperfection in this conversation is that I cannot, for the life of me, remember what Annabelle's last name was when first she slithered into town with what we've been led to believe was her first husband. And, I declare, I don't think I ever knew what her maiden name was. These are two important elements in deciding if Mr. Culpepper has ever encountered this—I'll use a biblical word here because sometimes you just can't do better than the Bible—this concubine."

Stella melted. It started with bowing her head until her chin touched her chest, then slumping her shoulders, followed by clutching at her stomach that was suddenly kicking her like an angry mule. Funny the things you think at times like that. She looked down at the black and white tile on which she was standing, the very place that had once been the deep end of the inside pool, and wondered if it was possible to stamp her feet hard enough to break the tile and fall through the floor into that old pool.

Chatty laughed merrily, one of his gifts. "I know what you're thinking, Stella Bankwell. I can read your mind. No one knows you better so let me just say this: when they took the old pool out, they poured loads of concrete in to fill it up. I know personally Charles Wesley Maycomb of the Maycomb

Concrete Company and, lawd, he told me all about what a terrible time they had. They had to bring it in the door by cupfuls because they couldn't get a truck in here. That makes it completely impossible for you to be swallowed up by the floor."

Leave it to Chatty to make her laugh in spite of herself. Pepper chuckled, too.

"Y'all, I am deeply embarrassed. Again, here I go making a scene in a public place. Please, forgive me."

Pepper leaned his head down in order to look her straight in the eye. "There is no apology needed. It's obvious that you are under a lot of stress. People don't think clearly under stress. You can trust me on that because I'm a bonafide law enforcement officer for the United States Government. Our branch of service has spent a lot of your tax dollars taking classes on this and becoming professionals on stress." He had the most encouraging smile she had ever seen in her life. It warmed her from her eyes to her toes.

"And that goes for me, too, Stellie," Chatty offered. "I have an uncanny ability to sense emotional stress. You know that for a fact."

Stella nodded and gave him a small smile. Chatty could always help return a good mood. He took her by the arm and gently pulled her a bit closer to him. Then, as if he were about to announce the recipe for the atomic bomb, he said out of the side of his mouth, low but not low enough that Pepper could not hear, "All of these unpleasant undoings of yours could have been avoided by getting a prescription of Xanax, just as I told you months ago."

Stella jerked her arm away, her foul mood returning, and cried, "Chatham!"

"Uh-oh," he muttered, stepping down from his stool, pulling a clip of money from his pocket, and laying three twenties on the bar. "I know when it's best to go. She only calls me by my Christian name when I'm about to be laid low. Mr. Culpepper, the drinks are on me. Please, do give me a call so I might invite you to drinks at my home on Sea Island. I live *next door* to Governor and Mrs. Burnett. They love me like a son. I'll invite them over and you can meet them." He winked. "And if Stella has forgiven me by then, she, too, shall be invited."

Chatty dared to glance at his friend then reacted to her expression by saying, "Oh my, I'm withering away. Very soon, I'll be like the wicked witch in Oz, melted into an oil spot." He scooted between Stella and Pepper and did not look back as he called out cheerfully, "Goodbye, dear hearts!"

Pepper, concern and compassion filling his face, began, "Stella, I…"

She cut him short. "Mr. Culpepper, here is a folder with three possibilities for your friend. One studio, a one-bedroom, and a small two-bedroom cottage. If one of these should meet your requirements, please call our office." She turned on her espadrille heels, the ones that had a rubber bottom so they did not make a furious clicking, and hurried away.

Again, she looked down at the floor and wished it could open up, swallow her, and make her disappear from the rotten mess that had become her life. From fairy tale to nightmare. It just kept getting worse.

Chapter Thirteen

It had been two days since Stella's latest public meltdown in the lobby bar of the King and Prince. She had spoken neither to Jack Culpepper nor to Chatty, though first thing the next morning, Chatty had sent an enormous floral arrangement made personally by Edward, the island's beloved florist.

Pepper, though, had made no attempt to reach out. He had called Alton, Marlo's father-in-law, on his cell phone—it was one of the numbers in the folder Stella had left with him—and, as has already been established, men are of little use in gathering information.

"Who is the apartment for?" she asked Alton, whom she had known since she was twelve.

"Marylyn."

"Who is that?"

Alton rolled his eyes. "I have no idea, except on the application it says she is Caucasian. On age, she said 'Guess.' She lives in Roanoke, Virginia, and wants it for a month. One of the possibilities is close to your cottage."

Stella rolled her eyes. Great. If Pepper's girlfriend ended up close by, at some point she was sure to meet them while they were holding hands and strolling romantically along the beach.

"Alton, what else did you find out?"

"I promise, as the Eagle Scout I am, that is all I know. Oh. I do know she's coming tomorrow."

Well, wasn't that a fun fact to hear? Something to really look forward to. Stella tucked her head and quietly went back to her desk. As she was digging in a drawer to find a rubber band, the phone rang.

"Good morning, Sloan Coastal Realty."

"May I speak with Mrs. Bankwell?" said a woman's voice with a heavy Latin accent.

Stella thought of hanging up, but something sounded vaguely familiar. Silently, she held the phone for a minute and then said warily, "May I tell her who is calling?"

"This is private business. I don't think I should tell." When Stella heard that, she knew it was their housekeeper, Lana, because that was a catchphrase of hers: *I don't think I should tell.*

"Lana Banana, this is Stella."

"Oh, Miss Stella! I've been worried so sick about you. You okay?"

"As good as possible. How did you find me here?"

"I know what I know. I just figured it out that you were with your friend." Stella could see her grinning, happy that she was so smart. Stella had learned from Lana that when folks come from other countries, like Lana's Brazil, it means a lot when they can maneuver the English language enough to figure something out. "I didn't know the name of the company, so I called each real property company until I found you. I thought, 'Well, if she's not there but she knows someone there, they will tell me.'"

Stella laughed. She loved Lana. Over the past year, as Stella suffered, Lana had made her delicious food and brought her cupcakes. They were very close.

"Lana, I'm sorry I left without talking to you. Or called. You mean much more to me than that. I'm just trying to avoid Mr. Bankwell. Please don't tell him where I am."

"I will not say a word. I'm just glad you're safe. But Mr. Asher, he is odd. He hasn't spoken of you except to say you were gone for a few days. Then last night…" She paused and took a deep breath. "Last night, he went into your closet, he got all your pretty things in several loads, then he took them to the fire pit in the backyard and he burned everything!"

Stella's stomach churned and her head began to swim. Material things weren't so important to her, but she was sentimental, and many of those dresses—those quite expensive dresses—had special meaning to her. She thought of the black dress she had worn to her daddy's funeral. Long-sleeved, below the knee, with a round neckline. It was a Stella McCartney, so simple and pleasing. The red dress she had worn when she chaired the American Heart Association Wear Red for Women event. The navy Gucci overcoat with stunning red buttons. Then, it came to her: the piece that she would miss for the rest of her days: the wedding dress that she and her mama had sewed together. The memories of making it were precious even if the wedding itself no longer was.

Stella swallowed, her eyes brimming with tears. She felt both invaded and sad that it had all come to this. "Lana, did he really burn everything?"

"Yes. Except he did have a woman over here—he called her Annabeth or Annadale—and he let her pick jewelry and handbags." Lana, who had been speaking quietly, now whispered loudly into the phone. "She took all the 'Shanels' and I saw her with several 'Tif-fa-ny' boxes."

Stella dropped her face into her hands on the desk. She would try not to dwell on this. She would try to remember what her daddy used to say: "Worry not about what hard work and money can replace."

Lana continued, "But Miss Stella, there are several things at Mr. Peterson's, the dry cleaner. I know that—how do you say 'spec-ti-cular' Armani overcoat is there. A few dresses and slacks. I will pick those up and take them home with me. I'll keep safe till you come back." She paused. "Or do you come back?"

In all that had happened in the last week, the idea of going back to Buckhead had never occurred to Stella. To be honest, she had no plans except for one: healing and getting back on her feet.

"No, Lana, I don't expect to come back. Are you calling from your cell phone?"

"Oh no. I not trust Mr. Asher. He is what, in Brazil, we call "shady." I call from my sister Espi's house. Call this number if you need me." She reeled off the phone number. Lana had never before mentioned not trusting Asher, but Stella wondered what it meant. Did she mean as a womanizer or a businessman or simply a man or all of the above?

Stella sighed. "Lana, there are a couple of things I'd like to have if you could mail them to me. My laptop and my Daddy's Bible, which are in my sitting room. Could you send those to Marlo's office?"

"With happiness. And I not let Mr. Asher know. I will sneak." She laughed with a merry chime. "If I find anything I think you want, I'll sent that, too."

"Thank you." After Stella gave her the post office address in Marlo's name, she said, "One more question: How is Neely?"

"Huh! Neely is still unkind, not obeying boy. Since you have left, he has worked for Mr. Asher at the airplane company."

Stella was taken aback. This didn't sound like an arrangement that either of them would like. But maybe Asher had decided it was better to keep your enemies close, even an enemy who was, at least for the time being, your son.

"Neely's mother called the other day. I don't know what but there was a great upset over that call. I heard Mr. Asher say, 'I'll get you the money. Be patient.'"

"I have no idea," Stella responded. "But then I have no idea about so much. Listen, Lana, I need to run. Thank you for calling. Let me give you Marlo's phone number, too. Call her if you can't get me at the office."

They hung up and Stella sat at her desk, lost to the world and staring at the people hurrying by on Mallery or into Strother Hardware across the street. She was shaken out of her trance only when Alton said, "Stella, I have an errand, if you wouldn't mind."

"Of course not, Mr. Alton."

He looked a little sheepish. "We have some folks coming in for a condo at the Beach Club tomorrow. Would you take a drive over and check it out? Please make sure all light bulbs work, heat/air, washing machine, TV, WiFi. We keep this rented out a good bit, but I don't know what is going to happen. The gentleman, Mr. Briscoe, who owned it as an investment property, just died. An elderly man. It's in an estate that Cager Burnett is handling, so as soon as the Governor knows something of the heirs' intentions, he'll let us know. Sometimes they sell the beach properties; sometimes they just fight over who's going to use it and when." He shrugged and smiled. "You learn a lot about people in the real estate business, and it's not always something you want to know."

"Do I need to check drawers and closets?" Stella asked, picking up her purse then her sweater from the back of her chair.

"Wonderful idea! Please do. The housecleaning staff is supposed to do that during each cleaning, but one never can tell."

"If it's okay, I'll drop by my cottage while I'm headed that way and let Spigot out."

"Take your time." He turned to go back to his office then stopped and turned toward her. "Stella, I know you're going through a hard time right now but know this: our family loves having you with us. It's just kinda sparkled things up."

She walked over and hugged him. "I didn't realize how much I was missing love until I got here. Thank you."

Jumbled up with emotions—her clothes burned, Annabelle in her house, the love that Lana and the Sloans had shown her—she was a bit distracted as she walked toward her silver Jaguar parked three spaces down from the office. She pulled the keys from her bag and pressed the button to unlock the doors. The beeping sound caused a man standing near the trunk to jump back.

"Oh!" he said. "That's you. Is this your car?" He was wearing navy work pants and a white button-up, short-sleeve shirt with "Homer's" embroidered across the pocket.

"Yes, it is. Why?"

With a no-nonsense look, he walked over to her, papers in hand. "I'm Jed from Homer's Towing. I have papers here to repossess this car."

"What!" she exclaimed. "This is a mistake. This car is paid for. I have the title at home."

"Yes ma'am, maybe it is paid for. But my orders to repossess don't come from a lender." He handed the papers to her, and she stared at them, trying to make sense of what she was seeing.

Finally, Jed spoke up. "Ma'am, that's a court order from the IRS. They're taking your car because of unpaid taxes."

Chapter Fourteen

Jed from Homer's Towing Service stood silent for several minutes as Stella tried to make sense of the document declaring that her car was being "seized." It was a frightful word, and though she was well educated and had been an executive in the days before she married Asher Jasper Bankwell III, she could not comprehend it.

She was frozen to the sidewalk on Mallery Street, gripping the piece of paper tightly. Jed was a bit hard-hearted due to his many years of repossessing cars for loan companies. It was not an easy job. Once, he had to take one from a nine-months pregnant woman whose husband had left her four months earlier. That one tore him up so badly that when he got home that night, he couldn't face a bite of dinner and told his wife he was going to have to find another job. Homer, though, paid three dollars more an hour than Jed could find anywhere else, so he had been forced to stay. As it was, it took every dollar he made to support his wife and three kids. The IRS seizures did not bother him, though, because he had no tolerance for people who lived the high life while not paying their taxes. He had to pay his taxes while living in a double-wide trailer and driving an old pickup truck. Whenever he seized a car for the IRS, it was always a fancy, expensive one like the Jaguar he was about to take. It was never an old beater or inexpensive car.

Something about this one, though, bothered him. In his gut, it felt more like the one he had repossessed from the pregnant woman. So when Stella found her voice and began to ask questions, Jed was patient and kind instead of using his normal brittle and clipped tones.

"I'm sorry, sir, I don't understand. We've always paid our taxes."

The "we" triggered Jed's understanding. He had seen this before with husbands doing things their wives did not know.

"Ma'am," he began gently. "Do you file a joint return with your husband?"

She nodded.

"Do you check over the returns before you sign them?"

She looked down at the pavement, apparently focusing on a paperclip that someone had dropped as she sifted through myriad thoughts. The answer was "no," she signed whatever Asher or their accountant put in front of her. She grew up in a trusting family and had reliable relationships in college and business. People who are trustworthy always believe the best in everyone else. When she finally looked back up at Jed, tears now brimming from her eyes, about to spill forth, he knew the answer. He took off his baseball cap as a sign of respect, then ran a nervous hand through his thick dark brown hair and shifted his weight from one leg to another.

"I'm sorry, ma'am. I have to do my job. I wish I could leave the car, but I answer to a boss who answers to the IRS."

It wasn't a loud, mournful cry that began filtering over Stella. At first, a fast stream of silent tears poured down Stella's cheeks, and she shuddered as if trying to stop them. Within thirty seconds, her whole body was shaking. Poor Jed. He didn't know what to do or say. He stood, sorrowfully, watching her until both of them heard someone say in a tentative, quiet voice, "Stella?"

Both turned to the man, who seemed to have been heading toward the realty office and stopped when he saw them.

Mascara ran down Stella's face as she huffed and cried. "Oh, Pepper. I don't know what to do." Then, there on the main street of St. Simons Village, the wailing began in full force. Another public meltdown for Stella Jackson Bankwell. Jed looked on helplessly as Pepper stepped closer to put his hands on her shoulders and steady her. Instead, she collapsed into his arms, sobbing and covering his white oxford shirt with mascara, lipstick, and tears.

"Hey, hey, Stella, whatever it is will be alright. I'm here to help you. What in the world is going on?" Pepper, being a seasoned U.S. Marshal, had seen plenty of people in distress. He was always calm and level-headed in these moments. In fact, Marshal Jackson Roy Culpepper was exactly the person one needed in such situations.

Stella couldn't speak for crying quietly. Jed spoke up and explained, gently prying the crumbled paper from her shaking hands and showing it to Pepper. As he held Stella with one strong arm, he read the paper. "Just give us a moment," he said to Jed, who stepped back and out of earshot.

⋙

Stella couldn't believe it as she stood there with Pepper's protective arm around her. She had made a fool of herself. Again. She could barely listen as Pepper tried to explain.

"I've seen this kind of document before," he told her.

He put his hand on Stella's head and soothingly stroked her hair. It was an intimate gesture which he would have not done normally but it felt instinctively right. After a minute or

143

so, he said softly, "Stella, sweetheart, I'm afraid you're going to have let this gentleman take your car. The papers he has are in order, correct and legally binding. Let him do his job and then we'll work on trying to get the car back for you." She sensed that he was not telling her everything, not the whole truth, but his calmness helped.

Now here, he was exaggerating a bit. Overly comforting. Once the IRS got a piece of property, it would take a very long time to straighten it out, and the chances were overwhelming that once that Jaguar was towed off, Stella would never see it again. He'd break that news slowly to her. He was a trained diplomat.

Her tears slowed, and she tried to ignore how people were staring as they walked by or slowing their cars to gawk at the redhead who was close to hysterics.

"I have strong contacts in the IRS," Pepper assured her. "Let me make some calls."

She pulled back from his chest, vaguely noticing the big smudge of black mascara, and nodded slowly. She was hiccupping her way to a stop. Pepper smiled and wiped her face with a handkerchief while she rubbed at her nose.

To Jed, he said, "Sir, while you get the car hooked up, I'd like to make a copy of this paper."

"Certainly," Jed replied. "Ma'am, if I could have the key, that would be easier."

Dazed, Stella replied, "I need my house key."

"I'll get it off the key ring," Pepper said.

"And my Winn-Dixie card. Oh, and the CVS card, too."

Pepper tried to hide a smile while he did as instructed and handed Jed the Jaguar key. He put his arm around Stella again and said, "Let's go in the office." As he shepherded her away, he called back to Jed, "I'll bring the paperwork right back."

"Is there anything you need from your car, ma'am?" Jed asked.

She turned and looked back him pitifully. "My hairspray."

❧

An hour later, Stella felt a bit calmer due to Pepper's comforting strength, Marlo's mothering, and a shot of whiskey from a dusty bottle that Alton scrounged up from the back of a closet. In between sobs, she told her story and filled in the pieces that Chatty had withheld, including Annabelle and the country club debacle. Her tears finally stopped, and she was beginning to think things through enough to have questions.

"How on earth did they find my car?" she asked, scooting forward on the green mid-century sofa in Marlo's office.

"Satellite," Pepper responded. He was sitting in an armless chair next to the sofa while Marlo perched on her desk. "All expensive cars have a system that communicates with the satellite in the event that they're stolen or in an accident."

"Or need to be seized by the IRS," mumbled Stella.

He nodded. "When the U.S. government wants you, they can find you. They got your tag number from the county tax office, ran the plates for the vehicle identification number, then used that number to trace the exact location through satellite."

"Now what?" asked Marlo. "How do we find out what's going on with the taxes and what Asher has been doing?"

"I have buddies high up, and since I'm a federal officer, it's not privileged information to me. I'll get to work on it tomorrow after I teach a training class at Glynco." Pepper leaned forward, placing his elbows on his knees, using a clever method to encourage confidence during a questioning. "How long have you and Asher been married?"

Stella sighed heavily. "Nine years." A troubling thought clouded her mind and her heart sank deeper. "That means nine tax returns." She touched Pepper's arm. "Could I go to jail? Just for being trusting and naïve? Stupid?"

The answer, of course, was "yes" but Pepper diverted from that answer. "Let's not get ahead of things," Pepper insisted. "All we know at this point is that your car has been seized." His voice brightened, like he was trying to cheer her up. "It could be a mistake." He knew it wasn't.

Suddenly, Pepper frantically looked down at his watch, a present from his grandmother. "It's almost four. I've got to get to the airport in Brunswick to pick up Marylyn." He took Stella's hand and squeezed it. "Try not to worry. I know it's hard, but I'm going to do everything I can to help you." He stood. "Marlo, my cell number is on the paperwork I filled out. Text or call if y'all need me."

"I don't have a cell phone," Stella admitted. "Well, I have one, but it's turned off." She smiled wryly. "I didn't want to be found through its tracking device." She shook her head, trying to clear herself of what seemed like a never-ending nightmare. "If I need you, I'll call from here or the cottage."

Pepper nodded and started to the door. He snapped his fingers. "Oh, Marlo, I almost forgot." He pulled papers from the back pocket of his navy pants. "Here's the signed rental agreement and a deposit check. I need to get the key. Marylyn will be there, starting tonight."

"Do *not* cry," Stella instructed herself silently. A bad day was getting worse. Almost as bad as getting her car seized by the IRS was knowing that a man who had caught her eye was on his way to the airport to pick up his girlfriend. She bit the inside of her lip and focused on that first pain rather than the pain in her heart.

"I have the key right here," responded Marlo, walking around the corner of her desk, opening a drawer, and pulling out an envelope. "The WiFi code is here and also the phone number for the unit. My cell phone and office phone numbers are there too. Don't hesitate to call."

He took the envelope and thanked her. "Same here. Y'all call me if you need me. Again, try not to worry." He flashed a dazzling but sympathetic smile as he left.

Stella looked at her friend, shaking her head sadly. "Just my luck." She blew her nose into the tissue she had been twisting in her hands. "If I had any luck."

Marlo eyed her carefully, weighing if she should drop the big news that she had been dreading to deliver to her. Finally, she took a deep breath.

"Would this be the wrong time to tell you that this Marylyn has rented the duplex across the street from you?"

Chapter Fifteen

For hours, Stella had been sitting on the navy velvet sofa, holding Spigot on her lap, lost in a whirl of thoughts and emotions. She was finished with crying. It had gotten her nowhere. Now was the time to figure out what Asher had been doing and to fight back.

She looked at the clock. It was 10 P.M. She had barely moved since Marlo brought her home a few hours earlier, promising that she and Tatum would drop off a car in the morning. Alton and Evelyn had an old Chevy SUV they called their "airport car." It was fifteen years old, so they didn't mind leaving it in the airport long-term lot or driving it over rugged terrain when showing property.

Stella was naïve and trusting, but she was not dumb. She had an excellent memory even when she wasn't paying much attention. Her brain seemed to take a snapshot and store it somewhere in the deep crevices of her mind. She was trying to relax and let those snapshots float to the front so she could piece together the puzzle of this mess.

"I never sign anything that I haven't gone over with my own eyes," Marlo had commented. "That's not to make you feel bad."

"Thanks," Stella mumbled. "I'll remember that."

One thing was for certain: if Stella ever got herself out of this fix, she'd never come close to this kind of disaster again. She stroked Spigot's head and said, "This is the kind of jam you get into by believing in fairy tales. I should have known that it was all too good to be true."

Thank goodness that Chatty, for once, chose his words carefully when she called to tell him the latest news. He was unusually sensitive, but probably because it was the first time he had heard from her since his Chatty Cathy act with Pepper at the King and Prince.

"Helloooo, my sweet Stella," he sang into his phone when she called. "The day is suddenly brighter and the air is sweeter. Though I did drive over to Savannah to have lunch at Gryphon's Tea Room with two of my distant cousins, so it was a nice day already. After all, we are the Chathams of Chatham County and the county seat is Savannah. The leopard print carpet in Gryphon's is marvelous. It would have looked terrific in the den of your former Ansley Park house, and you remember how—"

"Chatty," she interrupted. "You're not gonna believe what happened today." Then, she filled him in on the details while he punctuated her story with gasps and exclamations such as "Oh my!" "You don't say!" then, finally, "The devil is coming for Asher Bankwell. Mark my words. I have known this, without question, since the fourth grade when he untied the sash of Samantha Godsey's dress and sneakily tied it to the back of her desk. She ripped her dress when she tried to get up for recess. He's always been stealthy, that one."

Before he hung up, after he had layered on much sympathy, he promised Stella, "Now, you be of comfort my dear Stella. I will be there to help you always. Not today, because I'm in Savannah with the Chathams. But starting tomorrow, or even tonight, I'll be there for you."

The conversation woke Spigot from a deep sleep, and the dog began to wiggle and stretch. She licked Stella's hand and looked up with her soulful brown eyes.

"Do you need to go out?"

Spigot's ears shot up and she jumped down from the sofa to run to the back door. A worry stabbed at Stella. Someone, it seemed, had already trained Spigot. She certainly understood words like "goin' outside" and "treat" and "eat."

Stella found the newly purchased leash and snapped it onto the dog's collar. "Now, listen, I've got enough troubles without losin' you, my new friend. Don't you be leavin' me." Then she whispered a little prayer, "Please, Lord, don't let this dog belong to someone. I just can't take it. Not now."

Spigot raced out the door, pulling Stella behind her. Once in the yard, she sniffed every leaf her nose could reach, pawed at the ground in spots, and generally took her own sweet time. Through the fragrant night air, soft sounds of people talking drifted to Stella's ears, followed by the sound of a screeching screen door opening and banging shut. Spigot heard them, too, and pulled Stella from the backyard to the side yard, issuing a little yelp as she went.

Lighting is soft on St. Simons Island in order to encourage an environment for sea turtles nesting during spring and summer. When Marlo and Stella visited the island during the summers of their youths, they loved to roam the beach, looking for loggerhead tracks that led to the "body pits" the turtles dug out in the sand where they could nest and lay eggs. Both girls were fascinated by the turtles, who often returned to the same beach every year. Ever since she graduated from college, Stella had been an annual supporter of the conservation fund for the sea turtles. She was glad the island's lighting created a welcoming place for the turtles, but it was certainly hard to see clearly at night.

But, even in the dim light that fell faintly over the street, she spotted something she wished she had avoided. Especially on this most unpleasant of days. Across the street, at the duplex that her "good" friend Marlo had rented to Pepper's "friend," she watched as Pepper walked across the yard with a woman. He had his arm around her shoulders and it looked like her arm was around his. They crossed into the path of a low wattage outdoor light on the front lawn so that Stella could see that the woman had either light brown hair or dark blonde hair that was twisted into a messy bun. She was tall, just a bit shorter than Pepper, and thin. She wore jeans or pants and a long cardigan. By the time they got to Pepper's car and he turned to wrap her in a hug, Stella had had enough.

"C'mon on, Spigot." She gave a short jerk on the leash, and the dog immediately responded, turning to trot behind her to the back door. Once inside, she fed Spigot, remembering that she herself hadn't eaten since breakfast. She wasn't hungry. She was too distressed over everything. She pondered the situation of Pepper and his "friend" and allowed it to momentarily push from her mind the IRS woes and the loss of her car. Then, she did what most women would have done after the kind of day she'd had: she pulled a quart of mint chocolate ice cream from the freezer. And, with a big spoon, she dived in.

She did not stop until she had eaten the entire container.

Chapter Sixteen

Stella had "ice creamed" herself to sleep, having eaten an entire quart. She was sound asleep when she heard a phone ringing. She thought she was dreaming but it persisted, and finally she opened one eye and squinted to look at the old corded clock on the nightstand: 6:45 A.M.

Her mind, fuzzy from an overdose of rich cream and sugar, couldn't think clearly. Then fear shot through her: What if it was Asher? She was in no frame of mind to talk to him with this hangover. She pulled the covers to her chin, and Spigot, asleep next to her, opened her eyes for a moment and then slowly closed them again.

The phone stopped. In two seconds, it started again. It rang dozens of times before Stella decided to pull herself out of bed and cautiously approach. She had the presence of mind to think, "If it's Asher, I'll just hang up on him." Her hands shaking, she lifted the receiver, took her time putting it to her ear, swallowed hard, then said softly, "Hello?"

"STELLA!" the voice thundered. "What in the tarnation are you doin'? Are you still asleep?"

She gulped. "Uh, yeah."

"Good gracious, child, you don't have time to be sleepin'. You're in a mess and you need to be workin' on that." Cager Burnett had retreated back to his gruff self.

"Yes sir," she replied meekly.

"Get dressed and get over here in fifteen minutes. We gotta roll our sleeves up and go to work." He hung up.

Stella stood with the receiver in her hand for a few seconds and then gently replaced it. By that time, Spigot, faithfully, had leapt from the bed and followed her. There was concern in her eyes as she sat there watching Stella.

"Oh boy," Stella mumbled, and she knelt down to hug Spigot. "Another day. Another problem."

✑

McCager Burnett was grim when he opened the door twenty-five minutes later.

"I told you fifteen minutes," he grumbled.

"I had to walk the dog," she replied meekly, following him down the hall to his office.

His head spun around and he looked at her quizzically. "Dog? What dog?" Then, with his hand, he waved away the question. "Never mind. We have more important matters at hand." Across his desk was scattered hundreds of pages. He put on his black-rimmed glasses, sat down, and motioned to the seat where she had faced her last tongue lashing. "Sit."

Obediently, she did, just as Miss Alva brought in a tray of coffee. "When I heard his tone to you on the phone, I knew you'd need a cup." She set the silver tray on a nearby table and poured. "Cream?"

"Please."

Miss Alva handed her a cup, then poured one for her grimacing husband. "Y'all call me if you need me," she said as she slipped out the door.

Stella took a hot gulp, almost scalding her tongue. "Governor, what is this all about? My nerves are shot."

He swiveled the oak chair to face her. "These pages were couriered down to me last night from my office in Atlanta. Our corporate jet bought them down. I've been up all night, studying them."

She nodded, still not understanding. Cager Burnett, a distinguished graduate of Emory Law School, was the top estate attorney in Atlanta. All the finest families used him, paying over a thousand dollars an hour for his services. Asher's father, Jasper Bankwell, had been one of his clients and his good friend. The Governor continued to oversee matters for Miss Caroline.

"Chatham called. Obviously, I know about the IRS and your car." He took off his glasses and rubbed his eyes. "I'm too old to be pulling these all-nighters, but Asher is up to no good. I've suspected it for quite a while now." He picked up some pages. "I handle the larger financial affairs for Caroline, but she has access to her bank and brokerage accounts. There's a steady syphoning of money—tens of thousands a month—coming out of her account. Withdrawals. That's not the kind of money she spends because everything she has is paid for."

"Did you call her?" Stella asked.

"Good heavens, no! The first thing she'll do is tell Asher. She's always been a soft touch for him." He put both elbows on the desk and rubbed his forehead for several moments. Then, he looked up. "Stella, I need to see your tax returns. The accountant will drag his feet if you ask, so you should have your attorney demand them."

Her eyes widened with sorrow. "I don't have an attorney."

The Governor smiled. "I'm an attorney."

She looked hopeful then shook her head. "I don't have any money to pay you. You cost a lot."

"I'll take all my fees out in friendship. Deal?"

She jumped up, leaned over, and hugged his neck. "This is the best deal I ever made!"

≪

Asher Bankwell guided his black BMW down I-16. He'd just passed through Laurens County, stopping for breakfast at the Waffle House. Smothered and covered hash browns, bacon, eggs, waffles, and two cups of coffee made him feel much better, since he had left Atlanta at 4:30 A.M. He wanted to be there and waiting by the time the prison opened at nine.

What a mess. It was all Stella's fault, too. Had she not stirred things up with that gossip-provoking scene she made, he and Annabelle could have continued right along with no one noticing them. He had not meant for things to turn romantic with Annabelle. It started out as business, but she was downright impossible to resist when she set her cap for someone as she had for Asher.

He glanced over at some deer munching grass in a meadow. It occurred to him that perhaps it was Annabelle who was really to blame. After all, if she hadn't seduced him, if she had just stuck to business, then they wouldn't have built up passion, Stella wouldn't have had anything to notice, and they could have continued on with business just as they had done for years. He glanced in the rearview mirror at his reflection and looked away quickly. The strain was showing in the deepening lines around his eyes. He had always been so handsome and had always taken it for granted, but his looks were vanishing fast.

He was deep in thought as he pulled off Interstate 16, headed to Lyons. His world certainly had collapsed into pieces over the past two weeks, starting with Stella's meltdown and departure. He knew she had to be in one of two places: the mountains with her mother or St. Simons with Marlo. Neither woman was talking and, to be frank, so much had happened in the last three days that Stella was the least of his concerns. At 5 a.m the previous morning, IRS officials and U.S. Marshals had descended upon his house in Ansley Park, served him with seizure papers, and escorted him and Neely out of the house. He was placed under arrest and handcuffed for perpetrating fraud on the federal government.

His attorney and golfing buddy, Cooper Austin, took his own sweet time showing up, but when he did arrive at the jail four hours later, he was full of fire.

"What has the world come to when a fine man of character like Asher Bankwell is awakened from a deep sleep and hauled out of his bed in the middle of the night?" he exclaimed in his deep baritone. "Is this Russia rather than Atlanta, Georgia? The roots of his family stray not far from General James Oglethorpe."

The judge, an African American woman in her fifties, looked unimpressed.

Cooper pushed his luck. "The founder of the colony of Georgia," he explained a haughty tone.

She turned from being unimpressed to being just plain mad. Judge Amanda Wright-Moses had had enough of these high-falutin' socialites turning up in her court for playing fast and loose with their federal tax returns. For several seconds, she debated on whether to allow bail or not. She had the right to keep Asher Jasper Bankwell III in jail but it would be an overreach, and most decisions she made with an ultimate goal in mind: to be appointed to the U.S. Supreme Court. She made her decision.

"This court remands Mr. Bankwell to be at liberty until his trial. His bond is set at $500,000." She banged the gravel, signed the papers, handed them to the clerk, then left the bench without further word.

Cooper was stunned. He had been before her and other judges on tax evasion issues but had never seen a bond higher than $100,000. Asher's bank accounts had been seized, but Cooper knew where the money would come from.

"Our firm will arrange the bond," he said to Asher. "Since your assets are frozen, I will need your mother to present deed or cashier's check to guarantee bond."

Telling Caroline Bankwell what had happened was tougher than jail. Miss Caroline, though, could be baffling and hard to predict. Asher, of course, created a big story of a grave misunderstanding that merely needed clearing up. He had even said in a feigned voice of puzzlement, "You don't suppose that Stella has anything to do with this, do you? The timing, after all, is suspicious."

Miss Caroline had leapt on the opportunity to blame Stella, the person who had embarrassed her to the highest degree and left her standing in the Buckhead Country Club with Chatham's glass of Chardonnay soaking her hair.

"Asher, I am certain you are correct! She has an unseemly anger." She had walked over to her son, who was standing in front of the ornate fireplace in the great room. She put her arms around him. "Dear boy, we will fight together and get this whole mess taken care of." Then, picking up the phone, she called her trust officer and told him to arrange for a cashier's check to be sent to Austin and Associates.

Now Asher looked at the dash clock as he pulled his mother's car toward the prison gate, handed the guard his driver's license, then was waved into the parking lot surrounded by high chain-link fences topped with rows of barbwire. 8:55 A.M. Perfect timing. Visiting hours were about to begin at the U.S. Federal Corrections Institution in Jesup, Georgia. Asher stepped from the car, cleared his pockets of everything except his identification, and strolled toward the door. He was dressed in a deep gray pin-striped suit with a tailor-made, crisp, starched shirt and a red tie. The guard asked for his identification and gave him a sign-in sheet.

"Who are you here to see?" she asked.

"Bennett Sutton. He's expecting me."

Chapter Seventeen

The Governor and Stella had been at it for over an hour, digging through papers, trying to find something that might to lead to answers. So far, they had succeeded only in understanding better the pages in front of them and calculating that more than a million dollars had left Miss Caroline's accounts in the past two years.

Stella had also written a letter to the accountant, announcing that McCager Burnett was to be given full access to any documents that contained her name and social security number. That, along with the Governor's strongly worded demand of what he wanted and that he was to have possession by 5 P.M., was faxed at 8:45 a.m.

Just as they were taking a breather and sipping coffee, Miss Alva came to the door. "McCager, your office is calling."

"Yes?" he asked when he picked up the phone. He listened for a second and said in a courteous, respectful tone, "Howdy do, Miss Armstead. I hope you're having a fine morning." Miss Armstead had been his assistant for forty years. She was tall with slightly sloped shoulders, glasses that sat midway down her nose, and short salt and pepper hair that curled beautifully at the ends with natural wave. She preferred to wear navy, dark gray, or black. Often the, dress—never slacks, only dresses or skirts—was accompanied by a matching cardigan, and always with a short strand of pearls—a gift from the Burnetts on the occasion of her fifteenth anniversary of employment. She had never married and was utterly devoted to her job, the Governor, and Miss Alva.

After the niceties were out of the way, Miss Armstead continued. Stella watched the Governor, who at first looked thunderstruck. Then his face darkened and distorted.

"Tell George Madison to get copies of the legal papers, the check, anything else and fax it to me immediately. You call Cooper Austin and tell him that we are about to have a man-to-Cooper talk. Wait. Don't call Austin yet. Let me take a look at the papers. Thank you, Miss Armstead."

He set the phone down, hard, and looked at Stella. "Well, you're not the only one the IRS came a-callin' on yesterday. But they did look upon you with greater kindness than they had for Asher Jasper Bankwell III."

Her eyes widened and she jumped up from the dark burgundy leather sofa in the Governor's office.

"They showed up at Asher's at 5 A.M. yesterday morning, along with U.S. Marshals. Took him to jail, and he was arraigned on a $500,000 bond that Caroline instructed the bank to pay. Everything he's got, except the jet service, is locked up tighter than Dick's hatband. Apparently, it's a shell company owned by a shell company owned by another shell company, so they can't yet tie Asher to it. He's locked out of the house, his bank and stock accounts are frozen, and they took his cars, too."

All Stella could do for several seconds was look at the Governor, shaking her head. "What about Neely?"

"The boy was there and taken for questioning. But they didn't charge him so he disappeared, and no one has seen hide nor hair of him since."

"Where's Asher?"

"Up to no good would be my well-formed opinion after years of knowing him. But meanwhile, we know that Caroline took him in so he must be staying there."

The Governor rubbed his chin, staring blindly at the coffee table. A small smile began to creep across his lips.

"You know, Stella, I have a feeling that you're gonna come out of this mess looking like a champion." His smile grew into a broad grin.

≈

Bennett Sutton, age sixty, had been in the federal pen for twelve years after making off with an abundance of Buckhead money. He had been sentenced to make restitution to the victims as well as to serve fifteen years. And, since all his convictions were federal offenses, he would have to serve 85 percent of that time, which meant he had less than a year to go. He had entered the facility as a slightly built man, about 5'6" and weighing no more than 135 pounds. When he was arrested, he wore a size 29 pants waist. Those days were long gone. The high-carb diet they fed the prisoners, plus all the candy bars he was able to pay for from his 25-cent-an-hour job in the library, had taken him to a 38-inch waist. His belly spilled over, resting on his thighs and straining the buttons on his orange jumpsuit. He still wore a comb-over to cover his bald spot, and his hair had turned silver, no longer dyed a brassy blond.

Since the Jesup prison was a low-security facility, he was able to sit at a table across from Asher instead of talking by phone from behind glass. Two guards stood close. Asher and Bennett were not allowed to shake hands or touch, but they could put their elbows on the table and lean forward.

"It's a mess," Asher began. "And unless a miracle happens, it's not going to slow down or get better."

Slight panic flashed in Bennett's gray, watery eyes. He had been counting the days until he could get out and back on the golf course. In the time he'd been imprisoned, his daughter had graduated from high school and college. His son, who'd stopped speaking to him, had married, and his daughter-in-law had delivered a baby boy a year ago. The boy, who should have been named after Bennett, was called instead Charles Roger Sutton, named for his maternal grandfather.

"What's happened?"

"You heard about Stella's meltdown at the country club the other night?" A couple of other prominent Atlantans were serving time in the same prison, so if Bennett had not heard the news from his wife, he had heard elsewhere. When Bennett was sentenced, he had pressed Asher to look after his wife and children so they could live in the style to which they were accustomed. In exchange, he would not divulge Asher's role in the crime, and Bennett's wife Connie would agree to stay married. If she divorced Bennett, the deal was off. Of course, Connie had no idea who was seeing after her finances. She just knew that she was able to live in a million-dollar house purchased in her name after Bennett took the low road to Jesup in the back of a U.S. Marshal's car. The kids continued in private schools, and her devout patronage at Neiman-Marcus remained uninterrupted.

Bennett nodded. "I told you and Annabelle to keep it strictly business. No tomfoolery. Time and time again, I told y'all that."

Asher nodded slightly. It was hard for him to admit fault. But to himself, he'd many times over the last several days,

"Why, oh why did I do that?" To be honest, he hadn't thought much about it in the week after the country club blowup. At that point, all he could think was, "Oh well, I'll just divorce Stella and marry Annabelle."

This is the way a man thinks when he has gotten away with too much thieving, lying, and dishonesty for too long. He convinces himself that there are no consequences, that he is king of all he surveys.

Wrong. It turned out that the king over Asher's domain was the federal government, and they were as hungry for him as a German shepherd who has not eaten in a week. In looking back, he knew that he and Annabelle had pulled off some pretty sophisticated fraud. They, under the watch care of and direction of Bennett, they had made many fortunes and tucked them all away in offshore banks. Aw, but the lust of man is often his downfall, Asher thought. But he wouldn't say that out loud.

"Annabelle wouldn't leave me alone," he insisted to Bennett. "Finally, I crumbled."

"You're a fool." Bennett spat the words out bitterly.

"Now's not the time for us to be fighting amongst ourselves," Asher responded. "We've got an even bigger problem than the U.S. government and, granted, that's huge."

Bennett looked puzzled. "What could be a bigger problem?"

"Congressman/Governor McCager Burnett, that clever, mean, tenacious son-of-gun." Asher paused for a moment then dropped the bomb. "He's Team Stella."

Chapter Eighteen

After the letter was faxed to the accountant and the Governor's law office apprised of their required tasks, all that was left for the Governor and Stella to do was wait.

"I've asked Mrs. Puckett to make a late breakfast for you two," Miss Alva said as she gathered up her purse, preparing to leave for her weekly bridge game. "McCager, you have to get some sleep. You're not forty years old anymore, and your health will not stand up to these all-nighters."

"My adrenaline's pumping hard, Miss Alva," he replied, using his wife's name as a term of endearment and Southern courtesy. "I may be up for three days."

"I hope not!" She kissed him on the top of his head, and he looked like a bashful little boy as she did. It was a wonderful, strong marriage envied by many, including Stella. As Miss Alva whisked out the door, extremely spry for a seventy-two-year-old, Mrs. Puckett, their longtime housekeeper, came into the dining room with china plates of hot omelets.

"Well done, Mrs. Puckett!" The Governor clapped his hands. "A little more coffee, please, if you don't mind."

"This is beautiful," Stella said, looking at the three-egg omelet stuffed with sausage, peppers, onions, asparagus, and cheese.

Just as Mrs. Puckett picked up the silver coffee pot from the antique sideboard and started to pour into the Governor's cup, Chatham appeared in the arched doorway, bursting with joy and a big smile. He had let himself in the kitchen door. Years ago, he and Miss Alva had conspired to put in a beautiful iron gate, with a little bell that jingled atop it, between the two properties so he could come and go as he pleased. His body shook with jolliness and he dramatically spread his arms wide.

"From Atlanta has arrived the most glorious news! The devil has been cornered." He brought his arms into a big hug around himself and said, "Did I not tell you that a comeuppance was coming for Asher Bankwell?" He pointed to himself. "Right again." Then his eye caught the omelets. Like a sheepish boy, he smiled innocently. "Oh, Mrs. Puckett…"

"Give me a moment, Mr. Chatham, and I'll have an omelet for you." Like most, the housekeeper could not resist Chatham. Most everyone, with Asher being one rare example of the opposite, wanted to love on him and cater to him.

He smiled happily. "Thank you, Mrs. Puckett. Extra cheddar, please." He pulled out a chair directly across from Stella. The Governor sat in his usual place at the head of the beautiful English antique walnut table. "Asher was arrested for his no-good, conniving ways. A lifetime in jail."

The Governor held up a hand to slow Chatham's enthusiasm. "It is a most unusual circumstance, but you are delivering news that we already know. And besides that, Chatham, you're quite a bit ahead of things. He has only been charged. Not indicted by a grand jury and certainly not convicted. The legal system has a process. Remember, in America a man is still innocent until proven guilty in a court of law."

Chatty waved away such nonsensical talk. "Asher has not been innocent since ten minutes after he was born at Piedmont Hospital. He's been guilty his entire life of something, if only in using his good looks to fool people." He looked at Stella and smiled sympathetically. "Like my friend, Stella."

Stella pushed the corners of her mouth up into a smile. "Chatty, much good has come from my sorrowful bout with Asher. I have you and the Burnetts."

Chatty jumped up from his seat, scurried about the table, and threw his arms around Stella. "You are my sunshine, sweet Stella."

The Governor comically shook his head and rolled his eyes while Chatty repositioned himself in his chair, took a black linen napkin, and spread it across his lap. He leaned forward. "Listen to this delicious piece of information. They took him away in *handcuffs* in the back of a marshal's car!"

"Chatty, how on earth would you know that?" Stella asked as she cut a bite from her omelet.

"Because Mona Windsor was out walking that monstrosity of a dog of hers at 5:30 A.M. and she saw it. You know, she goes to bed with the chickens and gets up with the roosters. And thank heavens, she just happened to have her binoculars so she could look up that big, long driveway of yours and she saw everything!"

"That happened over twenty-four hours ago. Mona usually works much faster than that to spread her gossip," the Governor replied dryly.

"It was my error," Chatty admitted, looking ashamed. "I left my cell phone in my cousin's car in Savannah, and Mona does not have my home number here on Sea Island. First thing this morning, I had to meet my cousin halfway and get my phone. There were at least a dozen calls and texts. Mona was absolutely frantic to get in touch with me. The last time I talked on my cell phone was when you called yesterday, Stella, after the Feds had gotten your car. Then I turned it off and forgot all about it."

Stella suddenly jerked, stunned by what she remembered. "My job! I have a job and I forgot all about it." She looked at her watch. "It's after ten! I was supposed to be there by nine. Oh no, and after all the drama I caused yesterday."

The Governor, rarely rattled, calmly said, "Use the foyer phone, call Marlo, and tell her that you will be with me until further notice."

As Stella pushed back her chair to do as she was told, Chatty said merrily, "And be sure to tell her I'm here, too."

Chatty never liked to be left out, especially when it came to Stella.

Marlo, of course, was understanding, but she did have some news. "Pepper called here, looking for you. He said it's urgent."

"Great," Stella replied glumly. "Urgent news means more bad news, or at least it does for me." The thought of Pepper walking across the lawn the previous night with his arm around that woman, Marylyn, crossed her mind and burdened her heart. She didn't bother, though, to tell Marlo. "What's the use?" she thought.

"Here's his phone number. As a matter of fact, he left both his cell and his office number at Glynco. He said he's teaching a training class today, so if you're not able to get him by cell phone, have whoever answers the office phone pull him out of class."

Stella slumped. This was sounding more like horrible news than just bad news. Their call concluded, she replaced the receiver and dragged back to the dining room. Heaving a heavy sigh, she plopped into the dining room chair and explained to the Governor about meeting Pepper, the U.S. Marshal who was assigned for a few months to Glynco, that he had been there yesterday when Homer's Towing Service had shown up in the village, and how he promised to look into the matter.

"Governor, importantly, he is very handsome and eligible. As handsome as Stella is beautiful," Chatty piped up. "And, he has integrity. Asher Bankwell does not even know how to spell the word."

The Governor ignored Chatty's unnecessary commentary and said levelly, "Perhaps you should call Marshal Culpepper and tell him to come here as soon as he can arrange it."

❦

About an hour later, the doorbell rang at the Burnetts' home. Mrs. Puckett escorted U.S. Marshal Jack Culpepper into the drawing room where the trio awaited him. Both Chatty and the Governor stood in accordance with gentlemanly manners, while Stella sprung from her seat in the club chair and made the introduction to the Governor.

"And, of course, you remember Chatham Colquitt," she almost mumbled as she avoided Pepper's eyes.

"Of course." They shook hands and Chatty, in a big surprise, held his tongue. Stella hoped he was beginning to understand the seriousness of the situation.

"Please, Marshal, have a seat." The Governor gestured toward the chair opposite Stella's. "May I offer you anything to drink?"

"No, thank you, sir. I'm good."

"Let's talk then, please."

The four of them sat down, but Pepper shifted uncomfortably in his chair. "Before we begin, perhaps what I'm about to say should be kept just between us, sir. Just Stella and you." He looked at Chatham apologetically.

The Governor waved away Pepper's concern. "There's no reason to worry about Chatham as long as you tell him that it's confidential and should not be repeated. If told that, Chatham will carry a secret to his grave."

Chatham brightened and nodded cheerfully.

"It's when you don't issue that disclaimer that one should be concerned. Mightily concerned," he concluded. Chatham's brightness faded considerably. The Governor looked at him sternly. "Chatham, not one word said here is to be repeated. Understood?"

"Yes sir." Chatty looked like a scolded school boy.

"Very well," Pepper said. "I will take your word on that." He took a breath. "The U.S. Marshal service took Asher into custody yesterday on tax evasion charges."

Chatty smiled beatifically. "Oh, I already told them *that*."

The Governor shot him a warning look that caused Chatham to melt into his seat. "Sorry," he mumbled.

"Are you sure…?" Pepper gestured toward Chatty.

The Governor nodded. "Yes. Believe it or not, he loves Stella more than anything in the world and will never utter a word to harm her. On the other hand, he fears me more than anything in the world so he wouldn't dare."

Pepper nodded. "Of course, there are many things I cannot tell you, but this I have on good authority: everyone believes Stella is innocent, so if"—he looked directly at Stella—"you will cooperate, I believe this will work out favorably for you."

Stella tilted her head in puzzlement. "Cooperate?"

Cager Burnett reached over to pat her hand reassuringly. "He means with the tax returns. You did sign them, so legally you are culpable. But we can certainly make a case for your naivete in signing. Especially since Asher was the sole income earner during the years of your marriage."

"I'm sorry, sir," Pepper said to him, "I'm afraid the situation is much graver than that. The tax evasion charges are just the tip of a very large iceberg."

"M-m-meaning?" Stella stuttered.

Pepper waited several seconds before replying, as Stella's heart thumped so loudly that the sound exploded in her ears. He looked at her with great sympathy. Slowly, he found his words.

"It is thought, no, it is believed that Asher has been laundering money. This is much more serious than tax evasion. However, right now, evasion of taxes is the only concrete evidence that authorities have."

For once in his life, Chatty was struck speechless.

Chapter Nineteen

The normally unflappable McCager Burnett was, for the moment, a bit flapped. His mind raced to grasp what he had just heard, but then he looked over and saw that Stella had begun trembling from head to toe. He gathered himself completely, arose, and went over to sit on the arm of her chair.

"Stella, get ahold of yourself." He patted her hand. "We will figure this out. You're not guilty of anything and we will prove that." The truth, though, was that Cager Burnett was a seasoned lawyer of fifty years, a former congressman and governor, so he was well aware of the tangled web that government charges could weave and how difficult it could be for even the innocent to escape.

"Marshal Culpepper, I am certain you are a man of truth, but I'm stunned. Asher Bankwell laundering money? I've known him since the day he was born, and while I do not question a lack of honor on his part, I do question that he is smart enough to figure out how to launder money. It's a fairly complicated process."

"That's right," Chatty chirped up, having regained his voice. "When we were in the third grade, he couldn't add two plus two correctly. He said the answer was five. I remember that Mrs. Guest was very disappointed at that."

Stella was still nervous, but she was beginning a slight turn from fright to fight. Pepper's voice was soft and compassionate when he spoke. "He isn't in it alone. There are others."

"But not me, Pepper? Please say they don't think I'm involved." Tears welled in Stella's eyes.

Pepper got up from his chair and moved to stand closer. He squatted down beside her, took both of her hands, and looked in her teary eyes. "Stella, you are not suspected. Your only problem is that you filed joint returns and you signed them. The IRS might not be completely forgiving of that—or perhaps they will—but I don't believe you will go to jail." He shrugged slightly. "Maybe interest and penalties. I don't know. It's complex. But I, and I'm sure the Governor, will do everything we can to help you."

"And me, too," Chatty said firmly. "I shall never abandon you nor look away from my dearest of dears." Stella looked to her friend, mouthing a kiss. "As long as I have a dime, you'll always have a nickel." He paused, cast his eyes upward, and thought for a second. "I might even give you my entire dime."

It was a sweet moment that brought a bit of comic relief. Pepper stood, his handsome profile caught in the sun, and placed his hands on his waist as he looked out the tall bowed windows toward a giant oak. Ever since he was a little boy and watched the western *Gunsmoke* on afternoon television, he had wanted to be a U.S. Marshal. Whenever he and his friends had played as cowboys and robbers, he always insisted on being the marshal. He took pride in his job every moment of the day. Except for this moment. This moment stung. It hurt more than the time he was clipped in the arm by a bullet during a showdown. This was actually the worst moment of his entire marshal career. He had fondness for Stella. And a nagging worry.

He cleared his throat. "I need to get back to Glynco. Or FLETC, as they prefer to be called. Please remember, every word of this is confidential." He looked directly at Chatty, who nodded obediently. Then he reached out to touch Stella's shoulder. "Try not to worry. I know that in this room are three people who will do everything they can to help you."

"Governor Burnett, it's been a pleasure to meet you." Pepper stretched out his hand and the two men shook. Both the Governor and Chatty stood. Chatty, too, shook Pepper's hand and said, "Please help my best friend. Please." Tears began to pool in his eyes.

Pepper smiled. He was taking a liking to Chatty. "Stella is indeed blessed to have a friend like you, Chatham Colquitt."

"Yes, I am," Stella said firmly, standing up to give Chatty a tight hug. After Pepper left, the three close friends were silent for quite a long time. They sat in the drawing room, bathed by the morning sun but showered in cloudy doom. Cage Burnett, worn out from being up all night, finally stood.

"If you two will forgive me, I must take a nap so I can refresh my mind. Otherwise, I will be of no help in the resolving of this matter." He smiled weakly. "I'm not as young as I used to be." He pushed his shoulders back and winked at Stella. "Don't worry, my girl. I'm still as mean as a banty rooster when the mountains in me get riled up. And I'm plenty riled up." He turned to walk away then looked back. "Y'all stay as long as you like. Ask Mrs. Puckett for anything you want or need. Nighty night." He chuckled over the childhood expression as he headed to bed.

As soon as he was up the stairs, Stella looked at Chatty. "Where would I get a prescription for Zoloft?"

Chapter Twenty

On the sofa covered in quilts, Stella sat numbly with Spigot pressed into her leg, as close as possible. She stared at the prescription bottle in her hand, thinking about the half of a pill she had taken earlier. Other than occasional antibiotics for a sinus infection, she did not recall ever having a prescription.

Dr. Meehan, a general practitioner and Tatum Sloan's regular golfing buddy, had agreed to see her immediately. He was tall, slender, dark haired, and had an abundance of compassion in his brown eyes.

"This," he said to Stella and Marlo who had driven her over, "is not a case for Zoloft. It's more urgent than that. This calls for Xanax."

Bewildered, Stella had shaken her head, indicating that she did not understand.

"Zoloft is for chronic depression. It takes a while to work into your system. You need something to work immediately and calm your nerves."

Since the moment Pepper dropped the bombshell, she felt like she had not stopped shaking though it had tamed down from the initial violent shake. Her nerves felt tightly pinched, like constantly pulsing mini electrical shocks. Sworn to secrecy over the money laundering, she had told Marlo and Tatum only that it was much worse than they had imagined and there would probably be serious federal charges.

"Stella, do you drink?" the doctor had asked.

She nodded.

"How much?"

She shrugged. "It used to be hardly ever. I've never been drunk, but lately I'm getting closer. And more frequently. It's the only thing that calms my nerves."

"Listen to me," he said gently but firmly. "No drinking while you're taking this medication. Like angels, we need to be careful where we tread. You don't regularly take medication, and you've just started drinking significantly more than usual. Your system does not have a tolerance built up."

Dr. Meehan prescribed fifteen days of the lowest dosage possible, then told her to take half of one as needed, at least four hours apart.

He handed her the prescription along with another small piece of paper. "This is my cell phone number. Don't hesitate to call me. Don't be surprised if this medication makes you sleepy. Don't drive until you understand the full effect it has on you."

"Don't worry," she mumbled under her breath, thinking of her repossessed Jaguar.

Kindly, he placed his hand on her shoulder. "You have good friends in the Sloans, and now you have a friend in me. You'll be fine." Her worry eased considerably because his manner of compassion was genuine. He was a man she knew not, yet she felt comfort from his words.

She and Marlo stopped by St. Simons Drug Company and picked up the prescription, then Marlo dropped her at the cottage. Stella knew her friend was dying to know more, but she was grateful that Marlo didn't press her. It was enough for her to know that Cage Burnett was involved, that Pepper had delivered the news, and that Chatty was there but nothing more.

"Do you think Chatty is someone who should be armed with confidential government information?" Marlo asked cautiously as she put the car in park in the driveway. Even before Stella replied, she knew the answer. Anyone who knew how much Chatty loved Stella would know he'd never hurt her.

Stella nodded. "He would give up his trust fund, his house in Buckhead, and his house on Sea Island before he divulged one word that would hurt me and/or keep Asher from prison." She paused for a second. "Though I'm not sure he would give up the fraternity ring that supposedly belonged to Jefferson Davis."

The pair needed that moment of levity and laughed for several seconds. Chatty was so proud of that ring that he kept it in a safe deposit box rather than his home safe.

Stella continued, "After the initial shock wore off a bit and the Governor had retired upstairs, Chatty kept saying, 'Oh my. Asher in prison orange. Justice cometh to those who waiteth upon the Lord.'"

Marlo rolled her eyes comically. "There he goes, twisting the scripture to his way of thinking. Asher will receive payment for his vengeance, but Chatty, as usual, is thinking only of what he will get: justice for his darling Stellie."

Stella gave a small chuckle—not because she felt like it but because she was trying to be optimistic. "Let's just hope the eye of justice is clear and doesn't get fuzzy when reaping Chatty's vengeance. I'd hate to be captured in the harvest." She felt a sudden pang of guilt, thinking of all the times when she should have gone to church yet chose to sleep late. If the Lord gave her what she truly deserved, she'd be up the creek. Even though she was completely innocent of Asher's conniving, she had failed in other ways.

"Grace," she had said softly to herself as she stared at the budding azaleas.

"What?" Marlo asked.

Stella opened the car door and mumbled. "Just thinkin' out loud."

≪⑤

Now, two hours later, Stella was perched, immobile, on the sofa, having taken the afternoon off from the real estate company after her doctor's visit. The half pill she had taken was spot-on perfect. Her trembling had stopped and her nerve endings weren't firing off pops similar to firecrackers. She was not drowsy but relaxed to the point that, physically, she felt good. It was her brain that was on overload. She could not stop thinking.

"Asher? Laundering money? Why?" she asked herself. "He had plenty of money. Old money."

The sudden shrill ringing of the telephone snapped her out of her circling thoughts. She started to get up to answer it, but Spigot was so comfortable that she decided not to disturb her. She stroked the dog's head and thought of her mama's constant assurance: "The Lord always provides. He knows what you need before you need it and He will put it right there for the right time."

Stella smiled. "Little girl, the Lord knew I was going to need you before I did." Spigot pulled out of her lazy pose and sat up. Stella leaned over and kissed the top of her head. "You're better than Xanax any day." She laughed. "Well, almost. That little pill is helping a lot."

Sometime later, the dusk of day was pulling the sun toward its colorful setting over the gentle blue waves when a knock came at the door. Still worried that Asher might find her, Stella proceeded with caution. She peeped around the edge of the café curtain that hung over the front door and saw a muscular, familiar arm.

Pepper.

Her heart jumped. She ran to the tiny bathroom, fluffed her hair, and dabbed Dewy Pink lip gloss on her pale lips. By the time she returned to the living room, he was knocking again and Spigot was barking.

She opened the door, trying to smile brightly, which was harder than she expected because she was so relaxed.

"Stella, I'm sorry to drop by unannounced, but I tried calling earlier to check on you. When you didn't answer, I got worried. Marlo told me she dropped you off around four."

"That was you on the phone? Oh, Pepper, I'm sorry. Spigot and I were cuddled up and comfortable on the sofa so I didn't want to move. Please, come in." She pushed the screen door open.

He smiled gloriously and made a move to enter just as a feminine someone called, "Pepper!"

They both looked to see the pretty woman across the street, who was closing the mailbox. Smiling, she crossed the street.

"I thought that was you." She stopped at the edge of the yard. Stella saw a look of something special cross Pepper's face.

"Marylyn, come here." He gestured toward her, his smile stretching larger. He put his arm around the woman and gave her a half hug. "I want you to meet someone." He turned to Stella and said, "This is someone very special to me."

The moment the words were out of his mouth, her heart nosedived. Then she thought of the Xanax and Dr. Meehan saying that she could have another half when she needed it.

"Yep," she thought wryly. "The Lord always knows what you need before you need it."

She glanced back at the pill bottle sitting on the end table.

Chapter Twenty-one

Chief Deputy U.S. Marshal Jackson Culpepper was full of good joy, making happy chitchat with Marylyn, while Stella, standing on a small kitchen stool, dug through the cabinet to find two additional coffee mugs to join the red mug she used every morning.

Stella, by comparison, had resentful thoughts running through her mind, plus she was mad at herself for not being able to overcome her mountain upbringing. Where she came from, you always invited someone in for coffee and then, before they left, you gave them a little gift of some kind to thank them for visiting. At home, it was usually a jar of homemade jelly or chow-chow, a much-beloved relish side dish for a country supper of peas or pinto beans, vegetables, and cornbread.

"And now, Miss Smarty Pants," she thought, climbing up on her knees on top of the light blue tiled countertop, stuck head deep in the cabinet and straining to reach over drinking glasses to snatch the mugs, "you don't have anything to give them to take home. Maybe yogurt."

She pulled back from the cabinet, after finding two similar mugs: one was yellow, the other orange, and both matched the red one she used.

Admiringly, she held them out. "They're lovely! It's homemade pottery." She chuckled. A fake chuckle, of course. There was no true laughter in her heart. "They must go with the red one I've been using." She prepared to hop down from the counter, but before she could do it Pepper was by her side, putting his hands on her waist. He gently yet powerfully swung her down to the floor. Her heart giggled thrillingly. This both softened and hardened her. He had a girlfriend, but she couldn't deny that her heart, with a mind of its own, acknowledged her crush.

With coffee made, poured, and served at the round kitchen table scattered with red place mats, Stella made half-hearted conversation. When she had first moved to Buckhead, she tended to be the quietest one at gatherings until Chatty took over and schooled her on contributing to conversation.

"Now, I, of course, must admit that your beauty speaks for itself," he had said. "The men appreciate that and would rather look at you than hear you speak. But the women? Honey, your looks work so hard against you that you are going to have work double-time to get any authentication at all. Learn to make good conversation."

Stella, puzzled, had tilted her head. "Authentication? What on earth does that mean? It sounds like a Van Gogh being checked out to every little speck of paint."

Chatty nodded frantically. "Until the Buckhead women decide that you aren't a cheap replica of a high-class wannabe like, oh let's say for excellent example, here, Annabelle Honeycutt, you will be treated worse than a piece of bubble gum stuck to the heels of their Pradas."

Now Stella, determined to overlook her heart's pitter patter, reached up to tighten the back on her pearl earring, then pushed a casualness into her voice. It was harder than it seemed when she was close enough to see Marylyn's perfection— gleaming white teeth, full lips that had not been touched by a milligram of filler, long lashes, and hazel eyes that, to Stella's estimation, cast too much adoration toward Jack Culpepper.

"Marylyn, how do you like your cottage?" she asked. She threw a sweeping arm toward the living room and around the kitchen. "I love mine. I just moved in several days ago. This belongs to the Sloans, dear friends of mine. It's quaint and, to some folks, needs a facelift. But I'm quite happy with it."

Marylyn flashed a stunning smile, tucked a strand of hair behind her ear, and leaned forward as someone does when a confidence is about to be uttered.

"I couldn't be more delighted. It feels like the little house has thrown its arms around me and hugged me tightly."

Stella's smile dropped. She lifted the red mug and took a sip. "How lovely to hear that." Marylyn, unlike Stella who was attired in borrowed clothes that were several years old, wore a lightweight crewneck sweater in the season's trendiest color: hot pink with a touch of violet mixed in. The collared long-sleeved shirt underneath was white with checks in the same hot pink shade. To add insult to Stella's injury, Marylyn wore matching capri slacks and flats. It all showed off her slender figure.

A 14-karat gold necklace, with a tiny cross, peeped through the shirt and dangled over the collar. In Stella's mind—or so she thought—she rolled her eyes and said to herself, "Great. A cross. Now, I really have to rise to the occasion and act like the Christian I'm supposed to be."

But the eyeroll was visible. Marylyn's expression melted into woundedness and her eyes teared. Pepper looked at Marylyn, his face, too, registering hurt, and then turned to Stella, his eyes firing with anger. As for Stella, her heart sank. She was horrified. For a moment, no one spoke.

Pepper pushed the chair back from the table, stood up, and held out his hand to Marylyn. "I think it's time for us to go." With a hard look, he faced Stella, whose heart was thumping, and said, "I'm sorry we've intruded." Marylyn, squeezing his hand, took to her feet.

Stella stood, too, her hands clutched under her chin. Thoughts raced through her mind, and none had anything to do with her crush on Pepper. All she could think was what a rotten person she had become. She had just treated someone as unkindly as she had been treated. Well, almost as unkindly.

Before Stella could speak, she heard a cheerful voice cooing from the front porch screen. "Hellooo!" The screen door squeaked, indicating that it was being opened while Spigot gave a tiny bark, running to greet the surprise drop-in. "I have been raised with the most impeccable of manners. Mrs. Glaze would give me an F for coming by unannounced, and then to enter without invitation? Oh my. If she had not already left this world, she would now be deceased and her body en route pronto to H.M. Patterson, the funeral home for the elite of Atlanta society."

The unexpected guest stopped a few feet from the kitchen table and smiled beatifically. He looked around the cottage, and it was not a gaze of admiration for what he saw. Stella could see how he felt it was quite a step down from the heights to which his Stella had once soared. Yet his smile was so grand and comforting that the tenseness immediately dispersed. Stella had, once again, been saved by Chatty.

"Why, Marshal Culpepper, what a happy surprise to find you here!" He glanced toward Stella with a teasing, knowing look. He walked over and shook hands, adding a proper little bow. Smiling, he turned to face Marylyn.

"We haven't met. I know we haven't because I never forget such beauty. I'm Chatham Colquitt." She pulled her hand from Pepper's grasp and offered it to Chatty. It wasn't a full grasp he gave her but a delicate one, gently squeezing her fingers.

"I'm Marylyn Winston." Stella detected a slight tremble in her voice. Marylyn smiled weakly.

Pepper spoke. "Chatham, it is nice to see you again."

"Chatty. You may call me Chatty. I allow all of Stella's friends to call me that since she is my best friend." To Marylyn, he turned. "Ms. Winston, are you visiting St. Simons, or have you joined the many who have now seen the light and realize how marvelous our coastal Georgia is?"

"Uh, oh, no, I'm just here for a visit. I'm renting the cottage across the street."

"How darling! Well, you must join Stella and me for drinks at the Cloister one night. You, Marshal, are absolutely invited. We need security around such beautiful women."

Stella wanted to walk around the table and kick him in the shin. Hard. But she didn't need more trouble than she already had, so she restrained herself.

Marylyn swallowed. "That would be lovely. If time permits, of course. Thank you."

Chatty sniffed the air. "Coffee," he pronounced. Leaning down to pet Spigot on the head, he said, "Please don't rush off. Let's do sit and have a cup of coffee. Marshal, crime can wait. It waits all the time. One cup of coffee and a little conversation won't hinder much. Stella, remember: I like lots of cream."

Typical Chatty, expecting everyone to wait on him. Dutifully, she did as she was told while Chatty, unaware of what had just transpired, got the other two settled back at the table.

Stella scrounged for another mug and this time found a green one.

"My favorite color—green!" Chatty proclaimed as he took the mug and napkin from her. "Stellie, did you notice that I'm wearing my blue seersucker slacks? One of the joys of my Sea Island home is my wardrobe of seersucker." He sighed. "The wearing of seersucker seems to be disappearing except for in Southern cities with hot summers like New Orleans, Atlanta, and Charleston. I shall remain a devotee, always." He was blissfully unaware that any tension had existed.

Stella sat down in her chair while Chatty continued to dominate. "Now, please, Ms. Winston, if I might be so bold as to inquire, are you friends with Marshal Culpepper?"

A look of devotion crossed her face. She looked at Pepper and smiled warmly. "Yes, I am. A very close friend."

Chatty glanced at Stella. He knew that wasn't good news. She hoped he would watch his manners. Only uncivilized people questioned too much. He had to be mindful of how he extracted the answers he needed.

"For the sake of such a close friendship, it's most fortunate that you wound up on the island at the same time!"

Now, Stella, sitting next to Chatty, was able to kick him in the shin. He winced slightly but covered it.

"It isn't coincidence," Pepper replied. "I'm here on a stint to train new officers, and I invited Marylyn down for a few weeks. Marlo Sloan found the perfect cottage. The coincidence is that it is across the street from Stella's. I had stopped by to check on Stella while Marylyn was picking up her newspaper at the box and, suddenly, here we are together."

There was no reason, at least in Stella's thinking, for Pepper to add, "Marylyn and I met here on St. Simons. It will always be special to us."

Marylyn took a breath and nodded. "It's been over fifteen years since I was last here. It brings back a lot of memories." She cast her eyes downward. "Some memories so good they hurt."

Stella, realizing and accepting that she had lost yet again, joined Chatty in looks of puzzlement.

Pepper turned and looked Stella directly in the eye. "Marylyn's husband Curt and I trained together at Glynco. Then we served on four joint assignments."

Chatty couldn't help himself. He clasped his hands together over his heart as he always did when he was well pleased.

"Husband?" he asked sweetly. "It shall be my delight to meet him, too!"

Marylyn looked down at her orange mug and wrapped her hands around it. Pepper sighed.

"I'm afraid that won't be possible. Curt Winston, one of the finest men to ever serve the U.S. Marshals, was killed in the line of duty over two years ago." Pain pooled in his eyes.

For a moment, Stella and Chatty were stunned, absorbing the news. Then, without warning, Stella burst into tears and ran to the bedroom, where she threw herself facedown on the bed and cried so hard that the house rattled from the sobs.

⏤✍

After a while, the tears began to subside because Stella was wearing out. She felt a gentle hand on her back, patting her consolingly, while the consoler took a seat on the bed beside her.

"Oh, Chatty," she whimpered, raising up on her elbows and wiping her face. She took the tissue presented to her, blew her nose hard, and wiped some of the mascara-stained tears from her face. "I've gone and done it again. Embarrassed myself as if I had no raising at all."

"Now, dear, don't fret. If anyone deserves a good cry, it's you."

Stella's eyes flew wide open. All tears gone. Forgotten. Her breath stopped. For seconds, she was paralyzed. Her comforter was not Chatty. It was Marylyn. Hastily, Stella turned over and sat up. She tried to smooth her hair.

"Oh, Marylyn, please forgive me. You don't even know me and I've acted such a fool." She shook her head woefully. "Of course, don't take this the wrong way, but it's nothing special about you. I act a fool in front of people, lots of people, who know me."

Marylyn smiled sweetly. "Chatty explained a bit of what you've been through. Your husband. The country club. The IRS. As my daddy used to say, 'It'd drive a sober man to drinkin'.'" She laughed lightly.

Stella sighed heavily. "Leave it to Chatty. That's why we call him 'Chatty.'"

"Stella, he adores you. In the hour I've known him, he has made that clear. He didn't tell too much. Just enough. Besides, Pepper knew most of it, except he did seem surprised to hear about the Chardonnay that doused your mother-in-law."

Stella blew her nose again. "Oh yeah, Miss Caroline. I'd forgotten about that." She rolled her eyes. Which reminded her. "Marylyn, please forgive me for rolling my eyes. I thought

I had broken myself of that country girl habit, but you know what they say—you can take…"

"…a girl out of the country, but you can't take the country out of the girl!" The two women said it in unison and then laughed together.

"Here's something else—you can't take a country girl to the country club, either!" Stella was smiling but not laughing. "It wasn't about you. The eye roll. It's a terrible habit I've resumed in the last few weeks. It seems easier to roll my eyes than to cry. To distract them from tears!" She winked.

Marylyn took Stella's hand and placed her other hand on top of it. "I admit that I thought it was directed at me. And it did hurt, but all is forgiven. Don't think about it again." She studied Stella's eyes for a moment before continuing. She seemed to choose her words carefully. "Stella, when a husband is gone, when a marriage is over, it hurts, and the pain drives its way into the center of your soul. For those of us who lose a husband in a noble way, like Curt dying in service for his country, folks pile on a heap of sympathy. People don't take the time to be as sympathetic when the marriage ends in divorce. But the fact of the matter is that loss is loss. Love is gone. In a different kind of way, it is harder for someone in your situation. I will never see Curt again on this earth, but you will still have to deal with your husband throughout the divorce, and then, most likely, he will pop up from time to time. Perhaps one night you'll be out to dinner with a new love, having fun, laughing, with not a care in the world, and then suddenly he will walk in and the world will crash around you." She squeezed Stella's hand. "Dear girl, you cry all you want. Don't let any tear make you ashamed."

Calmness slid slowly over Stella. Here before her was a stranger, yet Marylyn understood completely how she was feeling. Stella nodded. "It's all so much to deal with, and now to find out that I may be a criminal of some kind…" She shook her head. "I can't comprehend it." She hugged Marylyn. "Thank you for your grace and kindness."

Marylyn winked. "Now, wash your face and let's have another cup of coffee. I have some cupcakes at the house. I'll run over and get them while you clean up. I believe that for every two dozen tears that are shed, a cupcake is earned!"

∽

Laughter returned to the little blue seaside cottage as Stella, Chatty, Marylyn, and Pepper talked lightheartedly and learned more about each other while a lovely wind blew through the screen door. Spigot, quite contently, was curled up under Stella's chair.

Marylyn had grown up in Birmingham, where she met Curt in high school. After college, they married and moved to Brunswick, just over the causeway, for marshal training. A few years later, he and Pepper had met again while working the G-8 summit held at Sea Island, hosting eight nations. Because of the long assignment, Marylyn had brought their daughter Harper to St. Simons for the summer, and there they had become close friends with Pepper.

"When we lost Curt, we were assigned to Washington, DC, and lived in Virginia," Marylyn shared. "Curt's parents had retired in Roanoke, so Harper and I moved there. As a paralegal, I'm able to find a job pretty easily. Now, Harper has decided to go to college in Birmingham at Samford, so she will be near my parents." Marylyn looked a little wistful as she stirred more cream into her coffee. "Again, I'm having to learn to live without someone I love."

Stella stood up, went over to Marylyn, and hugged her. "As someone wise once told me, 'Love is love, and when it's gone, it hurts.' But Harper isn't gone forever. She's just growing up so she can make you even prouder." A friendship had begun in the strangest of ways. Two women, one man, and uncertainty of who loved who. But a strong friendship between two high-minded women is stronger than a host of U.S. Marshals.

Watching the women, Chatty dropped a spot of cream-laden coffee on his starched white shirt. "Stellie, I need a sparkling soda water to get this spot out."

Stella threw him a comical look. "Chatty, we are not in Buckhead anymore. I don't have a pantry filled with luxuries like sparkling water."

He tilted his head, eyeing her quizzically. "That's a luxury? No, I think not. That's a necessity." He dabbed at the stain. "This is custom made, too. I got it from Savile Row the last time I was in London." He stopped dabbing. "That ghastly Annabelle. It's one thing to ruin your life, but why do I have to be dragged needlessly along?"

"Thank you, Chatty. It's poignant how much you care," Stella replied sarcastically.

"Marshal, we discussed that you're from Memphis?" Chatty asked, ignoring Stella's remark.

"Call me 'Pepper.' We've already been through so much together." They all laughed. "Yes, Memphis. On the Mississippi side, near DeSoto. Best barbecue in America, and don't let anyone tell you differently. There is none in Georgia nor North Carolina that can compare."

Chatty opened his mouth, and Stella knew he was about to say that he had never had barbecue and explain that if it couldn't be eaten with knife and fork, the European way, then he wouldn't eat it, but she spoke over him.

"Memphis." She studied the red bread basket atop the fridge as she tried to place a memory. "Why does my mind connect Memphis to Annabelle?"

Chatty forgot all about the spot on his shirt. It was time to rise to the occasion and to present the wealth of gossip, uh, knowledge that he had. "Because Annabelle came to Atlanta from Memphis. With her first husband who was a doctor, connected to Emory." He turned to Pepper. "Remember I asked if you knew Annabelle?"

Stella snorted a laugh. "Chatty, Memphis is a big town. Just because *you* know everyone in Atlanta doesn't mean that's the case in every city."

"Correction, Stella. I know those worth knowing in Atlanta. Then, if I need one of those not worth knowing, I call one of those worth knowing who always seems to know those not worth knowing."

Stella rolled her eyes and Marylyn pointed a finger toward her. "There you go again." She winked. A friendship was forming.

"Do you know Annabelle's maiden name?" Pepper asked. "There's always a long shot." He shrugged.

Chatty sighed. "Well, she has had so many that I doubt she can remember them all. Before she was a Honeycutt, she was a Clawson. No, wait. She was a Zimmerman. Before that, she was a Clawson. Some time or other, she was a Marcus. And it seems she had another name as she was coming to Atlanta and slipping in to marry that doctor. She's never long between husbands before greener pastures and bluer sapphires call. But her maiden name?" He tapped his fingers on the red woven place mat. "I have an excellent memory. An excellent memory and excellent manners." He smiled enticingly. "She told me once what name she was given at birth." He closed his eyes, humming softly.

"Chatty, what are you doing?" Stella asked.

He had gone into an almost trance-like stage. Phony or not. "Don't interrupt, Stella," he replied, without opening his eyes. "I'm conjuring up the memory."

While the three watched, interested, Chatty mumbled, his eyes still closed, "I see a lake. I'm at camp. A luxurious childhood camp where the finest families send their children. Fabulous sheets with a high thread count. There is a forest." Suddenly, his eyes sprang open. "Timberlake! That was her last name. Timberlake."

Stella shook her head in good humor, and Marylyn watched Stella watch Chatty, so no one noticed that a deep thought overtook U.S. Marshal Jackson Culpepper.

"Timberlake?" he asked.

"Yes, because I went to Camp Taki Taki Timber and it had a lake, a rather distasteful dark lake, but I have remarkable word association. When she told me, I put the two words together so here, years later, I remember!"

Pepper took a sip from his mug, lost in thought, as Stella and Marylyn talked about how young couples rarely registered for china and crystal any longer, and Chatty went out to the car to fetch a charger for his phone. After several minutes,

Pepper tumbled over the top of their conversation and asked Chatty, "Do you know her father's first name?"

"Oh goodness, no." The words were no sooner out of his mouth than he snapped his fingers. "I do remember her brother's name. That's because my parents spent two weeks every summer in upstate New York with the Whitneys—*the* Whitneys—in Saratoga. For the races. Horse races." He looked over at Stella. "In the world in which I was raised, racing refers to horses not cars."

Stella got up to retrieve the coffee pot and offer more to her guests. "Chatty, what do *the* Whitneys have to do with Annabelle's brother's name?" It was always helpful to have Stella around to translate Chatty's communication.

"Well, Jock Whitney was once married to one of the beautiful Cushing sisters from Baltimore. Gorgeous, they were. Babe Paley, who married William Paley of CBS, was finally retired into the Hall of Fame for Best Dress. Her sister, once married to one of the Roosevelt boys, was remarried to Jock, who, among his many contributions to humanity, was that of helping to fund the making of *Gone with the Wind*. Her other sister married an Astor."

"And?" Stella prompted.

"Annabelle's brother was called by the name 'Jock.' Nickname or Christian name, I cannot declare."

No one noticed. No one should have noticed. But Pepper felt the color wash from his face. "Jock Timberlake?" he repeated, clearly unbelieving.

Chatty clapped his hands joyously. "Yes! Jock Timberlake."

Pepper stood up abruptly. "Chatty, please see that Marylyn gets home safely. Stella, Marylyn, I'll talk to you later."

And with that he was gone. Not gone with the wind. Just gone for the time being.

Chapter Twenty-two

In the twenty-minute drive from Stella's cottage to FLETC—Federal Law Enforcement Training Center, but always fondly known as "Glynco" (for Glynn County)—US Marshal Culpepper made several official calls and had the ball rolling.

From Memphis, Tennessee, to Atlanta, Georgia, to Washington, D.C., federal officers began digging through files, both paper and digital. When Pepper heard the name "Timberlake," his gut kicked in. He was certain there was more to the situation than met the eye. Jock Timberlake. Until he was finally busted, Timberlake had run a ring of crime that stretched through Tennessee, Alabama, and Georgia. Big Jock Timberlake had to be dead by now, but perhaps this other man was his son. When it came to gossip and remembering someone's name because it was the same as an elite, well-known socialite, Chatty was not to be underestimated. Pepper had already figured that out. Maybe it was Little Jock, the son of Big Jock who used to tell his band of thieves, "Don't make Big Jocko mad. That is not a pretty sight to behold."

And it never was. In the circles of folklore and law enforcement, Jock Timberlake was legendary.

Pepper eased the black SUV, always clean according to regulation, across the causeway built originally in 1924 to join the island to Brunswick's mainland. He looked to the side where the marsh gleamed in golden beauty. Often, he thought of Roy Hodnett as he crossed because Roy and his wife Anne had become such good friends to him when he first came to train. Anne, a spitfire of a woman, who was dainty and pretty yet tough enough to be hired by the government to produce training films for officer training, took a liking to Pepper at once. The two struck up such a close friendship that he called her "Mom" and often enjoyed events with their family. Her husband Roy was without question the most respected and beloved man on the island. He had spent his life whole-selling crackers and cookies only to retire to the island when he was sixty and make himself a millionaire many times over through real estate.

Roy, amiable and kind, often reminded Pepper of his grandfather. Both had a Southern gentlemanliness to their manners and were generous beyond measure. They were so alike that when Pepper thought of one, he often thought of the other. Pepper had been with his Pop Pop at his weekly barbershop appointment when he first heard the name "Timberlake." Pepper was perhaps six years old, playing with his brown and white toy horse and a cowboy that he had named Marshal Patton.

Wendell, the barbershop owner, was clipping Pop Pop's hair and talking about a recent raid on an office across the street. "Yes siree, I sit right here and watched the whole thing. I was all by myself until Harry Pitchford came in and watched the commotion with me. They took Timberlake out in handcuffs, plus two other guys that come and go. It must've took three hours for all those officers to haul out the boxes. Dang, if they didn't have the whole sheriff's department, the state police, and the U.S. Marshals. There were more officers over there than there were people in town!"

When Wendell mentioned the U.S. Marshals, Pepper had stopped to listen. He had already decided he was going to be a marshal one day. His mama always reminded him that "children were to be seen and not heard," so he knew better than to ask questions. His patience was repaid by another man, waiting for a haircut, who lowered his newspaper and said, "Well, they say they've got him on all kinds of charges. For running gambling houses, running illegal moonshine, and"—he looked down at the little boy with his toys then back to the men— "they got him for those women, too. You know what I mean." Pop Pop and Wendell nodded. That was the first time Pepper heard the name "Timberlake," but it was far from being the last. People talked for years about Big Jock Timberlake and his criminal doings. The stories often began with "I know a man who…" and concluded with a gunfight, a killing, a robbing, or some such.

Then Timberlake became a case study as Pepper trained for the marshals. Big Jock was fifty-seven years old when he went to federal prison, and just when he was about to be released twenty years later, a person came forward with evidence linking Big Jock to the assassination of a federal prosecutor thirty years before. He was indicted, tried, convicted, and died in prison. His name became part of U.S. Marshal slang. If it was clear that someone might never leave prison without a sheet draped over his lifeless body, the saying was, "He'll get the Timberlake kind of justice."

As Pepper pulled to the first gate and showed his badge, his cell phone rang. He pushed the button on his steering wheel to answer the call.

"Hey, Pepper, this is Charlie Mitchell in D.C. I saw the order come through for some information you needed." He chuckled. "Jock Timberlake. You son-of-a-gun! Do you always make it a point of tying me into your investigations?"

Pepper laughed heartily. Charlie Mitchell, a fine and decent man who had grown up in Sevier County, Tennessee, and swore his daddy had once kissed Dolly Parton at the high school prom, was always a wealth of information for Pepper. He knew all the bodies and where they were buried.

"If only I were that smart," Pepper replied. "Because if I were *that* smart, you'd be on every assignment I pull. Then, I'd just sit back and watch you do your magic. We Tennessee boys have what it takes, you know."

"The Rocky Top fraternity. Did you see that basketball game the other night? I'm checking to make sure none of those seniors get a job with the Marshals. My son's sixth grade team could outplay them."

Pepper parked in a spot near his office and laid his head on the steering wheel and laughed. You had to look hard to find fun in law jobs, but Charlie Mitchell was guaranteed to bring it. Once for a company picnic, they were dividing up food and drinks to bring. Someone said to Charlie, "All you need to be worried about is bringing the laughter." And he did. He always did.

Once Pepper was able to stop laughing, Charlie asked, "Sure 'nuff, why are you looking at Jock Timberlake? You can't convict a dead man."

"Trying to see if he connects to a whole lot of craziness going on in Atlanta."

"Drugs? The high falutin' kind? That's pretty prevalent these days."

Clutching his phone, Pepper stepped out of the car. "Pal, you're right on that. Mighty right. No, it's something more."

The late February day was perfect in both sun and heat. He looked at the palm trees and hardwoods as he headed to his office. "I'm thinking back before you and I were old enough to tie our shoes. Do you know anybody who might have worked with Big Jock? He died years back, right?"

"Yeah, they found him dead in his bunk one morning. Autopsy showed heart disease, and hell, he was ninety-two years old!"

"That's a long time for the taxpayers to shoulder the bill for a lowlife like Jock Timberlake."

"Well said."

The two bantered back and forth about stories they had heard on Timberlake and how hard it had been to capture him. Finally, the Internal Revenue Service had started an investigation that allowed justice to be served.

"One of our colleagues in Memphis called me as soon as he got your call," Charlie said. "You could have cut out the in-between folks and called me directly."

"I'm ashamed I didn't think of that," Pepper said with a chuckle. "You must know something or you wouldn't be calling. Did he have a son named Jock?"

"He had two sons, and he named both of them Jock and called them First Jock and Second Jock. Quite an ego, that one."

"Since this kind of crime is generational, they certainly had to end up in the same life. Am I getting warm?"

Charlie laughed. "You're partly right. First Jock was gunned down when he broke into a house where the owner had a bigger gun. After that, Second Jock, who most called S.J., got a job at a tire store and eventually bought it. He died several years ago. Naturally. Cancer, I think."

"Oh."

Hearing the disappointment in his friend's voice, Charlie nudged him a bit. "Why such a sad voice? You don't like it when the crooked go straight?"

How was Pepper to explain his one-in-a-million hunch—that a woman once named Timberlake, who was from Memphis, was involved with a man in Atlanta who had gotten into the crosshairs of the IRS? White-collar crime was almost commonplace. It wasn't worth the pittance that the long-distance call was costing.

"I'm down at Glynco, instructing. I met a woman here who left her very wealthy husband in Atlanta who, it turns out, is having an affair with a woman who grew up in Memphis. Her maiden name was Timberlake."

"You're investigating this personally? Not professionally? Has the very eligible Jack Culpepper found someone who has caught his attention?"

Pepper's face flushed with embarrassment. He always believed the fact that he had no emotional ties—a wife or children—made him a more fearless law officer, while someone like Charlie with a wife and five children left the field for office work as soon as possible.

That was Pepper's noble reckoning—that he gave up having a wife and home so he could dedicate himself completely to his country. But others saw it differently. His mama always said he was afraid of commitment. His Aunt Miranda said that one day he'd wake up and smell the coffee and learn that being a solitary traveler on life's journey was a life ill spent. His cousin Buddy often asked, "Why can't you get married and be miserable like the rest of us?"

His college friend Diana had watched him change a tire on her car three years earlier and commented, "Pepper, you're so smart. You have such experience and knowledge. Your wisdom would rival that of an old man. It's so sad to me that you don't get married and have children that you can raise up with your smarts. We need more young people like that."

But it was Dr. Elmore Ragamore, a psychologist for the U.S. Marshals, who had, without frills or gentleness, laid it out in terms easy to understand.

"In a dangerous situation, with guns firing, bombs exploding, you are practically fearless. In fact, you may be the bravest lawman I've ever evaluated." Pepper had smiled, trying to hide the pride he felt. Dr. Ragamore allowed Pepper's self-worth to expand. He waited a moment longer and then said, "But the truth is you possess an enormous fear—you cannot make the commitment necessary to another person in order to have a fully satisfying emotional and physical relationship."

Pepper's smile disappeared.

"You think, Marshal Culpepper, that you are fearless. Not true. You fear something that is normal to most people and doesn't come with real danger attached. How interesting is that?"

Now, before answering Charlie, Pepper's thoughts filtered back over that afternoon of a routine evaluation after two officers had been killed during a massive man search commanded by Pepper. It was protocol for other officers involved to enter therapy briefly or for an extended time. He shook his mind loose of those thoughts and replied to his friend.

"No, no, not really. She's lovely, but there's no involvement. Charlie, you know the name Timberlake is legendary in Memphis, and when I heard she was a Timberlake from

Memphis and had a brother named Jock, it seemed like too much of a coincidence."

"Buddy, I just got a text to pick up my daughter," Charlie said. "I'll call you back in ten minutes. Hang tight." Before Pepper could say anything, Charlie was gone.

Eight minutes later—Pepper knew because he was watching the time tick off while pretending to grade test papers for the training class—the phone buzzed. It did not finish its first buzz before Pepper said, "Hello?"

Charlie chuckled. "Anxious, are we?" He wanted to make him squirm for a bit but he was already late for a meeting. "Jock Senior, the one killed in the robbery, had two children. His brother, S.J., raised the children. One was a girl, Annabelle, and the other was a boy named—get ready to be shocked here—Jock."

Pepper almost dropped the phone. Either from dismay or relief. "And is he a son who followed in his father's criminal footsteps? Bad blood breeds, you know." Already, Pepper's mind was racing to connect Jock Timberlake, Annabelle Honeycutt, and Asher Bankwell. What a score this would be!

"Not hardly," Charlie replied, sounding a bit sad to burst his friend's bubble.

"Oh, c'mon. An apple doesn't fall far from the tree. U.S. Marshal Rules 101."

"Well, according to the good folks at Bethel Baptist Church in Corinth, Mississippi, this Jock is a good apple." Charlie paused for a beat. "He's been their pastor for the last seven years."

Chapter Twenty-three

U.S. Marshal Jack Culpepper had taken up playing poker when he was training at Glynco to keep entertained during the winter nights.

Fairly quickly, he realized that the skills of bluffing and cool calculating were beneficial in his line of work. Too, when he went undercover, poker sometimes gave him entry into a game that often involved either someone with information or the culprit himself. A year earlier, Pepper had written up a syllabus for a class on poker and submitted it to the powers-that-be for inclusion in official training. To prepare himself to teach the first course, if approved, he had entered three professional tournaments. Two were in Texas and one in Las Vegas, where the toughest, most successful players gathered. No one knew he was a marshal. He had created a second identity for himself because the world is small and it gets much smaller when you're involved in niches like poker playing.

He bet with his own money, but his boss Virgil Lancaster had requisitioned $10,000 for the game in Houston. "To be taken seriously, you can't piddle with small money. And it will increase your skill. A good poker player has to be willing to lose it all without worrying about paying the next month's rent."

The suggestion made Pepper a bit nervous, but he could see the logic. With the $10,000 in his pocket, he had placed third in the tournament. He realized he needed to be good but not so good that people discussed him and checked on his background. It wasn't unusual for criminals to have enough sources to learn as much about the Marshals as the Marshals knew about them.

That's why Pepper took a minute to debate on whether his colleague was just ribbing him or it was true.

"Marshal, you still there?" Charlie asked.

"Yeah, I'm here," he mumbled, distracted for a second as he watched Anne Hodnett confer with an actor and cameraman on a training film being shot about forty yards from his office. It looked to be a sex-trafficking tutorial, one of the biggest problems the Marshals faced. He swiveled his chair around so the scene outside wouldn't distract him.

"Charlie, I ain't got time to be jokin' around. Many reasons for that, but the main is that I don't know if there's somethin' here to check out. In that event, I have plenty of real work to do."

"Understood." Charlie was stuffing pages into his briefcase, preparing to leave because Allison had to be picked up at piano practice. "That's why I'm *not* joking. This Jock Timberlake has been a minister for twenty years and served at seven different churches. All either in Alabama or Mississippi. His first job was in Scott County, Mississippi, where he worked while he went to preaching school."

Pepper chuckled. One of his favorite things about Charlie is that he could be such a country boy. He was both fun to his coworkers and disarming to those who didn't know him. Too often, someone underestimated him for a lack of smarts.

"Divinity school, I believe it is called." Pepper's mind flipped back to Ellis Auditorium in Memphis and a caper that was attached to the Jock Timberlake legend. The large, white, two-story building with a basement was within spitting distance of both Beale Street and the Mississippi River. Built in 1924 with a capacity for seating 10,000 people, for the next seventy-five years it had served the community as a concert hall—John Phillip Sousa was the first to perform there—a convention center, and athletic arena. Perhaps the biggest legend surrounding Ellis Auditorium involved the monthly Southern Gospel Music all-night singings hosted by renowned promoter Wally Fowler and including several well-known quartets. Once a month, groups like the Blackwood Brothers, who had captured America's fancy by winning the Arthur Godfrey talent show with their remarkable family, blood-related harmony, played at Ellis. Born in Mississippi, the Blackwood Brothers had moved to Memphis during years when they regularly performed there.

But while the group born in Mississippi became famous for many hit records, wins on the Godfrey show, and a tragic small plane crash in Alabama that claimed two key group members, it was the Statesman Quarter who planted a seed that would reap a worldwide harvest.

A poor young boy, born in Tupelo, had moved to Memphis with his family when he was around twelve in hopes of his father finding consistent work. Growing up in a small Pentecostal church, the boy fell in love with gospel music. He dreamed of growing up to sing with the Statesmen, which included lead singer and piano player Hovie Lister and the world record-setting baritone J. D. Sumner. One month, the boy, then fourteen, missed the all-night singing for the first time. Sumner worried about the boy until his group returned the next month and he saw him hanging around back, watching, as the groups unloaded sound equipment and instruments.

"Son, where were you last month?" Sumner asked. "I looked for you."

The handsome, dark-headed boy dropped his head, kicking at a small stone. "Sir, I didn't have the money."

Sumner put his arm around the boy. "Son, from now on, you're with me. You'll come in the back door with me."

A few years later, the Statesmen rejected the boy at an audition for a tenor replacement. But things eventually worked out fine for Elvis Presley, whose loyalty to J. D. Sumner was strong and unwavering. When Vegas beckoned and Elvis answered, J. D. Sumner and the Stamps joined him on stage to sing harmony and, always, to sing one of Elvis's favorite hymns.

At the same time that the gospel music groups were filling up Ellis Auditorium on a monthly basis, Jock Timberlake was never one to miss an opportunity to make a crooked dollar, even if he needed to unashamedly use the Lord and His work. He had the monthly dates of the singings circled in black magic marker on his desk calendar. Thousands of cars filled the parking lot at Ellis, including a dozen cars used by Jock's moonshine runners. In large Chevy or Ford sedans, they took out the back seat, then filled it and the trunk with two-quart and one-gallon containers. When the show broke—usually at about two or three o'clock in the morning after each group on the program had taken to the stage three times—and the cars began to file out and head home, Jock's men and their illegal cargo slipped right in line and waved at the police officers directing traffic. Within twenty minutes, they would outsmart Memphis and Tennessee authorities and be bound for numerous roadhouses scattered throughout rural Mississippi.

Now, here was Charlie on the phone, telling Pepper that Jock's grandson was not a disciple for the devil but an apostle for Jock's great enemy, the Lord.

"He could have gone to technical school to learn how to assemble the Bibles and then hand-tool the leather covers for all I know. I am certain, however, that he worked as a minor preacher while in Scott County and went to school. A buddy of mine was working Jackson, Mississippi, then and told me."

"Apprentice."

"Huh?"

"He was working as an apprentice to learn to preach."

Charlie grunted. "Well, one thing he didn't have to work at was finding good, modern tales of the devil's deeds. He just needed to go to family reunions and hear them firsthand. Look, I've got to pick up my daughter. You can always call me if you need me. Anytime. Even at Mrs. Seymour's Studio of the Music Arts."

"Thanks, my good pal. But it looks like my hunch has been crunched. Talk another time."

Pepper sighed heavily then walked over to open his window. Mindlessly, he watched two female officers seated at a picnic table drinking coffee and sharing a break. He couldn't shake the feeling he had. That was another way poker had helped him—outside of smarts, the best poker players had an unbeatable gut instinct when they learned to use it rather than walk away from it.

The Timberlakes. Asher Bankwell. Something crooked must have joined them at the pocketbook.

It was almost 6:30 P.M., and after three hours of coffee and cupcakes, Chatty, Stella, and Marylyn had become friendly with each other. They were comfortable enough that Marylyn shared the details of Curt's death and how Harper, barely a teenager, had hidden in her bed for two days, curled up with the blanket she had loved as a child. Stella teared up and admitted to herself that Pepper had picked the right woman, and he would get Harper as a bonus. Marylyn, on her side, was loathe to admit it to herself, but the beautiful Stella seemed to have caught Pepper's eye and she completely understood why—such beauty and compassion. And she wanted Pepper to be happy. He was wonderful in every way—plus, he kept Curt's memory alive for her.

"Oh, that's silly," Marylyn told herself as she watched Chatty and Stella tease back and forth. "She's too glamorous for Pepper. He has always been drawn to more ordinary-looking women like me. Attractive but not gorgeous." She tried to shake it off. But still, a tiny worry remained.

She was snapped out of this conversation with herself when Chatty popped the end of the table with three fingers. "Oh child a'mercy! We have about missed the cocktail hour." He looked at the Cartier 14-karat gold watch on his arm. "As McCager Burnett says in that mountain voice of his, using those odd hillbilly sayings, 'It's pert nigh gone.'"

Stella knew what this meant and didn't flinch. Marylyn looked quizzical, but Chatty waved away her concern. "Never you mind, dear. Let's pop over to the Lodge for drinks and a bite of dinner. We've already missed the bag piper who plays every night, but we can enjoy the upscale, rustic beauty of the Lodge and gaze across the water as the cargo ships and shrimpers come and go."

Stella looked down at her ragamuffin clothes. "Let me change into something a little better."

Chatty arched an eyebrow. "My thoughts exactly, dear one." He leaned over and lowered his voice, as if someone was eavesdropping. "Actually, that's why I chose the Lodge rather than the Cloister." He wrinkled his nose and shook his head. "I don't think you have the appropriate clothes for the Cloister. You know, we are going to have to remake your image totally from scratch after that little country club stunt of yours."

Stella, unamused—especially in front of Marylyn—threw a look at him that should have shut him up. It didn't.

"Now don't waste that look, precious darlin'. It will give you lines, and since you no longer have money for Botox you have to be careful." Stella reared back in her chair, about to drop his goose into a pot of hot water, when, as Chatty can perfectly do, he turned the conversation. He took her model-like hands in his and said, "Now, remember that as long as I have a dime, you will have seven cents. You will have plenty enough."

Despite herself, she laughed. "I thought it was a nickel. That as long as you have a dime, I have a nickel."

In his patented gesture, he crossed his chest with one arm, put his large hand against his cheek, and gazed at her thoughtfully for a moment. "Yes." He nodded. "Yes. That's what I've said. But I've increased your allowance. The sight of you in those clothes has broken my heart and put me in such a shape that I may give you everything I have before this nightmare ends!"

❦

208

The threesome climbed from Chatty's Land Rover at valet, thanked the young man who opened the door, and stepped into the two-story foyer covered in rich, dark paneling, handsome bannisters, and wide stairways. They passed the baby grand and the stunning eight-foot-high portrait of a mysterious woman that hung over the stone fireplace, then headed toward the bar and casual dining room.

Marylyn was still wearing the same clothes because Chatty had deemed her perfect enough, though he had whispered in Stella's ear at the first opportune moment, "I'm looking out for you, honey. You need to look better than she does every chance that comes your way."

In Marlo's cast-offs, Stella had discovered a simple, yellow silk Trina Turke—a popular brand at the beach for casual attire—and a cloth tie belt with tiny rhinestone balls dangling from the ends. Chatty had surprised her with a "cheer up" gift of expensive nude-colored suede pumps with a high heel. "Now, you will have a decent pair of high heels until this mess is sorted through."

Just as Chatty greeted the hostess, who, of course, he knew well enough to inquire about her frequent migraines, Arthur Adair, who had worked at the Lodge for years, hurried over.

"Mr. Colquitt, it is indeed good to see you again. Please forgive the intrusion, but Governor Burnett is looking for you. He asked that if I saw you I should instruct you to come to his house immediately and to bring Mrs. Bankwell with you."

"My goodness. This must be important. A summons from the Governor." He thought a second then looked at Marylyn. "It shames me to break my word, but outside forces prevent my keeping it. May I order a dinner for you to take back to your cottage? And Arthur, perhaps you could deliver Mrs. Winston to her cottage near the King and Prince?"

"Indeed, sir." Chatham Colquitt was known as a stout tipper. No one turned him down.

"Actually, I think I'll have cheese and crackers and a glass of wine for dinner," Marylyn replied. She smiled and winked. "But I'll hold you to dinner another time soon." She turned to Stella. "And you, too, my new friend."

From his pocket, he pulled his money clip and handed a hundred to Arthur. "Please, see her safely inside." He took Stella's elbow. "Now, we must see what is at the core of such an urgent request."

⁂

Alva Burnett was mixing martinis, so her husband answered the door. A bit irritated, he shook his head. "Chatty, when do you plan on getting into the modern age and getting a cell phone?"

Walking through the door, Chatty reached into his breast pocket. "I have one. But I don't know how to make a call on it. I just know how to answer when it rings. And, for the love of all my trust funds, I couldn't tell you the number if I had to. My house staff has it and so does Stella."

They followed the Governor into the den, where the martinis waited on a silver tray, along with a bright smile from Miss Alva.

McCager Burnett couldn't believe what had happened a couple of hours ago. It all started because Alva wanted a certain brand name spice that was not carried at Harris Teeter, the grocery store at the edge of Sea Island. For one reason or another, there was no one to go but him. He had to drive down Frederica Road, toward the village of St. Simons, to get to the Winn-Dixie. He parked in the large lot used by several businesses including four or five restaurants, a furniture store, and a dress shop. Across the street was the small airport where several jets were parked, regardless of day or time, waiting on owners to leave Sea Island.

"I won't go into the whole story," the Governor began, "but my lovely wife was insistent that I go to the Winn-Dixie..." His voice trailed off when Chatty almost spit out his first sip. Instead, he swallowed and got choked. This irritated the Governor.

"Governor, oh, Governor," Chatty began. "It is not fitting that you be seen at the grocery store. And if it is an absolute must, it should be, at least, a Publix. Most certainly not a Winn-Dixie." He lowered his voice. "That's where the common people shop."

Now, the Governor was mad. He *was* a common man, and he had been elected nine times to political office by common people.

"Chatham, you and I will discuss the blight of the common man in the eye of aristocracy at a later time. And I do mean that we *will* discuss." His voice was firm. "It shall not be forgotten."

The Governor put his arm around Stella. "Perhaps you'd better have a seat." He gently steered her toward the edge of the loveseat and sat her down. "Now. Take a big sip of that martini and hand me the glass." She did promptly as she was told.

The Governor walked over to the silver serving tray that Alva had set on the console and placed the glass there. He took a moment, gathered his thoughts, then sat beside Stella and put a comforting hand on her folded hands, which were beginning to tremble slightly. He looked her directly in the eye.

"Asher Bankwell is on the island."

Chapter Twenty-four

All night, Pepper tossed and turned. He had punched and plumped his pillow at least four times, thinking it would magically put him to sleep when he laid down his head. It did not. At 2 A.M., he had arisen and opened the sliding doors in the bedroom of his second-floor condo so he could listen to the gentle crashing of the frothy waves onto the beach. The tide was high, so it was hitting the stone retainer wall about twenty feet from the window.

Of course, Jock Timberlake was top on his mind, but, if he were to admit it, he was also once again rattled by thoughts of Dr. Ragamore. Pepper often went for months without thinking of the therapist's diagnosis of his fear of committing to a relationship. But when it did cross his mind, it always brought a heavy weight to his heart. He leaned against the doorframe and thought of Marylyn and Stella. Of Kristy Owens from two years ago. Before that, Tanya Wilson, and with her name he began silently counting. When he got to a dozen and knew there were several more to go, he quit. He had more important things to think about than women he had dated for no more than a month or two.

Pepper found something haunting about the endless darkness of a nighttime sea, especially when there was only a sliver of a moon, as there was on this late winter's night. As he cast his thoughts into the distance, it was black with no light. He mused over how hopeless it would feel to be lost in the midst of a bottomless ocean with no light around. The legacy of Jock Timberlake was much like that vast darkness. Untold were the number of lives Timberlake and his syndicate had taken by violence or the number of wives and children adversely affected by dollars lost to their lifestyle because Timberlake had coaxed men into using their money for gambling, illegal whiskey, drugs, or prostitution. It was too seedy and overwhelming to comprehend.

After his call with Charlie, Pepper had pushed aside the grading of test papers and searched high and low for any information pertaining to the Timberlake family. It was stunning to learn that Big Jock's grandson was an ordained minister. To any law enforcement officer with knowledge of Big Jock and his empire, that would seem to indicate that it was a clever cover. Pepper's first thought was that Rev. Timberlake was laundering money through the church collection plate. Trained as a law officer, Pepper always deciphered information through that teaching. It was 11 P.M. before he finally surrendered to the facts fact that the preacher was clean as whistle. There were no fewer than four IRS audits on him and seven on the various churches that employed him in service for the Lord, and nothing was untoward. In fact, one audit on the preacher revealed that he had even turned in gift money he received for Christmas and his birthday as well as the small cash envelopes he was given for performing a funeral or wedding. The auditing agent had noted in the file, "This is the first time I have ever seen cash turned in like this. The date and location of the services are dutifully noted."

Another audit revealed that Rev. Jock—as Pepper took to calling him to distinguish him from the other Jocks—was rightly owed a refund of $246.83 by the United States Department of Revenue.

For many years, the Feds had kept a watchful eye on this particular servant of the Lord, but in the last four or five years interest had trailed off, and the IRS had apparently turned their resources toward true criminals. Pepper sighed as he looked into the sea's blackness. Something still rattled his gut. Aloud, he said to the darkness, "What are the chances that there is not something awry with Rev. Jock's sister, Annabelle, being connected to Asher Bankwell, who is obviously in trouble with the IRS?"

He pressed his palms against his aching temples and shook his head, trying to forget the puzzle he could not resolve. He finally crawled back into bed and slept fitfully for two hours, then, at 5:30 A.M., tossed his sheets back and pulled up from his bed. Within minutes, he was dressed and running along the shoreline. Faster and faster he ran, trying to escape his questions and pushing himself toward returning mentally to his training classes. He was not paid to be an amateur sleuth. This wasn't even an investigation. It was all in his head. The sun was rising majestically over the ocean as he ran back to his condo. He passed Massengale Park and the Grand, where he could see that the light was on in the Hodnetts' condo. Miss Anne must be up and having her coffee. He returned home and decided to dress and pick up coffee at his favorite shop before he got on the causeway, telling himself that he needed to get to the work and return to those test papers. He had to prepare for his afternoon class.

At 7 A.M., he flipped on the light in his office and checked his secured email. He was awarded with a binging sound of an urgent message.

"We have received your request for information on Asher Bankwell. Please call me as soon as possible, regardless of time." The message was from Federal Bureau of Investigation agent Turner McGavin. Within seconds, the two men were on a call and all pleasantries dismissed.

"Marshal, are you working an active case on Asher Bankwell?" McGavin asked.

"No sir. The Department is not involved at all with this. Yet. I've stumbled across a situation socially. I guess you would say that it nudged my instinct. I'm on assignment at Glynco, down in Georgia, where I'm teaching a couple of training courses. Per chance, I met Bankwell's estranged wife, who is hiding, I guess would be the best description, on St. Simons Island. Her car was confiscated by order of the Internal Revenue Service. Something isn't right. Or at least, that's what my gut says."

Turner McGavin had recently celebrated his twenty-seventh anniversary as an FBI agent. A talented high school wide receiver, he had earned a college education with a football scholarship to Grambling State in Louisiana. He had been recruited by the much respected and much winning coach, Eddie Robinson. McGavin had grown up in the swampy back woods of the state where his hard luck family had survived on alligator meat and anything else they could catch or track. In the winters, they were cold, and the summers were so hot that McGavin and his brother had often slept on the ground outside the family's termite-infested shack, just to catch a bit of air, stale and humid though it might be. A rotator cuff tear suffered in the last game of his senior year had ended his dreams of professional football and left him stranded, looking for a new dream that would take him out of the Louisiana swamps.

Enter Andrew Malachi Swain, a Grambling State alum who was a football season ticket holder and a federal agent always looking for raw talent. He had admired McGavin's lightning feet and quick thinking for four years on the football field, and he was there on the autumn afternoon when a fierce tackle ended the young man's professional dreams. By Tuesday morning, after a call to university officials and a thorough background check, Swain was full speed on recruiting Turner McGavin for the FBI. It turned out to be a brilliant decision for both. Swain landed a young man who would go on to earn many honors, while McGavin would use his hard upbringing to fuel mightily the fight against white-collar crime. He refused to let the memory of his growing-up years fade. Instead, he used the experience to throw gas on his burning desire to put law-breaking rich men behind bars. Once you've known the heat, cold, and starvation of a Louisiana swamp, he'd told Pepper, there is little sympathy for those who live in ill-begotten mansions and, worst of all, have private jets at their disposal.

Turner McGavin had been on the trail of Asher Bankwell for almost four years. Just when his commanding officer was about to close the file, a fortunate call came out of nowhere. Now it turned out that Jackson Culpepper and Turner McGavin were two men looking for the lifeline the other could throw.

"Bankwell first came to our attention about four years ago when his name came up as a business partner with a guy from Savannah named Thomas Neal Richmond," McGavin explained. "This was one of the worst offenders I've seen in all my years. He had legitimate businesses fronting for all kinds of illegal doings, but his biggest moneymaker was laundering money and stashing it in offshore accounts. We had Richmond under indictment, and it was a solid case we were practically guaranteed to win when he turned up dead in a single car crash outside Highlands, North Carolina. That was eighteen months ago. We were about to abandon the case by force of the higher ups when I managed to link a $500,000 deposit into Bankwell's private account from a company connected to Richmond. It was many times removed from Richmond and was quite a pig trail, but we linked them. Based on that, we were able to get the Revenue Service to go after Bankwell." He paused. "You know what we say: if there's no other way, there's always the IRS."

Pepper chuckled. "Yeah. I've used that a time or two myself. Tell me, Agent McGavin, have you found any connection between Bankwell and a woman named Annabelle Honeycutt?"

Calmly, he replied, "I can tell you that they've been a romantic pairing for two years. Even before Richmond was killed. I can tell you the address of the apartment where they meet and the fragrance he orders for her from Neiman-Marcus, but we have not been able to link them in crime. Our entire department has tried and I've nearly worked myself into a divorce over it. I'm ashamed to admit that all I've come up with is failure. So far. Any way you can help us out on this?"

Pepper rubbed his hand over his brow. "Buddy, you know a lot more than I do at this point. This is my basic information: Bankwell's wife Stella took Annabelle down in a public undoing at the Buckhead Country Club. She came to St. Simons because her friend, Marlo Sloan, is here, and then her luxury Jaguar was confiscated. Oh yeah, and she's an emotional mess. My bet is that she's innocent in all this."

Turner McGavin, alone in his Washington office where he had spent the night on the love seat because his wife was tired of playing second fiddle to the FBI, had to laugh. Rich people acting "a fool," as his mama used to say.

"Yeah, we heard about the country club. Sorry I missed out on that one. It sounded entertaining." He tapped his forehead for a few seconds. "Well, let's agree to keep each other apprised on this. Maybe, together, we can solve this."

"This call is much appreciated. I'm happy to know that someone else thinks Asher Bankwell is a scofflaw in some way or, perhaps, many."

Half an hour later, Pepper still pretending to work on his training class while his mind wandered, was interrupted by Jane Collier, a fellow agent who stopped by on her way for coffee. They chatted about the weather, her father's seventy-fifth birthday party, and the observation that the month of February was always a rainy season on the island. Their conversation was interrupted by the ringing of Pepper's desk phone, so she mouthed "see you later" and he nodded as he picked up the phone.

"Culpepper," he barked into the phone.

"Is this U.S. Marshal Jackson Culpepper?" asked a polite male voice.

"Yes!" he barked back. He was in no mood for dancing around.

"This is Rev. Jock Timberlake," the man replied with a casual tone. "I hear you're looking for me."

Chapter Twenty-five

Stella opened her eyes and glanced around the room, at its pale blue wallpaper accented with tiny pink flowers. She snuggled under the down comforter and studied the carved pineapples on the tips of the four-poster bed. Her face felt dry and tight from all the tears she had cried lately.

Her eyes fell on the twin portraits of a shy little girl facing a bashful boy. Then she glanced over at the window seat draped in white lace curtains. She was so grateful that the Governor and Miss Alva had insisted that she spend the night with them. They had even gone the extra mile by asking Arthur at the Cloister to retrieve Spigot and bring her over. The moment the dog saw Stella's eyes were open, she crawled across the bed and teased her face with a cold nose.

"No question about it," the Governor had said with certain authority. "You are staying here. As the former Governor of the great state of Georgia, I am able to call upon a security detail. We will surround this house so that Asher Bankwell cannot get close."

As the four of them were gathered together in the living room, Chatty had spoken up. "Stella is my best friend in the world. I will not abandon her. Even if I must stand guard around her room, I shall fight heroically for my beloved Stella."

Miss Alva had lowered her eyes and fought to hide a smile. The Governor winked at Stella. Even though Chatty's house was next door, they all knew the truth—yes, he loved Stella beyond measure, but he was also afraid of Asher Bankwell and didn't want to chance that he and/or his thugs would break into his house and come after him.

"You shall be our guest also," the Governor replied, which Chatty accepted with a grateful smile.

Stella turned over on her back and stared up at the white ceiling with its elaborate molding and thought back on the revelation that the Governor had stumbled across. He was close to turning his Ford SUV into the Winn-Dixie parking lot when he spotted something over at McKinnon Field, the airport that served the Golden Isles. Private jets took off and landed frequently, usually right in the landing path over the Lodge, the smaller, cozier hotel owned by Sea Island. A stairs plank on a small Citation jet dropped as the Governor drove through the roundabout at the CVS and took the short jot to turn right into the parking lot. Putting his car in park, he saw a man move to exit the plane, his jacket collar pulled up to his ears. Even in the early evening nightfall, the Governor recognized that man.

Of course, Chatty had challenged him. Only Chatty would question the formidable Governor McCager Burnett.

"And just how do you know it was Asher? How can you be certain?" he had asked. Chatty was still frozen to the spot where he had stopped when he entered the living room, next to the antique coffee table. Stella, wide-eyed, looked between the Governor and Chatty. Miss Alva had quietly dropped into a comfortable club chair. The Governor raised his eyebrow and menaced Chatty with a stare before replying.

"Chatham, I am a former U.S. Marine. I am trained to know people by the length of their stride, the way they hold their shoulders or angle their head. Without question, it was Asher Bankwell. Do not, for the sake of our longstanding friendship or the memory of your fine parents, question me for one moment."

Chatty withered. He dropped his head and rounded his shoulders and his immense being melted into a puddle of humiliation. "Yes sir," he said simply.

Stella had felt her mouth go dry. Her heart sped up. "Wh—wh—what would Asher being be doing on the island?" she asked feebly.

"There's only one answer to that riddle," the Governor replied. "He is looking for you."

After a few more minutes of dwelling on the previous night's conversation, Stella tossed the covers back. She did not move immediately. Finally, Stella dragged herself from the luxurious bed. In the bathroom she splashed water on her face, dried it, then dabbed on a moisturizer that Miss Alva had left for her. Dismayed, she studied her face. "Another week. Another year older," she mumbled. Her thoughts stayed on her dissolving looks until she remembered she had bigger problems—Asher Bankwell.

"Oh Lord, help me," she whispered, and then she heard a light knock at the door.

"Oh, Stellie, are you awake? Your prince has arrived."

"Yes, Chatty, come in." She was attempting to detangle her golden red curls with her fingers when he appeared in the doorway, still in the previous day's seersucker, holding a larger platter with a silver coffee pot, matching creamer and sugar, tiny spoons, white linen napkins trimmed in lace, and delicate china cups rimmed in gold. Stella glanced in the mirror and saw the reflection of her beloved friend with his morning offering. Dropping her hands, she stepped over and kissed him on the cheek. He blushed bright red.

Pulling back, she clasped his shoulders with her hands. "Chatham Balsam Colquitt, you are—," she began but was interrupted by Chatty's reminder.

"—the fourth," he said. "Chatham Balsam Colquitt, IV."

It was times like these that he delighted her most. No one else viewed the world the way Chatty did.

"Excuse me. Of course. The fourth. Under any name, the truth is the same. You have been my best friend in the world. God bless you, dear Chatty, and thank you for loving me."

He blew a kiss in the air, then turned toward her bedroom to take the tray to a tiny table between two small antique chairs that looked like a set from a 1940s movie. The armless vanity chairs were covered in a blue and pink chintz that matched the wallpaper and had a wide ruffle around the bottom. Chatty poured a cup and said, "Here, dear Stellie, sit here and let's talk for a moment before joining the Burnetts downstairs. Oh! You need a robe. Darlin', it isn't appropriate to receive a gentleman into your boudoir without wearing a robe."

There were more important things to consider, but Stella knew she looked a mess in a brand new, oversized pair of pajamas that Miss Alva kept on hand for such occasions as a woman hiding from a husband who is trying to track her down his nutty wife. Chatty breezed over to the enormous wardrobe, opened the door, and found a white heavy, terry robe. He put it over Stella's shoulders, and she sat down and began sipping her coffee while Chatty dumped half the creamer in his own half cup of coffee. He stirred it carefully and without hurry before picking up a linen napkin and sitting down in the chair opposite her.

"Can you even taste coffee in that? With all the cream?" she asked.

He waved the question away. "There are matters of graver importance to discuss." He stopped to enjoy his first sip, and the happiness pulsated from his face. Then, he continued.

"Stella, have you ever suspected anything? Asher has always been sneaky but this goes far beyond what I ever thought him capable of doing." He tossed his hand through the air while saying, "Frankly, I can't believe he is smart enough to pull off any dastardly acts." He leaned forward. "You know, he was held back a year in math when we were in the fifth grade. He had to have a special study hall each day and a tutor. But they allowed him to proceed with our class." He sniffed haughtily. "I never believed that was the proper procedure. He should have suffered more. But there again, the Bankwell endowment saved him, I am certain."

"Perhaps that's why he has the hounds of hell on his tail," Stella replied tartly. "He's in over his head and he's not smart enough to figure his way out." Chatty chuckled as a knock came at the door.

"Stella, may I trouble you a moment?" It was the Governor.

"Yes sir!" She and Chatty stood as he opened the door. His expression was grave. He looked sorrowful before he spoke.

"Will you please dress and meet me in the dining room? We can all have a bite of breakfast first, but then I have some information to share. I have just received a call from the Attorney General himself."

Stella's heart fell, an emotion she had experienced too much lately. She nodded. "Yes sir," she replied quietly.

She was beginning to think that this waking nightmare would involve many more sleepless nights before it ended.

Chapter Twenty-six

Pepper was speechless for a few seconds. Rev. Jock Timberlake on the phone, calling him?

"Hello, there? Marshal, are you there?"

"Please forgive me. Again, who did you say this is?"

Rev. Jock was a mild-mannered, pleasant man and even, at times, quite jolly. In fact, his nickname among the children who knew him and his congregations was "Jolly Jock."

"Jock Timberlake. Too good to be true, huh?"

Pepper's mind began racing. His thoughts tumbled over how Rev. Jock Timberlake knew he had inquired about him. As though reading his mind, the good pastor provided the answer.

"Son, you don't get investigated as much as I have since I was fourteen without making one or two friends along the way. Someone tipped me off."

"If that someone is employed by the federal government, he has not only violated confidentiality procedures but has also broken the law." That's what Pepper said, but what he was thinking was how glad he was for that person and this phone call.

"Not to worry a'tall. The person who told me—and by the way, it might have been a female—strongly encouraged me to call you. That seems like to me that the person was working for the good of all concerned."

Pepper had to concur. "This isn't an official investigation. I'm poking into things out of my own curiosity. I'm sure you're aware that the Timberlake name is well known to criminals, law enforcement agents, and the general public. And, of course, folklore."

"Try living with the name," he replied in a tone more of sorrow than of sarcasm. "Marshal, this might not be an official investigation, but I believe that it rightly should be. Especially where my sister Annabelle is concerned. There are things I know that you should know. I welcome the opportunity to speak with you, but I think we should do it in person."

Pepper was interested in doing just that. "You're in Mississippi?"

"Corinth, near the west border of Tennessee. I guess you could say that's where all the evil started. Where are you?"

Pepper thought back to a movie he had watched as a child in which Sheriff Buford Pusser had set about trying to clean up all the evil doings in Selmer, Tennessee. It was a crime ring that stretched all the way to Phenix City, Alabama. Pepper recalled reading that the cleanup of corruption in Alabama alone had included more than 700 people.

"I'm on assignment at Glynco on the Georgia coast. In Brunswick." As he talked, he walked over to the enormous map of the United States that hung on the wall next to the door. He ran his finger across Georgia, the edge of Alabama, and into the corner of Mississippi. "Whew. It looks like we're about nine or ten hours driving apart from each other." His mind moved quickly. It wasn't an official investigation and therefore he couldn't take the time to go to Mississippi. He also couldn't request that Marshals from Memphis or Jackson, Mississippi, look into the matter, either. Rev. Jock interrupted his thoughts.

"I'm completely free today, but I have a funeral tomorrow and the next day. My congregation is an older one so I tend to do at least one funeral a week."

Pepper said, "If this were an investigation, I could request Marshals from nearby cities or perhaps even send a plane. But the way things are now…" His heart was sinking as he thought of what he might be missing. Then, Stella's beautiful face flickered across his thoughts. His heart wiggled a mite. Then he winced at how he was letting her down. This was what he had wanted since he was a boy—to ride to the rescue of a beautiful woman in distress.

"Plane?" Rev. Jock mused. "Now, there's a thought."

"It's out of the question. I can't requisition one."

"I may have a solution, though," the preacher replied. "I have a church member. A deacon. He owns several fast-food franchises across a couple of states. He has his own turbo prop. A King Air. He has pilots on salary but he keeps his license active, too. He told me at lunch a couple of days ago that he needed to get in some flying hours to keep his license up. Maybe I could get him to fly me over."

Pepper's heart soared. A solution! "That would be ideal!" Then, always looking for the downside in every opportunity, he warned, "But I can't even get his fuel reimbursed."

"Don't worry about that," Rev. Jock replied. "It's a matter of pennies to him. Let me call him. I'll get right back to you."

For the next half hour, Pepper nervously awaited and read the documents that Turner McGavin had sent after their conversation. Asher Bankwell's name popped up, but as the FBI agent had warned, there was no evidence tying him to anything. Asher couldn't be that smart, could he—that he was masterminding a money-laundering scheme yet wasn't connected? Deep in thought, Pepper jumped when the phone rang.

He grabbed the receiver. "Culpepper."

Rev. Timberlake was quick to the point. "We shall land in Brunswick around noon."

"I'll meet you there." Pepper replaced the receiver and mumbled to himself, "What on earth could the good reverend know that is so important that it be delivered in person?"

∽

Stella felt like a fragile child as she timidly entered the Burnetts' dining room, a marvel of old-fashioned grace and good taste. In the center of the long, antique walnut table with a satinwood inlay and scallop border was an enormous silver bowl with fresh flowers—surely Edward, the island's beloved floral designer, had delivered them—and silver candleholders on each side. On the mahogany sideboard, a morning buffet was set up and beautifully displayed in silver chafing dishes and crystal bowls. Stella sniffed the air—that familiar scent of a Sterno flame can. It was a unique smell and always brought back a flood of memories. Today, for some strange reason, she thought of a hospitality suite she had set up at the Indy 500 when she was working her old job. That triggered memory boosted her spirits because it reminded her of how successful she had once been when she was on her own. She did it then, and she could do it again.

Four places were set with Royal Crown Derby Regency in crisp turquoise bordered in gold. It was so beautiful and serene that it brought an additional peace to her spirit.

"My grandmother had this same china pattern and, as a child, I did love it so," carried on Chatty as he was dishing up Mrs. Puckett's amazing grits. He paused for a moment. "I wonder what happened to that exquisite set?" He studied on it for a second then snapped his fingers. "I believe it may be stored in my china cabinet right here on Sea Island. I need to bring it out soon and have a dinner party."

Miss Alva smiled sweetly. "Chatham, if you need additional place settings, you can borrow anything we have. Of course, I hope that goes without saying."

He smiled beatifically and nodded like a child, just as the Governor, dressed in gray slacks, a white dress shirt, and a yellow cardigan, shuffled into the dining room. He was limping slightly because all the recent stress was causing his gout to flare up. His big toe was painful. Chatty noticed the crippled walk.

"Dear Governor, it appears that you are having trouble with your gait," Chatty commented.

"Blooming gout. The disease of kings." The Governor tossed down a folder of papers and looked at Stella, who had slid into a chair and was determined to act brave. "Stella, isn't it a wonder how a mountain boy can come to live like this?" He waved a hand around the room. "This isn't me." He looked at his beloved Miss Alva and smiled. "And it isn't really who Miss Alva is, either, but the lawyering business has brought us a lot of money, and with no children we had to pile up the money or spend it somewhere."

Chatham was savoring a bite of the eggs scrambled with cheese. He swallowed, dabbed his mouth with the linen napkin, and said, "Please don't feel obligated, but I certainly would appreciate these dishes bequeathed to me in thy will. These should pass to someone who appreciates the perfection of this turquoise." He said it with such a comical tone that the others laughed. A laugh they needed. They rested in the luxury of the moment before the Governor turned to Stella.

"Now, for matters more serious than death and fancy china."

Stella nodded, tears standing by to fill her eyes if needed. It didn't seem like the Governor had good news. She swallowed. "Yes?"

"The state's Attorney General called. He has used his full authority to dive into these tax matters. But there is a separation of state and federal government. He knows this much: the Feds have an ongoing investigation into Asher and his business dealings. The state's having trouble finding chargeable offenses there, but the IRS has found some serious flaws." He took a deep breath. "Asher is in deep trouble, and they are going after him fiercely."

Chatty laid down his fork and knife and leaned closer to listen. Stella fought to hold back the threatening tears. There were things McCager Burnett was not going to tell her. There was more than enough to cause panic. She could tell he was trying to choose his words.

"And?" she whispered.

"Your signature is on every return. In the eyes of the law, you are as guilty as he."

The tears sprang forth and spilled over followed by Chatty, who leapt to his feet and ran over to hug her and console her. Then the tears suddenly stopped. She had to act stronger than she felt. Sure, it would take some time, but if she didn't start now, she'd never become a more resilient person after enduring this unimaginable moment in time.

"What should I do?"

McCager Burnett rubbed his brow worriedly. "If I were you," he began in a level tone, "I'd get the security team situated around this house to escort you over to the chapel at the Cloister, and then there, in the midst of that stained-glass beauty, I'd get down on my knees in that altar and I'd pray. Hard."

Chapter Twenty-seven

Pepper was taken aback at Rev. Jock Timberlake's movie-star good looks. For no reason in particular, he had expected a portly, bald-headed man, perhaps wearing a rumpled suit. He couldn't have been more wrong, or as Pepper's six-year-old nephew Skip liked to say, "wronger."

The Rev. Jock was about six-foot-two, with broad shoulders that made a V as his torso tapered down to a slim waist. He had a large, welcoming smile, dark brown hair with a few strands of gray, and smiling blue eyes surrounding by a crinkling of lines that showed he smiled a lot. At first, Pepper mistook him for the church deacon who had flown him over. He hesitated in the waiting area of the private terminal since only one man stepped off the plane.

The man grinned broadly. "You must be Marshal Culpepper." He laughed. "I figured that out by the monogram on your shirt. I won't even ask for identification."

Pepper, stumbling over his miscalculation, pointed to the badge hung on his belt. "Yes sir! But you can never be too careful." He reached in his back pocket and pulled out his official identification. The two men shook hands. "My car is outside. Shall we go back to my office? And what about your friend?"

"He's staying here," Timberlake replied. "He's toting around a large briefcase, claiming he has a lot of work to do."

Once the two men were settled in the office at Glynco, Pepper started to relax and realized that he was gaining an affinity for the preacher. Whenever something like that crossed Pepper's mind, he always stepped back. A law officer couldn't afford to be fooled. He offered coffee but Timberlake asked for water.

"You may be in the best shape of any minister I ever met," Pepper commented.

"It's how I deal with the stress. An hour of working out every morning in my basement gym. Then, if it's been a very bad day, I go for a run when I get home. In the morning, I finish working out by 6:30 then study the Bible for an hour or so. I have a small church with only a part-time assistant, so most days I just work from home. Every day after lunch, I visit those in the hospital or those at home. Occasionally, I visit an unreformed sinner at home."

"Unreformed?" asked Pepper as he pulled out his desk chair. He sat down without taking his eyes off his visitor.

"We're all sinners," the reverend said with a grin and a bit of a twinkle in his eye. He smoothed down the black and yellow striped tie he was wearing. His navy blue jacket hung on the back of his chair. "Some of us have asked the Lord's grace on us, others haven't." He looked Pepper directly in the eyes. "Marshal, the only difference between me and my grandfather is the size and multitude of our sins. And the fact that I daily ask for forgiveness of mine. Unless he had a deathbed conversion, which I hope for but doubt, he didn't come to a good end."

Pepper nodded. "I appreciate that you've gone to so much trouble to be here."

"I'm glad you came looking for me before I had to start looking for the law. When you have a name like mine, you want to avoid that."

The Rev. Jock Timberlake, like his sister, had grown up as an orphan in their Uncle S.J.'s home. The uncle was a kind man who taught by example. He worked hard at his tire business, came home for a family supper, then attended every event that his three girls, Jock, and Annabelle chose to participate in. His daughters were in debate and theater, Jock played baseball and basketball, and Annabelle, who always depended on her good looks, entered every beauty pageant she could find. She didn't win many, but she was always either first or second runner-up. Jock was six and Annabelle was three when their father was killed and they moved in to live with their uncle. The two were in their early teens before they knew the truth of their father's death and that their mother had died of an overdose of heroin, perhaps self-inflicted, after his killing. It grieved Jock deeply and made him want to do something that would bring a better reputation to his family name. Annabelle, however, seemed invigorated by the news. Jock told Pepper that it seemed like the excuse she needed to be the person she wanted to be.

After this bit of background, the reverend said, "Well, Marshal, let me get straight to the point, then I'll be getting on back to Mississippi."

The story that the good Timberlake laid out was fascinating—nothing like anything Marshal Jack Culpepper had heard in all his years of law enforcement. When Jock and Annabelle had learned the truth about their family heritage, Annabelle had become an out-and-out rebel, always in trouble of some kind, while her brother dove deeper into his church involvement—he was there on Sunday morning, Sunday evening, Wednesday night, and any time that his Sunday school or youth group met. Annabelle skipped her senior year of high school to marry for the first time while Jock was already in Dallas, studying theology. He had a plan. One he faithfully followed. In more than twenty years as a church pastor, he had only accepted positions with churches in communities that were in the throat of his grandfather's crime ring.

"I've served as pastor for seven churches. Not large ones but, still, those meaningful to their towns. You can walk through the graveyards of those churches and see headstones from the 1950s, '60s, '70s." He looked down at the floor, regrouping a bit, yet his voice had a tremor when he continued. "Most of those headstones belong to men who died in their twenties, and only a few lived into their thirties. They all died with their shoes on." He studied Pepper for a moment. "Do you know what that means?"

Pepper had never heard that expression, so he thought about it for a moment then gave a small shrug. "No. Not for certain. But I take it that it means that they didn't die in a hospital or a bed."

Rev. Jock nodded slowly. When he did, Pepper noticed for the first time a round spot of gray hair, about the size of a nickel, behind his left ear. It was such a perfect circle and so odd that Pepper almost got distracted, but he quickly pulled his attention back to hear the preacher saying, "To the man, they were all murdered because they were caught up in some wrongdoing—running whiskey, drunk and in a fight, found with the wrong woman by the right man, racketeering. I researched them all. Talked to their families. So what I'm about to say, I don't guess at. I know. My grandfather was involved in some way in each of those deaths. Either directly or indirectly. Sometimes, those men died in one of the roadhouses that my grandfather owned."

This was a new one for Pepper. He had seen family members sorrowful over the evil doings of their kin, but no one had ever gone to this extent. Jock explained that he kept a list of those churches. Over time, he let the deacons at each church know that should the opportunity arise, he'd appreciate consideration as their pastor. Church search committees can be tough, always looking for a reason not to sanction a candidate.

"I was always straightforward. I told them who I am and why I wanted to serve their churches. In every sample sermon I did so the congregation could decide, I told them. I've been elected with 100 percent of the vote each time. I do all I can to help that town, then I move on to another on my list."

Pepper, despite himself, was gaining respect for Jock Timberlake. He scooted his chair closer, folded his hands, and placed them on his desk. "That's admirable."

The preacher shook his head. "Not admirable. Necessary."

"Your name has a lot of baggage with it."

"True. I thought about changing it, but then I would become a liar like my grandfather. I would have just colored it up to make it seem noble."

Pepper had to agree. If the minister had changed his name, it would have eventually been discovered, and then his incredible work would have been destroyed forever. Rev. Jock gave a brief resume on the good works that he and his wife strived for, including a regular revolving door of foster children. He talked for a moment of how hard it could be but also rewarding.

"The rewards are small compared to the trials, but in the end we believe fostering is worthwhile. I always think of the young kids who got roped into working for my grandfather. I feel certain that none of them came from caring, loving, godly homes. Most people don't choose the devil if they know there's an option." A lopsided smile slid up his handsome face. "That's why I'm paying for the sins of the father. I know there's an option. The Bible says that the son shall not suffer for the iniquity of his father. So I'm not running down this path to escape trial and tribulation. I am doing this to make right the many wrongs of my father and grandfather. I was taught that by my Uncle S.J."

"In this line of work, we encounter a good many criminals who were abandoned in childhood," Pepper commented.

Rev. Jock illustrated his point by talking about a wonderful young girl whom his family fell in love with and wanted to adopt. "Her drug-using parents refused to give up their rights, he said. "She was finally forced to go back to her mother, but my wife and I stayed in touch and are helping her get through technical school. She's studying to be a hairdresser."

He talked, too, about one young man who had stolen from them and bullied their children as well as kids at school. "Where that boy was concerned, it was trouble every day. Finally, we had to ask family services to remove him from our home. It hurts to fail like that." Rev. Jock took a long swig of water, a ploy he was using to get his thoughts together before he delivered the big news. "We have a seventeen-year-old kid now. I'm very concerned. That's why I'm here."

This news surprised Pepper. He hadn't foreseen that. "How so?"

"He's disrespectful. In trouble at school constantly for beating up kids, taking their money. A month ago, he was caught selling opioids on the school grounds."

"That's bad, but how would that involve the U.S. Marshals?" Pepper was used to people thinking that any branch of law enforcement could investigate any crime.

The preacher explained that the boy, Shane Conroy, had left his laptop at his cousin's house where he had spent the weekend. Needing to do his homework, he had asked Rev. Jock if he could borrow his laptop, to which the preacher readily agreed.

"The day that Shane returned it, I was working on helping a church member untangle a problem between his social security and military payments. I began to type in 'benefits' in the search engine, and you know how it will come up with a predictive search? Usually relating to something you've recently searched for?"

Pepper nodded. "Yeah. Sure."

"I typed in the first three letters for 'benefits' and the name 'Bennett Sutton' popped up." He stopped there because he saw an odd look on Pepper's face. Pepper glanced all around the room, a habit of his when he was trying to pull something from his memory. He finally settled on a small cobweb in the corner of the room. He had heard that name. Where? When? He was pushing to the back of his mind but couldn't find it.

"Bennett Sutton," he repeated half to himself, half to Rev. Jock. "I've heard that name recently but I can't recall where."

Rev. Jock gave him a moment to study on it and then offered, "Intuitively, I knew it meant something since Shane had just used my laptop. I did a lot of research and read many newspaper articles. Bennett Sutton was an accountant in Atlanta who is in federal prison for fleecing a lot of wealthy people."

What felt like an electrical shock surged through Pepper. Stella! She had mentioned Bennett Sutton at the real estate office the other day. He snapped his fingers. "I heard that name from Stella Bankwell in passing." Pepper eyed him. "Do you know your sister, Annabelle, is believed to be having an affair with a guy named Asher Bankwell?"

The slightest light of surprise crossed Rev. Jock's eyes but, quickly, he replied. "That's the MO for my sister. She gets married for a year or two. Always to a wealthy guy. Has an affair with another wealthy guy. Divorces, gets a big settlement, then marries her paramour. Marshal, I think we may have just stumbled on another big clue here."

"What's that?"

Rev. Jock explained that after he discovered that Shane was checking out Bennett Sutton, he took his laptop to a friend who could crack Shane's password and allow access to the boy's email.

"Shane is not only participating in drug trafficking; he is into a phone scam that is bilking senior citizens. This Bennett Sutton is involved." Rev. Jock paused. He wanted his next words to have a calm but dramatic delivery. "It appears that Shane's partner is someone named Neely Bankwell. You think there is a connection between Asher Bankwell and Neely?"

Pepper absorbed the words, nodding slowly as he put his thoughts together. "Absolutely. They're father and son." He tapped his fingers on the desktop. "And I'd lay a year's salary on the odds that your sister, Annabelle Honeycutt, is in the midst of this."

He picked up the phone and called Jane Collier. "Would you please find a phone number on Sea Island for Governor McCager Burnett? Then pull all records on convicted felon Bennett Sutton. I need to know the prison where he is serving time."

Replacing the receiver, he said, "You may have just made a big turn in a case involving the U.S. Marshals, the FBI, and the IRS."

"If that's true, maybe I'll get off the audit list of the Revenue Service!"

Chapter Twenty-eight

Stella Bankwell did not know how to explain it then or later. All she could do was quote something her mama had often said: "All a'sudden, it just come all over me." Just like that, her despair and tears evaporated. The mountain strong cat in her arose from the tips of her toes to her head. Her tears and despair disappeared. Her fortitude and fight burst forth. She would no longer shiver and shake. She'd fight tooth and nail to save herself, her reputation, and on top of all that, she refused to worry about going to jail. Or to a mental institution. Asher had no idea that he had just met his match. This was not the woman he had married. Or maybe it was. Maybe she had been playing a role for the last nine years.

While Stella, Chatty, and the Burnetts were quietly finishing breakfast, Marlo had dropped off a box with two new outfits that she had ordered from a boutique in Jacksonville. When Stella went upstairs at the Burnetts' to shower and change into a casual red dress with a flounce skirt and matching flats that had a bow with a rhinestone in the center, Chatty went to his house next door to shower, change, and get a spritz of cologne. He had sweet-talked Mrs. Puckett into going with him "because it would be best if I'm not in the house alone, just in case that low-life Asher is up to his usual no good." Spigot, who had made good friends with Mrs. Puckett, tagged along.

When he returned, he smelled heavenly—his cologne was gorgeous. Waiting for Stella, he fiddled with his new cell phone. He had finally agreed to give up his flip phone after many years. So far, he could only occasionally answer but not call out on this new contraption.

"These are the most uncivilized gadgets known to man," he grumbled. "Manners are bad enough but this only accelerates it."

Stella came down and tried to show him how easy it was, but, irritated, he waved her away. "I will continue to call from an attached land phone inside my homes. I will only use this to answer calls. If I can."

She smiled indulgingly at her friend. "Well, do whatever works for you. Just remember this: if you get into trouble, dial 911 and hit this round button on the screen."

"And they will find me how?"

"A satellite pings your signal to a tower and tells them where you are."

His eyes widened. "This is feeling Orwellian to me! I proclaim now that I will never have an emergency that would cause people to trace me." He took the phone and stuck it in the back between his pants and shirt.

Stella studied him for a moment then asked, "Why are you putting your phone there?"

"Because if I put it in my pants or the shirt pocket of my jacket, it will ruin the line of the clothes. The way a person's clothes hang speaks volumes to that person and his tailor." It was all quite logical to Chatty.

The newly reborn Stella chuckled. "That's my Chatty." Then, with all her recently acquired calm, she told Chatty and Miss Alva of her new resolve and explained that she would not run away from any problems but straight toward them. She just had one thing she must do first.

Later, after a light lunch, Stella took the Governor's advice and asked the security detail to drive her the three-quarters of a mile to the Cloister's Chapel. The last time she had been in church was at a funeral back in the summer, which took place at the Methodist church on Peachtree Road. The Governor was right—prayer, especially words whispered in the small, picturesque chapel, was a good place to start.

"And, of course, I shall accompany you," Chatty proclaimed. "You need a praying partner. Besides, I'm on better terms with the Almighty because I donate my time for senior bingo. You've looked askance at Him too many times."

Two security detail were waiting outside the Burnetts' home. They agreed that one, Malcolm Lomax, would drive them while the other, Kirk Putnam, would stand guard at the house. Stella and Chatty settled down into the backseat of an SUV with darkened windows.

"St. Simons brings me peace from the moment I cross the causeway and smell the marshes," Stella commented.

"And the paper mill," Chatty added.

"When I come onto Sea Island, cross the marsh again, and pass the guard station, I feel even greater peace and security."

The words were no sooner out of Stella's mouth than she glanced over and saw that they were passing the entrance to the Cloister that led to the chapel. She leaned forward to Officer Lomax.

"Excuse me, sir. You've just passed the chapel."

Hard brown eyes looked at her from the rearview mirror. He hit the accelerator a bit harder and sailed over the marshes, away from the Cloister and toward Frederica Road. He said nothing.

Chatty exclaimed, "You've missed the chapel! Please turn around and go back. This is taking us to St. Simons and away from Sea Island."

Lomax stopped at the red light at Frederica and Sea Island. Then he turned left. "We are not going to the chapel," he said. "We're going elsewhere."

Newly minted warrior Stella Bankwell did not panic. Very calmly, she turned to Chatty. "Asher. He's taking us to Asher."

At that point, Chatty panicked enough for four people.

ᥖ

Jack Culpepper was on the move. He had called the Governor to tell him about the connection between Asher, Annabelle, Neely, and the foster kid Shane. He was unhappy to hear that Stella and Chatty had left the Governor's house.

"They've just gone to chapel," the Governor replied. "They have a security detail. They'll be fine."

Somehow, Pepper didn't think so. His gut. But he attempted to shrug it off. Marshal Jane Collier had told him that Bennett Sutton was in prison in nearby Jesup, Georgia, and Pepper could be there in ninety minutes.

"Please call the officials and tell them I'm on my way and would like to meet with Sutton around four," he said to Jane. It was winter, so the daylight would begin to fade by then.

Pepper had seen Jock off at the Brunswick airport, jumped in the sedan, and immediately headed to Jesup. Bennett would probably be the person to solve this. They could offer him early release in exchange for his testimony. With one phone call,

Pepper's boss had launched an official investigation and promised that the U.S. Marshals and the FBI would work together to put the criminals away.

❧

Meanwhile, the black SUV driven by the phony security guard was waved through the gates of McKinnon Field.

"Uh-oh," Stella thought, "they're going to put us on a plane and take us off the island." She looked over at Chatty, who had begun to sweat profusely. For the first time in all the years she had known him, Chatty had not one word to say.

A cold rain and dark, cloudy skies made for the perfect day to be kidnapped and, perhaps, something more. Stella reached over and squeezed Chatty's hand. She mouthed, "We will be okay."

❧

Halfway to Jesup, the phone rang and, as usual, Pepper answered, "Culpepper."

"Marshal, I'm Jack Pierce, the warden in Jesup. I've got some news for you."

"Good, I hope."

"No, not at all. We just found Bennett Sutton in his cell. Dead. From hanging."

Jackson Culpepper slapped the steering wheel and screamed the worst obscenities he knew. After he had calmed down, he said, still with a bit of an edge in his voice, "I'm forty minutes away. I'm still coming."

Five minutes later, another call changed all that. "Marshal, this is Cager Burnett. Stella and Chatty are missing. The GBI is here now, investigating, but it appears that one of the security men sent to guard us was cleanly removed—murdered or otherwise, we don't know now—and replaced by someone in Asher's camp. They left here to go to the Cloister Chapel hours ago. No one has seen them since."

Pepper, traveling the somewhat vacant four-lane road, wasted no time. At a rather fast speed, he turned across the median, spinning grass and mud flying about. He hit the lane that headed back to St. Simons while the Governor was still talking.

"Governor, it'll take close to an hour," he said, "but I'll be there as soon as possible. Keep me posted."

He hung up the phone. Nothing, he said to himself, could happen to Stella. He just wouldn't allow it.

Chapter Twenty-nine

McCager Burnett was riled up. He knew he shouldn't use his anger on the two Georgia Bureau of Investigation agents who had taken Kirk Putnam, the other security guy, into custody for questioning. They were sitting at the dining room table while Mrs. Puckett poured coffee.

"What in the tarnation is taking y'all so long? Either put the guy in the Glynn County jail or let him go. We need to find Mrs. Bankwell and Mr. Colquitt."

The Dignitary Protection Section of Georgia Public Safety had provided the security detail. They had attested to Putnam's validity. About an hour later, the Governor had received a call that the original security officer, Malcolm Lomax, had been found, floating under the dock at the marina, by a fishing boat captain as he returned from a day's work. He had been shot once. In an unusual turn of events, the two officers had not driven down from Atlanta together. Lomax had been guarding the state Speaker of the House at an event in Savannah. As soon as that detail ended, he drove Brunswick to meet Putnam at the State Patrol Office, where another officer would drive them to the former Governor's house. Putnam, newly assigned to the Protection Section, had never met Lomax, so he didn't question the man's identification. The imposter Malcolm Lomax even had a couple of stories he told, including a funny one that had happened to him and a state patrol officer whom Putnam knew.

"Governor, please," said one of the GBI agents. "I assure you that other investigators are on their way."

The Governor heaved angrily and stomped off to find Miss Alva, who was doing what she always did in a high-pressure situation—finding a way to stay calm by doing something normal. She sat at her writing desk in a small alcove that she had claimed for her private place. It was in the back of the house and was originally a storage room for silver. She had the shelves removed, wallpapered it in blue French toile, put in a comfortable chair and ottoman covered in matching toile fabric, and added a floor lamp for reading. At the little walnut writing desk, she handled most of her correspondence. There she sat, writing a condolence note to her former assistant whose mother had recently passed away, when her husband stormed in. No one except Alva Ryan Burnett knew how to handle him when his anger grew so large.

"Confound it! They're in there twiddling their thumbs while Stella and Chatty are missing. This is serious." His hands clasped behind his back as he paced the few steps back and forth across the tiny room. This was the most telling sign of his angst. "On top of that, our current governor is sending more security to keep *us* safe. They should use those resources to find them."

"Hello, dear," Miss Alva said as she proceeded to finish the sentence that she was composing on pink stationery with an embossed official emblem of the state of Georgia. She signed her name, then turned to her husband, who was truly ravaged with concern. She knew how deeply he loved Chatty and Stella. She was worried, too, but if she got upset, Cage would be beside himself. She stood up, put her hand on his shoulder to stop his pacing, took his hand, and said, "McCager Burnett, you are a former Marine who dodged bullets on the battlefield. As a congressman and governor, you faced hard times and bitter enemies. Now, use all that experience to calm yourself and think how best you can help. What would you do if you were in charge of the situation?"

Her words fell on eager ears, sank deep into his thoughts, and weaved their way out of his mouth.

"Alva! Magnificent idea!" He grabbed her shoulders in a hard grasp, kissed her quickly, and hurried out of the room as fast as his gout-infected foot would allow. Alva pulled her worn brown wool cardigan tighter around her and smiled, pleased that she still knew how to work her beloved, cantankerous husband.

Then, she heard something that sounded familiar in Cager's office. She scurried off to find exactly what she feared—the Governor had opened his gun safe and was pulling out guns, checking each one, then finding the ammunition that went with them.

"McCager Burnett! *What* are you doing?"

He didn't look at her. He continued with his mission, pulling out his prized possession—a .45 caliber Colt, 1873 single-action, pearl-handed revolver. It was identical to the two—one on each hip—that the legendary General George Patton had carried in World War II. Patton was the Governor's military hero. He screened the movie *Patton* at least once a month in their small theater room in the basement and kept it on their television, recorded, in case he woke up at night and couldn't sleep. He loaded bullets in the gun and put more in his shirt pocket.

He took out a .38 caliber midnight special, placed it on top of the safe, then reached in and took out his .357 Magnum.

With authority, Miss Alva marched over and took the gun away from him. She was specially trained in firearms, something the Governor insisted on when he won his first congressional campaign, so she could protect herself.

"Oh, no, you're not."

"Alva, this blasted gout might get in the way of me moving as quick as I need to. I require a gun that shoots big bullets."

"Outside this door are at least four security men who can protect you."

He smiled slyly. He had a plan. "Someone has to look after you." To please her, he replaced the .357 Magnum in the safe and pulled out a high-powered Remington hunting rifle with a scope that he had last used in South Dakota, years ago. Inside the safe hung an ammunition vest. He took it out and put more bullets in its pouches. He left the ones in his pocket because he would know, in a flash, that those went in his Patton-like revolver.

He kissed his wife on the cheek. Miss Alva, though she looked genteel and fragile, was made of pure steel. Never had a tougher man met his match more than Cager had with Alva. She was used to these rough guy maneuvers. He handed her a .22 Ruger, loaded and winked.

"In case someone gets by the guys outside."

She looked at the tiny pistol in her hand. "A lot of good this piddling thing will do."

"Aim low." He laughed, heading toward the door.

"McCager."

He turned and looked back.

"Where are you going? You have no clue where they are."

His eyes widened slightly. That was the first time he had thought of *that*.

Chapter Thirty

Stella tried to gather her thoughts as the SUV passed the Huddle House, the post office, the bakery with such remarkable cupcakes, and Redfern Village. Chatty was still sweating profusely, holding her hand tightly, and at times looking like he might burst out in a wailing cry at any moment.

The newly calm Stella remarked, "Did you know that Redfern is named for a pilot who took off from here in 1927, looking to set a world record by flying to Brazil? He was never heard from again."

The driver ignored her and Chatty whispered sarcastically, "Thank you for all your well-intentioned encouragement." He rattled his head in disbelief.

"It wasn't meant to be encouragement. Just a piece of history. Paul Redfern knew Amelia Earhart." She smiled pleasantly. Chatty glared at her.

Her new resolve kept her from looking too far ahead but, rather, focusing on five minutes at a time. The huge vehicle glided like silk around the roundabout. It took her back to the Governor's story of seeing Asher while headed to the grocery store after he passed through the roundabout.

The driver went left on Demere Road, then took an immediate right into the airport. Stella's worst fear. He stopped at the key pad and punched in a number, and the gate opened to allow entrance. To herself, Stella said, "Well, so much for keeping the criminals out."

She craned her neck to look at all the jets lined up, trying to see if she recognized any of the tail numbers. Asher and a couple of others jointly owned a small Citation with the identification of ACB 715 (for Asher, Caroline, Bankwell, and the Babe Ruth home run record that Hank Aaron broke while playing for the Atlanta Braves). It wasn't there.

The driver pulled into a parking place on the side of the terminal and switched off the SUV. Lomax turned toward them in the back seat and raised a .357 Magnum. Chatty began to jerk as though he was going into an epileptic seizure.

"To avoid attention, I will leave your hands free. Walk in, holding hands as if you're a couple. If I see you break your handhold, I'll shoot." He narrowed his eyes. "And I won't stop at whoever I have to shoot. Innocent people could die because of you two if you aren't careful."

Chatty looked at him in disbelief. "That would not be a very nice thing to do. Or Christian. I go to church every Sunday and I organize bingo for our seniors. I'm an authority on these types of matters."

Stella rolled her eyes. Chatty unintentionally alternated between exasperation and comic relief.

"I have no manners," Lomax grimly replied. "Remember that."

He looked down and saw Stella's purse lying between her and Chatty. "Give me that!" He rummaged through it with his big hands. No phone. That was a surprise. A dark pink Kate Spade billfold, tissues, and two tubes of lipstick. He pulled the three twenties, a five, and two ones from her billfold and stuffed them in his pocket. He took out her driver's license, credit cards, and even her library card so there would not be a name left behind. Then, he crammed her beloved Chanel bag far under the seat.

"Now, you," he said to Chatty. "Give me everything in your pockets." Chatty handed over an Italian-made leather billfold with three one hundred bills and several twenties.

"I had that handmade when I was in Rome by the finest leathermaker in all of Italy." Even in a situation like this—one where death surely was waiting shortly—Chatty could not resist a boast.

Lomax snapped, "Shut up! Empty out your pockets for me to see." Chatham, more beads of sweat forming on his brow, did just that. All jacket and pants pockets. He had three quarters in the front pocket of the pale seersucker pants. He was trembling and praying that this criminal would not find the phone tucked in his belt under his jacket. Good fashion sense, his mother had always said, is worth the price of rubies. In this case, it might be the price of their lives.

As instructed, the two piled out of the car, and Lomax felt Chatty's pockets but missed checking the belt. Stella noticed that this man was at least 6'7" and 280 pounds. He had a nondescript face beginning to sag with age and a buzzcut of dishwater brown hair. Remarkable for his size but for nothing else. Walking behind them, he nudged them toward the small terminal.

"Oh please," Stella prayed to herself. "Let it be Harry on the desk. He knows me and will know something is wrong."

But Harry had the day off, according to twenty-five-year-old Ross, who said that Harry was his uncle.

"We need a private room for a meeting where we can wait until the pilots and two other passengers arrive," Lomax said.

"Yes sir," Ross replied. "I have one you can use. Do you know if a flight plan has been filed yet?"

"Most probably."

"Which is the plane and to where?"

"RDS161. Seychelles."

Ross flipped through a notebook of flight plans for the day. "Ah, here it is. Sir, I'd like to see your passports and make copies. Since you'll be using FBO facilities. Otherwise, you wouldn't need to show your passports until you land in Seychelles."

Stella felt a surge of joy. Their kidnapper wouldn't have their passports. Hers was at the cottage. But then the beefy man set a large satchel on the counter, the kind that lawyers use during trials requiring a lot of paperwork. He pulled out three passports—all fake, but resembling the three of them standing there.

Chatty peeped over his shoulder, and being Chatty he could not resist saying, "I am insulted. I weigh nine pounds less than that."

Stella elbowed him and Lomax turned and said with a pleasant smile, "We didn't have time to update it since your recent weight loss. But we will get it handled before your next trip."

Chatty looked even more worried, but Stella frowned at him to keep quiet. To himself, Chatty thought, 'A passport for heaven?' For once, he wisely kept it to himself.

The fake security guard, acting pleasant and likable to Ross, said, "Okay, friends, let's go into this room and run over the details for tomorrow's meeting."

Like robots, they followed, though Chatty did make a strange face at Ross that looked something like a possum begging for food. Ross shrugged. He was used to strange people, and often the strangest ones were on the biggest planes.

Lomax, like the gentleman he was not, opened the private room, waved them in, then closed the door. Bottles of water waited in a silver-plated bucket, and a pot of coffee set on a warming plate.

"May I have a bottle of water?" asked Stella.

Wordlessly, he handed it to her and then told her and Chatty to sit down. He put the enormous brown satchel on the table. "That's a heavy 'un," he mumbled.

He took off his jacket, loosened his tie. "I suspect you know what has brought you to this unfortunate time?"

Both shook their heads, with Chatty especially wide-eyed like a child who couldn't understand why he was in trouble.

"You've brought too many law enforcement eyes on us. It all started…"

His words were interrupted by the door flying open, and there stood Stella's worst nightmare—Annabelle Honeycutt. Behind her, with a look of discomfort, was Asher Bankwell. While Stella was attired in a casual, inexpensive pink dress, Annabelle was beautifully dressed in Balmain couture, a black and white houndstooth double-breasted coat dress with black buttons. Over the dress, she wore a red and white houndstooth shawl-collared coat, completing the ensemble with red patent shoes. She carried a black Birkin purse—worth at least $20,000 with a red silk scarf tied to a handle—and a diamond of 30 or 40 carats was on her left hand. Stella slumped a bit in her seat, feeling embarrassed by the simplicity of her clothes.

Annabelle looked at Stella haughtily and smirked because of how ridiculously clothed Stella was. She seemed almost gleeful as she walked toward Stella with heavy purpose. Stella was happily surprised not to tremble at the woman's approach.

Annabelle stopped, looked into Stella's green eyes, then slapped her with such force that Stella felt a muscle stretch in her neck.

Stella, unflinching, looked at Annabelle and said not a word. Annabelle smiled. "That's for the embarrassment at the country club."

"I don't apologize," Stella responded calmly.

Chatty kicked her chair from behind, leaned forward and whispered, "Apologize! We will never get out of this."

Annabelle's beautiful, silky white complexion reddened from her neck up to her hairline. She slapped Stella again then leaned forward, placed her glistening, red-nailed hands on the arms of Stella's chair at the conference table, moved within inches of her face, and said in a deceptively sweet way, "And *that* is for making me have to see that you're killed."

She glanced over Stella's shoulder to Chatty's ashen face. When she spoke, her voice was hard, snarky and smothered with hatred. "And, oh Chatty, how Atlanta is going to miss you and your busybody ways."

Chatty started shaking so hard that his entire chair shook and Stella could feel the ground moving.

Chapter Thirty-one

No one had ever told Jack Culpepper—mainly because there was no reason for it to be discussed—that the four-lane between Brunswick and Jesup had little cell phone service. He was going nuts, anxious to know what was happening. The marshal car he was in had no radio to call headquarters.

If Bennett Sutton was dead, he had been killed. Plain and simple. Turner McGavin had dug deep until he discovered that Bennett had been paid to take the fall for several folks and that his family had lived comfortably during his years of imprisonment. Under ordinary guidelines, he would have been out in a year or so. He had been in a position for a bargain deal if he helped the authorities, which meant he could have been released almost immediately.

Yep. No question. He had been killed. By someone in the prison, maybe a guard who was earning extra money for his family. Just as he crossed into Glynn County, Pepper's phone buzzed with a message, meaning it had finally found a signal.

Marshal Jane Collier had left him a voicemail. "Warden Jack Pierce called. An autopsy is being performed, but one of the attendants who assisted in putting Bennett Sutton into an ambulance smelled chloroform on his mouth." That's strange, thought Pepper. It evaporates and can't often be smelled. Jane, in the message, answered his question. "Apparently, one of the EMTS has hyperosmia, a heightened sense of smell. Additionally, they used a good bit of it to put him to sleep before hanging him, so there was enough left to inhale. There you have it for nearly certain: murder."

Jack Culpepper had long ago gotten to the place that when these tiny treasures of evidence came along, he was plenty grateful. Otherwise, they'd be waiting months for the autopsy and trying to find a lead elsewhere.

Suddenly, he heard the scream of sirens and looked in his rearview mirror. It was almost dark but he could see the metallic blue of two Georgia State Patrol cars. One driver pulled up beside Jack and rolled down his window. "Marshal, we're here to escort you to St. Simons. The Governor's house. I'll lead and the other car will follow you."

At a speed close to ninety, Pepper took off behind the flashing lights in front of him, grateful for the trooper car behind him.

❦

Asher, the coward he was, didn't try to intervene for Stella other than to say tentatively to Annabelle, "Is that necessary?"

She swirled around, her eyes flashing with fight. "Asher Bankwell, I run this organization. Not you." She walked over to him and looked him steadily in the eye. "There are things about to happen, so I will not have you creating hysterics and disturbing what is to be done. Understood?" Then she turned back into the vixen they all knew so well and smoothed the lapels of his sports jacket. "Lovey pie, don't be mad." She winked. "This is business, but when it's all done, we'll celebrate for days. You know what I mean?"

Unbelievingly, Stella stared as she watched the man she had considered strong and capable transform into a coward who made Chatty look like Braveheart. At that moment, Stella felt her years of love for Asher Bankwell melt away like inches of snow in a hot sun's glare. He was still handsome. Tall, slender, and well dressed. And there in the center of his left cheek was that dimple she had long loved. He had been confident, bold, always with the manners of a perfect Southern gentleman—at least until things began to change. Here, before her, though, was a weasel who looked like he might jump if he saw a house cat. Somehow, he was an unknown personality in a well-known body. He looked at Stella with such regret in his eyes. She hoped he knew he had destroyed the most incredible life that a man could possess. He had thrown it away in a haphazard mess of greed and lust, wrongly thinking that he would have greater power, but the joke was on him. Stella could see that Annabelle was the brains and the power. She was the one who had figured out how to launder racketeering and drug money in offshore accounts, then got Neely involved with that foster kid named Shane.

Between them, they were bringing in more drug money from opioids and cocaine sales than the rest of the guys put together. Asher's son. His only child. He had stood by and allowed him to become a junior kingpin of drugs. If death was indeed coming for Stella, then she could die knowing that she took her last breath without an ounce of love for Asher. That was something meaningful.

᠅

Cager hoisted himself up into Chatty's Mercedes SUV and winced at the pain of his gout. But moments later, as he pulled out of Chatty's driveway with a self-satisfied smile on his face, he no longer felt the pain.

"This old Marine's still got it," he said aloud. Quietly, he had slipped out a back door that opened into Miss Alva's sewing room. A security guard, responsible for that side of the house, had been smoking a cigarette and talking to another agent. Cager slipped from tree to tree in their backyard, then opened the gate that Miss Alva had installed so Chatty could come and go. He held the bell so it would not chime. The Burnetts had a key to the car that Chatty kept at his Sea Island house. That's how Cager slipped away from the guards and off the island.

Instinctively, he turned left at the entrance of Sea Island and headed toward St. Simons. Huge trees with moss moved gently in the breeze. It was now in the early hours of darkness, and McCager had no idea where he was going, but he trusted his instinct to take him there. In Vietnam, in Congress, in the Governor's office, it had never failed him. He believed it would not fail him this time. But as the saying goes, "There are no atheists in foxholes." He had advised Stella to pray, so now he took his own advice. "Dear Lord, please lead me to Stella and Chatty. You know where they are. Please show me."

"It's time to get going," Annabelle said, checking her Rolex. "Where are those idiots with the rest of the cash?"

Lomax answered. "Five minutes away. We can go ahead and load the plane." He looked at Stella and Chatty. "Same plan as before. I'll walk behind you with my gun. Annabelle and Asher will walk in front. Don't try anything."

They both nodded. They left the room and walked through the door leading to the tarmac and a spectacular jet.

"Oh my!" Chatty said quietly, throwing his hand over his lips. Whispering outside the corner of his mouth, he said, "That's the biggest jet that Gulfstream makes." He waited a moment. "Really, Stella, you can't blame him." He threw his head toward the jet. She frowned then stuck her tongue out at him.

Before they got to the plane's airstairs, a black, custom-made, bullet-proof SUV pulled up. Two men jumped out. When the back door opened, Stella glanced in and saw a machine gun posted on a stand so the gun could be fired from that position.

Her heart choked her throat. Before, she only *thought* it wasn't good. Now, she was certain it wasn't. She stopped for a second and looked around at the island she loved so much. She took a lungful of sea-tinged air, looked across the street with trees heavy with moss and then toward the Lodge, a place she had loved for so long.

Nothing compared to seeing them for the last time.

Chapter Thirty-two

Pepper and his entourage passed a popular liquor store on Highway 17 and he could see ahead the left-hand turn onto the causeway. On the right-hand side was the enormous billboard that had been there for years and was used for community service. This time, it advertised an upcoming play presented by the Island Players.

Pepper flashed his lights to the trooper in front of him, turned on his left blinker, and pulled into Parker's Convenience store, which shared a building with a donut shop. When the three cars stopped, Pepper swung his long legs out and stood while both troopers came to him.

"Listen, I think we should part company here. Turn off your lights and go on over to the Governor's on Sea Island. I'm a good bit more discrete." He threw his head in the direction of the unmarked navy blue four-door sedan. "This island is only twelve miles long. Maybe I can sneak up on something."

The three men punched each other's cell numbers into their phones and agreed to call if any of them saw something suspicious. Pepper waited a couple of minutes until the marked cars pulled away, then he headed toward the causeway. He thought of the injustice of a well-liked teenager killed on that causeway by a drunk driver many years ago. It was a story he had heard when he was training at Glynco. Those were the kinds of stories that drove Pepper as an agent. He wanted to prevent any senseless killings today. He had come to enjoy

Chatty very much, and, frankly, he wasn't sure exactly what his emotion for Stella was, but it felt like something was digging into his heart.

༽

As Cager had realized earlier, he didn't know where he was going or how to begin. Yes, it was a small island, but there were a lot of places to hide. Pepper wasn't much of a praying man but suddenly he remembered his Vacation Bible School teacher, Miss Violet, who had told his ten-year-old class one summer, "If you don't know what to do, pray about it, then relax and prepare to receive an answer."

That's what he did.

He headed toward the sweet seaside village, taking the roundabout at the Lodge. For no reason, he whipped into the entrance, passed multi-million-dollar houses, and came to the guardhouse. The guard stepped out. Upon seeing Pepper's badge and identification, he waved him through. Pepper rode through the grounds, circled the drive in front of the small European-style building backed by the golf course, then cruised out through the centuries-old oaks. Just as he came to the roundabout, his phone rang.

"Marshal, this is Lt. Hulsey of the State Patrol. We've arrived at the Governor's house to find that he has disappeared."

"Disappeared?" This was a nightmare, only getting worse. "What do you mean by 'disappeared'? There's a complete security detail at his home."

"Mrs. Burnett said that her husband took several firearms from his gun safe and went out the back. She told no one until we arrived and inquired."

263

Three people, now including a former federal Congressman, were missing. On a tiny island. They had all vanished while several law enforcement agencies were tasked with protecting them. This was not good.

Before he had time to react, he looked straight at McKinnon Airport, which was surrounded by a chain-link fence. In the early darkness, he could see two jets, about fifty feet apart, with both set of stairs lowered.

"Call me back if anything further develops."

He edged around the roundabout in front of the Lodge and headed to the airport.

⤜

Cager Burnett guided Chatty's car through the roundabout on the opposite end of the road, the same one that Pepper was negotiating. The airport triggered Cager's thoughts of seeing Asher there the previous night, so he turned left, and in seconds he was pulling up to the airport gate. He had a special code for entry because he often met friends there who had flown in, or he had used it when he and Miss Alva were flying chartered jets. Suddenly, the driver behind him flashed his headlights. The Governor reached over and took the .45 caliber Patton special in hand as someone got out and walked up to the SUV.

Through the darkened glass, he could see the shadowy figure. He rolled down the window. "Marshal Culpepper, what are you doing here?"

"Looking for the most wanted man in Georgia. You. I saw the license plate that reads 'Chat.' I was hopeful it was him." He added with a hint of wistfulness. "Perhaps with Stella, too."

"I evaded security, went to Chatty's house and got his car. I had a hunch this was a place to look." He pointed toward the huge Gulfstream G800. "A lot of jets come in and out of here, but we don't see many of these long-range jets. That plane can fly fourteen, fifteen hours without stopping for fuel."

"Game plan?"

"Yeah, park your car in the parking lot at the industrial fish packing company next door. Come back and jump in with me." The Governor paused. "Bring every gun you have."

In less than a minute, Pepper jumped into the back seat, and the Governor punched in the code then pulled toward a little shed to the left, so dark that few would have known it was there. He backed the car in so no one else could see the license tag that played ode to Chatty's ego. The men hurried out while Pepper took a second to gather himself as he saw the Governor, in his ammunition jacket, pull out two pistols and a hunting rifle.

"Use that lately?" Pepper asked, pointing to the high-powered rifle with the scope.

"Shot a moose with it in South Dakota three years ago."

Pepper worried that the Governor, especially at his advanced age, was in over his head. What he did not know was that McCager Burnett had been the number-one ranked sniper shooter in the entire Marine corps when he retired from service. Over the years, he had kept up his shooting skills with regular practice. As he often said, "Don't work hard to develop a skill if you don't plan on keeping it."

"Follow me," the Governor whispered. The two men—Cager forgetting all about his painful gout as his adrenaline soared—sneaked into the shadows around the airport office. Thank goodness for the turtles and the soft lighting on the island. It was excellent camouflage. At the back corner of the airport FBO, they saw two planes, airstairs down, preparing to receive passengers. One was the Gulfstream G800. Two men, obviously pilots, had just finished prechecking the aircraft and turned in the paperwork. They were climbing toward the plane's cockpit to prepare for takeoff. The plane's incredible high-definition circadian lighting system began to flicker like a shimmer across the huge jet. Two guards—one with close-cropped black hair and a longish beard was known as Black-beard and the other with a ruddy complexion and strawberry hair was called Crude—had just finished loading trunks into cargo and were slamming shut the compartment just as the back door of the terminal office opened. Annabelle, in all her four-inch heeled glory, sashayed toward the plane. A cowed down Asher Bankwell followed her. The Governor shook his head. "Just as we thought."

A few seconds later, Stella and Chatty emerged, with Lo-max, a gun discretely in his hand, following them.

"Stella," Pepper said so softly that it was only to himself.

The Governor looked back toward him. "Hope you're a good shot." He glanced down to see that Pepper was holding a .357 Magnum. He had come armed for serious business. Thank goodness Pepper didn't have a wife like Miss Alva.

Blackbeard and Crude finished with the cargo loading, walked over to Annabelle, conversed for a minute or two, then Crude got into the SUV and drove off to a parking space outside the tarmac. Within moments, he was walking back toward Blackbeard, who was very large and barrel chested. Asher set down the enormous brown satchel then offered his hand to Annabelle to help her onto the first step.

The Governor's mind raced. There was no time to think it out or ponder the whats or ifs. He fired two shots into the air from the rifle—he didn't want to the waste the pistol bullets—the unexpected explosive sounds in the quietness of the serene village threw Annabelle, Asher, Stella, Chatty, and the guards into a frenzied state. McCager knew that the island was swarming with agents from every department possible and also that someone inside the airport office would immediately connect to the Glynn County Sheriff's department by an emergency button. Private airports were under strict protocol after the 9/11 tragedy. Soon, law enforcement would be everywhere, but it was the next three or four minutes that would count most.

◈

Annabelle raced up the steps and Asher, newly minted coward he was, ran behind her. She stumbled on the third step from the top, but he helped her up and held her tightly until they were inside the plane. Lomax was the closest to Stella, so he grabbed her and put a gun to her head.

Chatty couldn't stand it. Not his Stella. Oh, no. He wouldn't let this happen.

He grabbed the heavy satchel from the ground, took the handle, and swung at Lomax's head with all the might of his formidable size. Knocked unconscious, Lomax crumbled to the ground while Blackbeard raced over, grabbed Chatty, and held him in a chokehold.

"Run, Stella, run!"

She paused for a second then ran toward the gate. Crude, a former track star, easily outpaced Stella and grabbed her, holding her off the ground while she kicked and threw her arms around with all her might. Once she had taken a defense course, never expecting to use it, but as she flailed in Crude's arms, she was close enough to reach Blackbeard, who was choking Chatty. She raked her nails across his eyes, stunning him enough to release Chatty. The instructor had always said, "Go for the eyes first."

So caught up in saving their lives, Chatty and Stella did not realize that the stairs of the plane had folded up, the engines were firing, and the G800, positioned to lift off from the westward runway, was gingerly rolling toward a takeoff. What they did not see, the Governor and Marshal did: the suspects with a cargo full of evidence were about to fly away and out of their jurisdiction. Annabelle had prepared for such a time as this. Though she would hate to do it, she was prepared to have the pilots drop the cargo as soon as they were far enough away over the Atlantic Ocean. She'd rather lose twenty million dollars than spend twenty years in federal prison.

There was no time to waste.

The Governor and Pepper stepped out of the shadows. "Chatham, here!" called the Governor as he tossed the .45 caliber pistol to Chatty. Wide-eyed, he caught it and jiggled it around as if he had a hot potato. He had never held a gun in his hands. He had no idea what to do with it.

"Just point and shoot," yelled the Governor. "Pull the trigger. Don't let that one get away."

Crude, holding Stella with one arm, was fishing in his holster for the gun he carried. The Governor showed no mercy—except that he didn't let Pepper use the Magnum, and that was mercy in itself. He raised his hunting rifle, looked down the scope, and shot Crude clear through the shoulder, avoiding any harm to Stella. At the same time, the second guard, Blackbeard, still stunned by Stella's attack on his eyes, got up and started to run. Chatty pointed, closed his eyes tightly, and fired, hitting the guard in his leg. Chatty started jumping up and down like a little boy. "I did it! I did it! Governor, did you see what I did?"

Pepper hurtled toward the plane, which was picking up the speed necessary to lift the monster off the ground. He stumbled slightly but gathered himself up as he raced toward it. Even though it was now dark, Pepper, fifty yards from the back of the plane, saw the front tires begin to lift. Within seconds, Annabelle and Asher would be airborne and out of reach. He stopped where he was, put himself into shooting stance, and prepared to make the best use possible of the .357. For the briefest moment, he felt gratitude for the high-definition circadian lighting that made it possible for him to see the black tires in the ink-dark night.

"Boom!" The first shot shattered the night and missed its mark. The front tires were now a foot off the tarmac. Then, in rapid repetition, Pepper fired. The second shot hit the left rear tire and immediately began to pull the plane toward the side of the tarmac. The third shot missed, but the fourth shot ensured that the plane was maimed and could not lift off. The fifth and sixth shots exploded the right tire, causing both front tires to hit the ground as the nose buried deep into the tarmac, and the plane slid until it flipped on the tip of its long wing.

Just as Governor McCager Burnett had hoped would happen when he fired those two shots into the dark night, sirens were now screaming all around the airport. U.S. Marshals, GBI, FBI, and Glynn County Sheriff cars had the field surrounded, and several pulled onto the tarmac. In less than two minutes, armed lawmen surrounded the plane and two snipers stood in place on the top of SUVs.

The plane had flipped on the door side, so it would be a while before Annabelle, Asher, and the pilots were captured. Four fire engines and three ambulances stood close by and ready, lest a fire break out or someone else get injured.

Stella ran to the Governor, who hugged her and said with authority, "It's all over, Stella." The nightmare had ended.

Pepper, heaving with heavy breath, walked over and shook hands with the Governor.

"Well done, Marshal. That's quite a trick to bring down a plane like that with a .357." He chuckled. "Maybe that's why my wife doesn't let me use one often."

Pepper shrugged. "I owe you an apology."

"Good heaven sakes alive. Why do you owe me an apology?"

"Because I didn't think a man your age could shoot like a Marine Corps Scout Sniper."

"Once a top sniper, always one." He pointed his finger at Pepper. "As long as you stay in practice. Now, don't forget that."

Pepper laughed, more out of relief than anything. McCager still held Stella close to his side with his free arm. Without realizing what he was doing, Pepper stroked Stella's pretty red hair. He was so grateful that she had not been hurt. She smiled at him sweetly. Then she gently pried herself from McCager's arm, hugged Pepper's neck, and kissed him lightly on the cheek.

"Pepper, thank you so much."

A genuine moment of emotion bubbled between them. "I'm so relieved that you weren't hurt," he replied.

Chatty, meanwhile, had been standing with his gun poised on Blackbeard as the medics attended to his shattered kneecap.

"Whoa, this may be the worst I've ever seen," commented one of the paramedics. "This will call for a whole new kneecap."

This, of course, threw Chatty into absolute glee. He was so proud of himself. McCager walked up behind him and took the pistol from him. "Chatty, give me that before you hurt someone who doesn't need hurting."

Stella, her arm looped through Pepper's, ambled over to her best friend and hugged him tightly. "Chatty, I love you so much. You are the best!"

Excitedly, he began spewing out words. "Stella, it was me. I saved the day! I hit the guy over the head so you could get away from him, then I shot that other no-good character in the leg. He may never walk again. I. Am. A. Hero."

She laughed. "Chatty, I can always count on you." She hugged him again.

"Group hug," Chatty said. "We need a group hug, y'all."

The Governor, unloading Chatty's gun, replied dryly, "I don't do group hugs."

Pepper smiled comically and tossed his head toward the Governor. "I'm with him on this one." He patted Chatty on the back. "Good job, Chatty. You were brave and incredibly helpful tonight. You helped the U.S. Marshals, the FBI, the GBI, and the Revenue Service."

Chatty grinned from ear to ear. He loved to be bragged on. After a few seconds, he tilted his head and asked seriously, hopefully, "Marshal, do you think I'll get a medal or two for such courageous service?"

The other three laughed, but Chatty was mystified by the laughter.

Chapter Thirty-three

On her cottage bed, Stella laid out five dresses with tags and studied them thoughtfully. It wasn't herself that she was trying to please but rather Chatty. The Burnetts were hosting a dinner party of twelve for Chatty's birthday. Since he always viewed her as an ornament of his, she wanted to please him. This, she viewed as particularly important since he had recently helped save her life.

Spigot was asleep in the cozy chair by the window, so she was not too interested in the process. Stella picked up each dress, held it in front of her, then reviewed it in front of the full-length mirror. Finally, she settled on a soft yellow brocade damask with a thread of silver running through the fabric. It was sleeveless, with four rows of rhinestones around the neckline, and long waisted with a bubble skirt that dropped just above her knees. This, along with new silver evening shoes—also trimmed with rhinestones—and a matching clutch purse, was perfect. Chatty would fully agree.

Miss Caroline had been so gracious. Of course, she was horrified when she discovered that both her son and grandson were involved in embezzling, racketeering, drug trafficking, and, by association, murder. So she took to her bed as she had done when Eleanor had run off and left Asher and Neely. This time, though, Dr. Avery worried that her heart might give out; after all, this wasn't just society scandal. It was bigger than that.

Why, one night, it had even been announced on the BBC in London.

A couple of days after Asher's and Annabelle's arrest at the St. Simons McKinnon Airport, McCager Burnett, Miss Caroline's old friend and the attorney who handled all of her business as he had for Jasper when he was alive, called her.

"Caroline, this is a bad situation. For once, this might be a story that is worse than what the news says. I have some advice for you: Don't hire a slew of high-priced attorneys to try to get Asher and Neely out of this. Hire one good attorney for each. Don't spend an exorbitant amount of money on forensic accounting. The prosecutors will do that. I caution against giving either of them bond money." A well-placed source had called the Governor and told him that, though it wasn't certain yet, it did appear that Asher had been involved with all of Bennett Sutton's schemes. That meant he had stolen funds from most of Miss Caroline's socialite friends as well as from his own mother. As clearly and gently as he could, Cager explained this to a woman negotiating the five stages of grief. She still had one foot stuck in the denial stage.

"Cage, please remember that Asher was also a victim of Bennett Sutton. He, too, had money taken."

The Governor's tone was one she recognized. It was his this-is-the-law-and-the-gospel-so-do-not-dispute-me tone. "Caroline Bankwell, he stole from himself so he would not be suspected. How would it have looked if he had been the only one of Bennett's clients who did not suffer?"

"I do not believe I'm up to this discussion today," she said weakly. "Jenson Avery is tremendously concerned with my heart."

The old Marine was not to be deterred. He was taught early in the military that when things were their hardest, you rose to the occasion. You didn't lie down to them.

"Then it's even more important that we talk. I would recommend that you rewrite your will, allow Asher to use his trust fund to pay his attorney, and amend Neely's so he can hire an attorney." He let the pause hang long in the air. When she did not reply, he continued. "Stella does not know that you have a modest trust set aside for her to inherit when you have met your fullness of life. You're quite an extraordinary woman." He was easing in to his sales pitch. Though Miss Caroline did not devour the praise as Chatty did, she was open to being charmed. "You are generous and kind. You will come out of this with your dignity in full."

"Oh, Cage, I'm not certain of that. It's difficult to see where I've failed as a mother. I thank God that Jasper did not live to see this. Our church friends, his golfing buddies, my bridge partners, all stolen from by our son. How can I ever show my face in public again?"

Aw, just the opening the Governor was looking for. "I have a suggestion. And if you do as I advise, you will be almost as big of a hero as Chatty."

"I can't imagine what that could possibly be. It all seems so hopeless."

"You have a stock account that goes back to Jasper's father, who bought telephone, oil, and Coca-Cola stock. It's a bloomin' fortune."

"I am unaware of any such account," she replied briskly.

On the other end of the phone, the Governor rolled his eyes and took a moment before responding. "Oh yes, you are. I mentioned it many times and you sign a tax return for it every year. That's my point—you have so much money you don't even know how much you have. Would you consider taking that account and setting it up as a victim recovery fund since Asher was involved with Bennett? It would win a good deal of grace for you with our friends and neighbors, plus it would most likely help Asher in sentencing. If he is convicted, the judge might look favorably on a lighter sentence."

"You think this could make things right?"

"Better, definitely. It's the right thing to do. I can say with full confidence that's what Jasper would do."

"Excellent. Then we shall."

"Wonderful! And once it's done, I'll even call Mona Windsor myself, just for extra insurance that all Atlanta knows for certain!" That pulled a tiny chuckle from Miss Caroline's pinched lips.

It was during that conversation that the Governor intervened and suggested that she help Stella. "This could be viewed as a conflict of interest, so I can't negotiate this, but please call another attorney and get advice."

The attorney she called, Tim Casper, had been at the country club and was an eyewitness to Stella's meltdown, and of course he knew all the news. Caroline was kind and willing, so he went to work quickly. Now, a new glistening pearl-white Cadillac Escalade sat outside. Casper had set up an LLC for Stella and put the car title in it so the IRS could not take it, and then he had sent her a black American Express card to use in replacing all that Asher had burned. With Miss Caroline's blessing, he had also set up a trust fund from which she could draw a monthly allowance until she turned fifty-five, when she would be given the full amount of the trust.

That's how Stella came to have the five pretty dresses laid across her bed. She and Marlo had taken a day's shopping trip to Jacksonville, ninety minutes away, and had the most delightful time. In the two weeks since the shootout at the airport, each day had brought with it more peace and reconciliation. Chatty, through his self-aggrandizement combined with the actual truth, had become a surprise hero in the eyes of Atlanta and Sea Island society. Miss Alva, who delighted in his joy, threw a celebratory gala in the largest ballroom of the Cloister. Chatty selected his favorite custom-made tuxedo and then, the afternoon before the big event, he knocked on the screen door of the cottage.

"Yoohoo," he called, letting himself in. Stella came out of the kitchen, wiping her hands on a towel. Chatty peeped over the top of the four boxes he held. "My love, this is for you so you can look beautiful tomorrow. It would harm my image if the damsel I saved weren't the most spectacular creature at my soiree."

The boxes contained a Valentino red gown in silk and lace that was stunning, matching evening slippers, a purse, and a pair of ruby earrings.

"Now, remember," Chatty reminded her as he was leaving, "you must tell everyone how brave and daring I was. Don't forget to mention that the Governor and Pepper were *my* backup. Not the other way around."

"I will, my dear," she replied, kissing him on the cheek. "And I shall not fail to mention how Asher quaked in his shoes when he saw you."

"Perfect," Chatty responded. "Because that is exactly what happened." He was serious.

Tonight was another party—this time to celebrate his birthday. Chatty liked parties that were in his honor. As Stella was hanging up the four dresses she did not plan to wear for the dinner party, she heard a knock at the door. Spigot jumped down from the chair and ran, tail wagging. Stella followed her. When she opened the door, there stood Marylyn with a bakery box in her hands.

"Please come in. How are you?" asked Stella as she pushed open the screen door.

"I'm a little sad. I'm packing to leave. I've been here for a bit and it's been so nice. It brought back some sweet memories that I needed to remember." Marylyn handed the bakery box to her. "This is a little thank-you for all the kindness you've shown me." She winked. "Cupcakes."

Stella laughed. "Then let me make some coffee and we will enjoy one together."

After the arrest of Asher and Annabelle, Stella's crush on Pepper had grown. There, in the early evening light of McKinnon field, when she had seen U.S. Marshal Culpepper in charge and authoritative and, at the same time, witnessed Asher's meek cowardice, it was hard not to swoon over Jack Culpepper. But she kept her guard up. He and Marylyn, of course, had been invited to the gala because Chatty said it was only right.

"Pepper didn't do much to help me, but he wrangled the authorities and did the legal part, so he should definitely take part in the celebration of my heroism," Chatty had said, beaming happily.

In the last couple of weeks, she had seen Pepper and Marylyn together several times but, truly, not more times than he stopped in to see Stella at the cottage or the real estate office.

Twice, he had stopped by the office and taken her to lunch. She was wary and held tightly onto her crush, refusing to let it grow. She did not need any more hurt. Too, Marylyn was exceptionally nice and easy to like.

Over coffee, Marylyn explained that her daughter, Harper, was coming home for spring break, so she needed to ready the house and buy groceries to cook her favorite foods. "She loves burnt toast," Marylyn said, laughing. "I don't know how on earth she acquired a taste for that!"

Stella swallowed a bite of her coconut cupcake. She tried to speak nonchalantly. "I know you'll miss Pepper, too." She smiled sympathetically.

Marylyn smiled warmly. "I will. He brings such happy memories to me." She sat her coffee cup down. "But Stella, I have to be honest."

Stella nodded, encouraging her to continue.

"My husband has been gone for over two years. It was a hard grief to overcome. About three months ago, I met someone. He's an ER doctor, so he's on the opposite end of wounds and pain. I like that. We had been out several times before I came down here." Stella tried to keep her face stoic yet interested. Inside, her heart began to beat rapidly. "While I've been here, I have realized how much I miss him. He calls me almost every day and we have such fun conversations. I talked to Pepper about it and he strongly encourages me to let go of the past and build a new life. I'm going to take his advice. And, to be candid, I can't wait to get home and see him."

The first real flush of happiness that Stella had known in so long swept over her. Pepper was a free agent! He wasn't tied to Marylyn. This was impossibly joyous. Stella reached across the table and put her hand over Marylyn's.

"Pepper is exactly right. Go out there and do just that: make yourself a new life with a new man. A doctor? How wonderful is that!"

Marylyn smiled, then bit her lip as if she had something to say that she didn't want to say.

"What's wrong?" Stella asked, wiping crumbs off the table and dropping them back into the cupcake box.

"I don't want to overstep," she said quietly.

"Overstep," Stella commanded. "You're talking to someone who has had no boundaries for months! People have been overstepping on me for ages!"

Marylyn sighed. "Pepper is the loveliest guy. The most devoted friend possible." She reached out and took Stella's hand. "Be careful, though. He can put a big hurting on a girl's heart. I've seen it a few times. Maybe that's what makes him so irresistible. He's hard to get. I don't think it's on purpose. I think something beyond his control keeps him from committing."

Stella's face clouded. She was stunned and trying to make sense of what she was hearing and why she was hearing it.

"Marshal Jackson Culpepper only has one flaw as far as I know," Marylyn said. "He can't commit. Not to a woman. Not to a cat. Not to a potted plant. He belongs heart and soul to the U.S. Marshals." She paused. "You've been so kind to me that I wouldn't feel right not warning you."

Stella nodded, cleared her throat, then changed the subject. "It's going to feel like Lonely Street around here without you." Soon the two women were off onto other subjects.

When Marylyn left, Stella hugged her extra tight. She was grateful for the gift Marylyn had just given her, and she wasn't thinking about the cupcakes. Perhaps this woman had saved her from another broken heart.

~§

Chatty was full of high spirits and good cheer as his best-liked and most-beloved friends gathered to celebrate his birthday and make much ado over him. He was in his glory. In addition to Stella and Pepper, the Burnetts had invited Marlo and Tatum, Edward Armstrong, who had also created the most beautiful flowers for the evening, Laura Mancel, who owned a lovely bistro, the Petersons and Strothers, who were friends and neighbors on Sea Island, as well as Bess and Shannon Thompson.

Pepper had not yet arrived as the group mingled in the living room for cocktails with a fire to fight off the slight March chill. Stella was radiant. Her burdens had lifted tremendously, she had returned to her normal weight, which helped her self-confidence immensely, and it was, for once, a perfect hair night. Every woman understands that. The group had broken into three small groups to chat, with Chatty moving between each group and bringing the attention back to himself before flitting off to others. Stella excused herself to go to the powder room down the hall. She smiled as she walked toward it, thinking of when she had sat in the Governor's office during his lecture, calculating how long it would take her to make it to the powder room before getting sick. So much had changed for the better over the past month.

She was coming out of the powder room, slathering lotion on her hands and watching carefully to avoid getting it on her rings, when she heard a long, admiring whistle. She looked up to see Pepper, resplendent in a dark suit, crisp white shirt, and cheerful green tie. He was stunningly handsome. Her heart sputtered while he took a moment to gaze upon her glorious appearance. Marylyn's warning flew right out of her head.

"You are beautiful." He said it with sincerity, almost in a sense of wonder. She blushed and lowered her head slightly.

"Thank you." She smiled and turned the moment lighter by saying cheerfully, "You're quite handsome yourself."

Pepper reached out and took her hand, still slightly wet with lotion, and after another moment of admiration he said, "Could we go somewhere to talk privately?"

She nodded, wondering where that would be. "We could step out onto the patio." She motioned toward the back of the house. While the others gathered in the living room, they slipped into the dining room and then through the enormous French doors to the beautiful patio with its greenery, including gardenias that were anxious to spread their blooms and stonework that was as artistic as anything in Italy.

Stella wasn't sure what she expected—it had only been a few hours since she discovered that Pepper and Marylyn weren't romantically involved and that he was a catch without a hook—but what happened next was something she never would have imagined, even if she had days to think about it. She shivered slightly in the light chill, and immediately Pepper removed his jacket, threw it over her shoulders, and asked, "Is that better?"

She nodded. "Thank you."

"Stella, late this afternoon, I had a video call with all the law agencies involved in this case." He paused. His face gave nothing away, and she felt herself holding her breath. He took both her hands and squeezed them tightly.

"Stella Bankwell, you are the hero of the entire law enforcement of the United States of America."

She looked quizzical. "Me? Why?"

"Because you provided us with the rock-solid evidence we needed to put away Asher, Annabelle, and the whole kit and kaboodle. What we had was mostly circumstantial and could have been argued down, perhaps. The cash. The flight plan to Seychelles. Rev. Josh Timberlake's suspicions. But you, *you*, dear Stella, have sealed this case. Without question."

As she processed his words, trying not to focus on his strong hands holding hers, she knew what he was saying. Stella was in possession of a remarkable memory, one that wasn't exactly photographic but one she referred to as "sticky." She could glance at something and it would stick in her mind. Then, later, to her own surprise, she could summon it forward, sometimes amazed that she remembered it. People commented on this ability so often that she worked on keeping it active. She memorized phone numbers then punched them into the phone without calling up a directory. An oft-used trick came from her days of working in sports marketing, when she knew the jersey numbers of players, both current and historical—she always assigned the number seven to Mickey Mantle, who had worn that number as a New York Yankee—and race car numbers. In a way, she turned the numbers into actual people.

One day, about six months earlier, she had been digging through a desk drawer at the Ansley Park house to find an ink pen. She picked up an old, used envelope and started to discard it when she realized a series of numbers were scrawled on the back. For no other reason than to test her brain, she studied the numbers. After a moment, she said, "Richard Petty, Peyton Manning, Al Unser, Michael Jordan, and Johnny Parks." Johnny was a friend from high school whose football jersey number was 24. She put the envelope back and never thought of it again. The numbers stuck, though, and a week ago it had occurred to her that perhaps they had something to do with Asher's offshore money laundering, so she had shared them with Pepper.

"Those numbers you gave us made up the account number where they were storing the money. Names aren't used. Only numbers. It's incredible that he would write them down then toss them in the drawer, but he left off the last two numbers, probably thinking that made it safe. However, in Annabelle's billfold were two numbers written on the back of a grocery store receipt. We thought they were worth a try. We combined the numbers and found all the money, flight plans coordinating to dates of deposits, and people who will testify that it was Annabelle who made the deposits." He grinned. "She isn't the sort of person who won't be noticed or remembered."

Stella gave his hands a tiny shake. "That's wonderful! So you have what you need?"

He laughed. "You have done what all the powers of the United States have been unable to do. You will be responsible for putting an entire crime ring out of business!"

This was even better than the way Annabelle and Asher had looked when the authorities managed to get them off the wrecked plane and into custody. Annabelle was wildly disheveled, barefooted, her overwrought makeup smeared, and her fabulous dress split all the way down the back, proving again that Chatty was right about her opposition to underwear. Asher did not look much better. His hair was standing up and he had a cut under his eye that was certain to leave a scar on the previously perfect face. He had a handful of Annabelle's hair dangling from his hand, several inches of extensions.

"Well, well, well." Chatty the Hero had glowed as they, hands cuffed behind their backs, were ushered by. "Asher, I'm not sure if you grabbed her hair to save her from a toppling plane or to yank it out for how she's ruined your life. But the joke's on you—her hair is just as fake as everything else about her!"

Annabelle had glared furiously at Chatty while Asher released the wig extensions, letting them flutter to the ground, as his head was pushed down and he was shoved into a police car. That had been a delicious moment in time, but this news from Pepper was even better.

"Pepper, this is wonderful," Stella declared.

She released his hands and swirled around, her hands clasped to her chest. She felt like a young girl again, the way she had felt before the world taught her some hard lessons. Her twirl completed, she threw her arms around Pepper's neck and hugged him, and he hugged her back for a long moment. Suddenly, a serious thought crossed her mind. She pulled away and looked at him.

"Oh, Pepper, perhaps we shouldn't make too much out of this because of Chatty. He is so enjoying his newly minted hero status. I'd hate to take anything away from him."

He laughed. "You and Chatty. Always thinking of the other." The affection he felt for her grew. "Tell you what—we won't mention it tonight, but at some point he has to know. We will do it gently and protect his hero status as we tell him." He winked.

Her heart swelled. They took a long moment to look fondly at each other. Then, he leaned in to kiss her. The beating of her heart thundered in her ears. Then, just before his lips touched hers, one of the French doors opened.

"Oh, excuse me!" Mrs. Puckett exclaimed. "I'm so sorry. I had passed the doors a moment ago and saw you two here. I had been hoping to catch a moment with you, Marshal Culpepper and Miss Stella. Alone. The three of us."

Pepper, disappointed enough for both of them, cleared his throat. "Quite certainly. What may we do for you, Mrs. Puckett?"

She began to wring her hands fretfully. "My nephew works on Sapelo Island. He works there through the week and comes home to St. Simons on the weekends. Today, I received news that he has been arrested and charged with murder!"

Stella moved quickly toward the woman and put her arms around her. "Mrs. Puckett, I'm so sorry!" Mrs. Puckett was trying to sniff away tears.

"Miss Stella, he is a fine boy. I promise. He says he didn't do it and I believe him, without question. He's in a jam. Is there any way y'all can help him?"

Pepper, smiling and nodding, walked over and put a caring hand on the back of each woman. "Mrs. Puckett, you have come to the right place. Between Stella Bankwell, amateur sleuth, and the U.S. Marshals, we can put our investigative skills to your service." Then he chuckled, his laughter warming the early spring night. "If we're really lucky, we can get Chatty to throw in his heroic efforts, too."

Impulsively, Pepper leaned down and planted a kiss on top of Stella's golden red hair, surprising both himself and Stella. She looked up at him with a dreaminess in her eyes while Mrs. Puckett sighed with relief.

Maybe, Pepper thought to himself, I can get a permanent transfer down here.

Suddenly, Chatty burst through the doors. "What are y'all doing out here, without me? This is the celebration of the day that the good Lord put me on this earth. Remember, this night—March 12—is all about *me*."

Pepper rolled his eyes comically. "Chatty, I am beginning to learn that *everything* is always about you!"

Chatty nodded, smiling happily. "That is true. Do not you forget that."

The story hadn't ended. Instead, a new beginning had risen up.

Acknowledgments

It is not without risk to offer gratitude to many people because, inevitably, someone vital will be left out. I humbly beg forgiveness, in advance, if someone is mistakenly overlooked.

My ninth grade Program Challenge teacher, Jo Carter, introduced me to St. Simons Island and to author Eugenia Price. Right there, in Christ Church cemetery when I met Ms. Price, an epiphany struck me—I was going to write books. I found my calling on St. Simons Island.

Many years later when Kevin Lokey invited me to speak to his Rotary Club, after I had begun my publishing career, he reintroduced me to the island I now love so much. He also offered to introduce me to Buff Leavy of the *Brunswick News* who picked up my syndicated column. It has run there for twenty years. To all the editors at that newspaper, who have come and gone, I am grateful, and to Lindsey Atkinson who edits both my newspaper column and Golden Isles magazine column these days.

I am equally grateful to all the newspapers who publish my columns and to the many editors and publishers who have become cherished friends.

Roy and Anne Hodnett took me in and made me a part of their family. My love for them was as strong as the fiercest hurricane that could hit our beloved island. Pat Hodnett Cooper, her children Kelly, Luke and Kelly's husband, Robbie, have become family. They all know every inch of that island and they have shown me so much through their eyes.

Bess Seiler Thompson, my college friend, colors the island for me in beautiful shades. It is her gift to see it with a discerning eye.

She is also a docent at Christ Church so she can always help with a piece of information I need.

Frankie Strother first introduced me to the The Cloister on Sea Island and she was one of only three who witnessed my wedding vows to John Tinker in the Cloister's stunningly beautiful chapel. Parra Vaughan and the entire staff of Sea Island always make Tink and me feel loved and cherished.

The first part of this book was written from a beachfront condo at the legendary King and Prince. It is one of the most historical hotels in America. I have tried to share some of that history in this book for it is fascinating. My thanks to Bud St. Pierre, who always dreamed of having a book written that included the King and Prince, as well as Michael Johnson and Bart Johnson.

I have already dedicated this book to Edward Armstrong but I must admit here that he inspired the most delicious parts of Chatham "Chatty" Balsam Colquitt IV. Edward's tendency toward lyrical words and Southern phrases brought about Chatty. My husband says, "He's one of the most fun characters I've ever read."

And, my husband, John Tinker, has seen many entertaining characters for he is an Emmy-award winning television writer. Quite simply, without him, this book would never have been finished. I got halfway through and laid it aside for other work. Yet, Tink talked often of how he missed Chatty. Tink is always my warrior and encourager. I am blessed to call him my husband and I wish every woman had a husband who thinks she is amazing and pushes her as hard as Tink pushes me.

Then, there was that phone call with Allen Wallace of Mercer University Press. I called him with a question about a newspaper and, in the conversation, he discovered I had this half-written mystery novel. The next day, Marc Jolley, Mercer publisher, was writing to ask, "May we have it?" "How soon?"

For the last few years, I have said, repeatedly, that Mercer University Press is one of the finest publishers in America. I have published with several New York giants so I consider myself an expert on that. The Mercer catalog is diverse and wonderful. To every hand at Mercer who has touched this manuscript, I thank you mightily.

My family. Without them, I would be a much poorer storyteller because they are all such fine storytellers. I never leave the Sunday dinner table without a new tale. Louise, Rodney (one of my favorite storytellers), Nicole, Jay, Rod and their families, thank you. Thank you to Selena for her photography including the photo here.

Thank you to Karen Kingsbury, Janette Oke, and Jeff Foxworthy for the giving of their time to read this and to offer endorsements. I am also indebted to my "big brother" (since he calls me his little sister), Don Reid for his incredible story songs about small town life and the nostalgia we always feel when we look back. I spent hours, as a teenager, studying his lyrics, structure, and twists and turns. His written words have influenced my storytelling more than anyone. Thank you, dear Don for that and for bringing Debbie into our lives.

The Bible says that the last shall be first. And, with that, I thank my Lord and Savior, Jesus Christ, for the gift of writing that I so enjoy and for the remarkable opportunities He has put before me. It has been my childhood dream come true.

To the more than one million readers who have read my words over the years and, especially those who have passed them on to others, God bless you. I thank you from the deepest part of my heart.

No person is self-made. I vigorously believe that. I have been made by all the people mentioned above and dozens more who touched my life in some way, believed in me, mentored me and loved me.

Thank all y'all. I shall remain forever grateful.

The Author

Ronda Rich, whose Georgia roots were planted around 1750, is the best-selling author of several books including *What Southern Women Know (That Every Woman Should)* and *The Town That Came A-Courtin'*, also a television movie. Her weekly syndicated column about Southern life appears in forty-seven newspapers across the Southeast. Learn more about her at www.rondarich.com.